Fair Warning

"Stop it," Tristan ordered hoarsely. "Stop looking like that."

Madelaine's eyes widened. "Like what?"

"Like a woman yearning to be kissed," he said.

Madelaine studied him solemnly. "I hadn't thought of it," she informed him. "But now that you mention it, what could be more perfect than to experience my first kiss on this most perfect of nights."

"The night may be perfect; the man is anything but," Tristan stated flatly. "I have done everything you suspect me of and more than you can imagine. I am the last man on earth with whom you should share your first kiss." Then, as she moved closer, he said, "You are playing with fire, lady."

She did not stop, she moved still closer, and with a groan, he lowered his head and covered her lips with his. And Madelaine discovered that all his warnings had not prepared her for what his kiss would do to her . . .

The Misguided Matchmaker

by

Nadine Miller

A SIGNET BOOK

SIGNET
Published by the Penguin Group
Penguin Books USA Inc., 375 Hudson Street,
New York, New York 10014, U.S.A.
Penguin Books Ltd, 27 Wrights Lane,
London W8 5TZ, England
Penguin Books Australia Ltd,
Ringwood, Victoria, Australia
Penguin Books Canada Ltd, 10 Alcorn Avenue,
Toronto, Ontario, Canada M4V 3B2
Penguin Books (N.Z.) Ltd, 182–190 Wairau Road,
Auckland 10, New Zealand

Penguin Books Ltd, Registered Offices:
Harmondsworth, Middlesex, England

First published by Signet, an imprint of Dutton Signet,
a division of Penguin Books USA Inc.

First Printing, May, 1997
10 9 8 7 6 5 4 3 2 1

To Ilse Noren—a dear friend whose affection
and support have seen me through many a rough
spot in my writing career

and

Dee Gibson—a new friend whose generous
loan of her magnificent Regency library
has provided a world of fascinating research
into that complex historical period.

Author's Note

The *traboules* of Lyon still exist, as they have since the powerful Medici family first utilized them in the fifteenth century. Rumors still abound of the Black Mass being celebrated in the *traboules mysterieuses*—and even today tourists and Lyonnais alike often find themselves lost in the maze of covered passages and alleyways.

One

Like a magnet, the massive black funeral wreath spanning the door of Winterhaven Manor drew Tristan Thibault's eyes. "So, the old reprobate who fathered me really is dead," he said aloud, reining in the tired nag that had carried him up from Dover through a bitterly cold rain.

He shook his head in amazement. The lecherous Fourth Earl of Rand had finally cocked up his toes, and his passing evoked no feeling whatsoever in this particular by-blow except a firm conviction that the fires of hell must be burning ever hotter with Dickie Ramsden as the netherworld's newest resident.

The fading light of the winter afternoon lent a grim ambience to the graceful, porticoed entrance of the three-storied stone manor house he'd called home until the day he'd turned two and twenty. Even the rows of narrow, mullioned windows looked dark and uninviting—almost as if the family had given up expecting him.

Mentally, he reviewed the cryptic note he'd received from his half-sister apprising him that the earl had quit this earthly vale. "Please come home," Carolyn's nearly illegible scrawl had begged. "Father was killed in a gambling hell brawl and we are in desperate trouble." A contradiction if ever he'd heard one. The old man's demise could be nothing but a blessing to his long-suffering wife and progeny. Every problem that had ever plagued the Ramsdens, including Tristan's own illegitimacy, had stemmed from the Fourth Earl's excesses. With his shy, sober-minded son, Garth, as the Fifth Earl, life at Winterhaven had to improve.

Tristan frowned thoughtfully. He half suspected Caro's frantic plea for help would turn out to be much ado about nothing; she had always had a tendency to fly into the boughs at the slightest provocation. Still, he hadn't dared ignore her note—hadn't even wanted to. It was the first word he'd received from home in the six years he'd lived on the Continent, and he'd devoured every word with an eagerness that was embarrassing to a man of his age and temperament. A British secret agent posing as a citizen of Napoleon's France had no choice but to sever all personal contacts. But the war was over at last and the Corsican safely on Elba—and once again Tristan could turn his thoughts to Winterhaven and the people he had come to think of as his family.

He looked around for a groom to lead his horse to the stable, but strangely, none was in sight. Stranger yet was the absence of the usual footman hurrying down the shallow stone steps to take his saddlebags. Feeling his first twinge of genuine uneasiness, he secured his horse by looping the reins around a winter-bare shrub, hefted his bags, and made his way up the steps to the massive oak door.

Before he could lift the heavy brass knocker, the door burst open and a small, golden-haired whirlwind launched herself at him. "Tristan!" she shrieked. "I knew you'd come. I just knew it."

Tristan dropped his saddlebags and crushed his slender young sister in a fierce bear hug. "Of course I came." He chuckled. "Though I've a strong suspicion I've been well and truly diddled by your dramatic missive, you little scamp. Not that I care. If the truth be known, I was ready to come home and settle down on that small holding Garth promised me years ago."

Carolyn wound her arms about his waist and pressed her cheek to his chest. "Oh Tris, how I wish I had exaggerated our troubles—but I haven't." Her voice broke. "It's like a dreadful nightmare from which one prays to wake and never can."

Tristan put her from him and stared into her face, shocked by what he saw. Gone was the rosy-cheeked, mischievous child he'd left six years earlier and in her place a pale young woman whose solemn blue eyes were underlaid with dark smudges. Gently, he drew her down onto the night footman's bench which stood against one wall of the entryway. "Tell me all about it, including how in holy heaven you managed to in-

sert your note into an official Whitehall packet addressed to
Lord Castlereagh at the Congress of Vienna."

"I have a friend who is a clerk at Whitehall," she said simply. "He'd heard rumors you were with Lord Castlereagh, so
we thought it worth a try, though it would surely be the end of
his career if anyone learned he helped me contact you, so
never ask his name." A lone tear trickled down her cheek. "I
didn't know what else to do. Neither Garth nor Mama know I
sent for you."

Carolyn slipped her hand into Tristan's and, rising, drew
him up beside her. " Mama is in her sitting room. We should
go to her; she'll take such comfort in your presence, and it's
best you hear the story from both of us at once. It's not one
you'll want to hear again."

So saying, she led the way up the stairs to the countess's
private suite. Tristan followed, his anxiety increasing by the
minute. They opened the chamber door to find Lady Ursula re-
clining on the chaise longue, covered by a feather quilt.

A gloomy pall hung over the usually cheerful room. The
small pile of glowing coals in the fireplace added little
warmth, and the only light came from a single candle sputter-
ing on the Chippendale writing desk beneath the window.

Carolyn advanced into the room, a determined smile on her
face. "You'll never guess who's here, Mama. It's our own dear
Tristan, come to help Garth sort out our problems."

Lady Ursula Ramsden turned her head and surveyed them
from red-rimmed eyes. "Tristan? Thank heavens you're home
at last." She sat upright. "Well, that's that then. I absolutely
refuse to worry one more minute. Between the two of you,
you're bound to come up with a solution to this dreadful bumblebroth."

She brushed a lock of faded golden hair out of her eyes. In
all the years he'd known her, Tristan had never seen a single
strand of her hair out of place. Today she looked strangely un-
kempt, as if she'd somehow escaped her faithful dresser's
careful vigil.

Her pale blue eyes surveyed him from head to toe. "Good
heavens, I'd almost forgotten how exceedingly tall you'd
grown or how stern of countenance. I'd scarcely recognize you
as the dear little fellow I used to tuck into bed each night."

Carolyn nodded. "Mama is right. With your long black hair and sun-bronzed skin, you look more like a pirate than our own Tris."

"I've been called worse." Tristan chuckled. "One old flower lady at the Marché de Paris went so far as to cross herself each time I looked at her with my 'devil's eyes.'"

"What trials you've suffered—what trials we've all suffered since last we were together." Tears welled in Lady Ursula's own expressive blue eyes as she opened her arms to Tristan— a gesture evoking bittersweet memories that made his heart twist painfully in his chest. In just such a way had this generous-hearted woman greeted a frightened six-year-old who'd arrived on her doorstep with a note claiming he was the bastard son of her profligate husband. "Lord Tristan," she'd directed the servants to call him, and "Lord Tristan" he'd been ever since, though he had no more claim to the title than the lowliest denizen of the Rookeries, from whence he'd come.

Tenderly, he knelt, clasped the slender, middle-aged countess in his arms, and placed a gentle kiss on her forehead. She clung to him, as Carolyn had, with the fervor of a drowning person who'd just been thrown a lifeline.

"Now what is this about problems Garth must sort out?" he asked. "Where is the new earl? And why have the servants let the fires go out? This chamber is colder than my cabin on the channel packet ship."

"The new earl is here, my brother," a familiar voice declared from the doorway, "as is the wood for Mama's fire, but the servants are all gone except our loyal housekeeper, Mrs. Peterman, and the old head gardener, who stayed on without pay."

Tristan's mouth dropped open in shock at the sight of his brother, the Fifth Earl of Rand—his face haggard, his clothes dirty and disheveled, and his arms laden with firewood like the lowliest tenant on the estate. "What the devil is going on here?" he demanded.

Garth deposited the wood on the hearth, then turned to face Tristan. "It's a long, sordid story and I won't burden you with the details. Suffice it to say I sold out my commission once Boney was defeated and returned home to find our father, may he rot in hell, had managed to gamble away everything he owned before he was sent to his just reward by some Captain Sharp he'd tried to cheat at Hazard."

"Everything?" Tristan choked.

"Everything. The hunting box in the Midlands, the London townhouse, the farms in Suffolk, even Winterhaven and all its furnishings." Garth ran his fingers absentmindedly through his thick blond hair. "His sole legacy to his heirs is the collection of vowels he owes various London gambling hells, which add up to nearly twenty thousand pounds."

Tristan stared at his brother in disbelief. The old earl had always been a wastrel, but it would take most men two lifetimes to gamble away such impressive assets as the Ramsdens had once owned. An icy rage gripped him and he swore softly in the gutter French he'd picked up in the Paris slums. He had learned to fend for himself during his years in France, but these three gentle people he loved had no concept of how to survive without the wealth they'd always taken for granted.

Still reeling from shock, he tucked the quilt around Lady Ursula, then moved to the fireplace to build up the fire with the wood Garth had delivered.

Garth watched him with listless eyes. "There's more," he said in the same dull monotone with which he'd recited the first part of his incredible tale. "The mortgages on the properties, as well as Father's vowels, have all been bought up by one man—Caleb Harcourt."

Tristan looked up from his task. "The wealthy cit who owns Harcourt Shipping?"

Garth nodded. "And the Harcourt woolen mills and two of London's finest hotels and God only knows what else. I wonder if the fool thinks that by owning the properties of the Earl of Rand he may somehow acquire the title. Rumor is he's been negotiating with Prinny for a baronetcy in exchange for the blunt to pay off his most pressing debts."

"I think it is safe to assume Caleb Harcourt is no fool." Deep in thought, Tristan stirred the coals with the poker until they ignited the dry wood. "He must have a reason for going to the trouble of searching out the earl's creditors and paying them off—though God knows I cannot think what it might be."

"Nor can I, but it is something I intend to ask him when, at his request, I call on him tomorrow morning at his place of business on the London docks."

"When *we* call on him. We will beard the lion in his den together," Tristan said, his heart aching for Garth. He could imagine how bewildering it must be to go from a position of undisputed wealth and respectability to abject poverty and disgrace in the blink of an eye.

"Is that wise, my dears?" Lady Ursula's small heart-shaped face lacked its usual mask of calm serenity. "The man is a common cit, for heaven's sake, regardless of his enormous wealth. How can a gentleman hope to reason with someone so far below his social level?"

Garth moved away from the fireplace, pulled the chair out from under the desk, and sank onto it, obviously exhausted. "What choice do I have, Mama?" he asked with a touch of impatience. "Thanks to Father's penchant for gambling, this common cit currently owns everything that should be mine. I am at the fellow's mercy." He raised agonized eyes to Tristan. "I cannot even deed you that unentailed estate in Suffolk I promised you. It went the same way as the rest of my holdings."

Tristan hid his bitter disappointment behind an indifferent shrug. "Not to worry. I'm not certain I was cut out to be a sheep farmer anyway." He forced his lips to form a semblance of a smile. "As for dealing with cits, I have dealt with nothing else during my six years in France—including the infamous Citizen Fouché, Napoleon's Minister of Police. By and large they are no better or worse than their counterparts in the titled gentry. We will simply take this English interloper as he comes and proceed accordingly."

It was a foolish speech which said nothing and promised even less, but he could see from the two pairs of hopeful feminine eyes turned his way that it had the desired effect on the countess and Carolyn.

The bleak expression on Garth's face said he wasn't fooled by such blithe sentiments, but after a telling look from Tristan, he seconded them. No use cutting up the ladies' peace of mind any more than they had to. Moments later the two brothers took their leave, claiming they needed to plan their strategy for the coming meeting.

"Does Lady Sarah know of your problems?" Tristan asked as they made their way to the book room. The daughter of their neighbor, Viscount Tinsdale, had dogged Garth's footsteps since they were children growing up together. Both families had always taken it for granted the two would someday marry.

"I have not yet steeled myself to terminate our 'understanding.'" Garth's pain-filled voice trembled noticeably. "Everything else in this miserable bumblebroth pales beside the anguish of knowing I must hurt the woman I love—and in the worst possible way. Sarah has waited so long for me to officially declare myself that she is almost past the marrying age, and now I must tell her all the plans we made are for naught."

Tristan scowled. "I know Sarah too well to believe she will stop loving you simply because you're no longer rich."

"Of course she won't, any more than I will ever stop loving her. But think you Viscount Tinsdale will give his only daughter to a pauper, even if that pauper carries the title of earl? Or that I love Sarah so little I would ask her to share my life when I have nothing to offer her but shame and deprivation?" Garth shook his head vehemently. "No, once I know the very worst of my situation, I will find the strength to cut my ties with her."

Garth straightened his narrow shoulders in a proud gesture that made Tristan ache all the more for his unfortunate brother. He found himself grateful that his was a heart inured to such longings. From what he had seen of love, the pain of it far outweighed the joy.

"What you need right now is a stiff drink to dull the pain," he declared decisively. "And I am not the least bit adverse to helping you drown your sorrows. What say you we raid the cellar in the hope there may still be a stray bottle of French brandy lying about? I've acquired a taste for the stuff in the past six years."

Garth's's smile looked a bit ragged at the edges. "A splendid idea," he said somewhat too heartily. "But first, I have something I want to give you." He pulled a gold pocket watch from the drawer of the library desk and handed it to Tristan. "It is one of only two personal items our father hadn't disposed of at his death."

Tristan viewed the ornate timepiece with distaste. "Thank
you, but I have no desire to keep a memento of the old liber-
tine who never even acknowledged me as his son."

"Keep it in the same spirit I keep his jeweled snuffbox,"
Garth said grimly. "As a reminder of everything that is evil
and depraved—everything I am determined I shall never become."

The offices of Harcourt Shipping Ltd. were housed in a nondescript two-story warehouse overlooking the sprawling
Billingsgate fish market. Tristan and Garth had driven in from
Winterhaven in the old earl's sporty phaeton—not the easiest
of vehicles in which to wend one's way through the milling
crowds of lower-class housewives and upperclass servants
haggling with the stall owners over turbot, salmon, lobsters,
and eels, as well as the various other fruits of the sea served on
London dinner tables.

The pungent aroma of fish was everywhere. It overrode the
stench of the ancient, refuse-covered docks and the masses of
unwashed humanity crowding the busy market, and it set Tristan's already queasy stomach to roiling dangerously. The nocturnal search Garth and he had made of the Winterhaven cellar
had yielded not one, but two bottles of vintage brandy, and
they'd managed to consume them both before the cold gray
light of dawn reminded them they had an appointment with
Caleb Harcourt in but a few brief hours.

Now, with a wintery sun torturing his bloodshot eyes and
the voices of the fish hawkers thrusting javelins into his aching
head, Tristan gritted his teeth and prayed as much for a settled
stomach as a clear mind when he and Garth faced the powerful
cit who held the fate of the Ramsden family in his hands. With
shaky hands, he pulled the phaeton to a stop before a door with
a discreet brass plate bearing the name Harcourt Shipping Ltd.,
tossed a coin to the urchin who acted as carriage tender, and
helped his exhausted brother alight from the passenger's seat.

A moment later, they entered the building and to their surprise found the inside to be as elegantly austere as the outside
was shabby. The massive waiting room into which they'd
stepped was complete with colorful Axminster carpets, Hepplewhite chairs, and a collection of paintings as impressive as

that in the gallery at Winterhaven before the Fourth Earl de-nuded it to finance his addiction to the ivory turners.

Blessing of all blessings, the aroma of fish had not perme-ated the walls of Caleb Harcourt's tasteful *sanctum sanctorum.* Instead, a spicy fragrance teased Tristan's grateful nostrils— the source of which was explained by a sign, "Harcourt Fine Spices and Exotic Herbs," at the foot of an open staircase lead-ing to the floor above. He pointed it out to Garth. "You were right. Shipping is only one of Harcourt's enterprises."

At least two dozen men, in identical dark coats and breeches, stood in small groups about the room conversing in the hushed and nervous tones one might expect of men await-ing an audience with the Regent at Carlton House. All conver-sation instantly ceased when Tristan and Garth entered the room and removed their high-crowned beavers. The reason was patently obvious. Though their coats of fine marsella were drab and outdated by *ton* standards, next to these somberly clad men of the merchant class they looked like two peacocks in a flock of barnyard geese.

The door had barely closed behind them when a wizened lit-tle man, dressed all in black with a bagwig on his thinning gray hair and what looked suspiciously like house slippers on his feet, shuffled over to them. "My Lord Rand?" he inquired, peering from Tristan to Garth over his wire-rimmed specta-cles.

"I am the Earl of Rand," Garth said stiffly. "And this is my brother, Lord Tristan."

"Of course. Ephriam Scruggs at your service, sirs." The lit-tle man bent over in a bow that threatened to land him flat on his face at their feet. Righting himself, he declared, "The cap'n's been waiting for you. Turned meaner'n a snake when you wasn't here an hour ago. I'll just nip in and tell him you've arrived." Turning on his heel, he shuffled back across the room and disappeared through a heavy oak door. Moments later he poked his head out and crooked his finger at Garth and Tristan.

Garth's already ashen face blanched a shade whiter. "What kind of madhouse have we stumbled into?" he whispered.

"Courage, brother," Tristan whispered back as they crossed

the waiting room under the scrutiny of dozens of watchful eyes. "I've a feeling the worst is yet to come."

Caleb Harcourt's small private office was even more elegant than his anteroom, but the giant of a man who stood behind the carved rosewood desk looked as if he would be more at home on the deck of one of his ships than in his present surroundings. His deeply tanned face had the look of old leather, his salt-and-pepper hair was unfashionably long, and his black topcoat, while superbly cut, looked as if he'd slept in it. He surveyed them with frank curiosity. "Which one's the earl and which the bastard?" he asked in a booming voice.

Tristan saw Garth stiffen in anger. "I am Tristan Thibault," he said quickly. Harcourt was obviously an insufferable boor, but he held all the aces in this particular game; to rile him now would be sheer stupidity.

"Castlereagh's favorite spy, or so my sources tell me." Harcourt's shrewd gray eyes held an odd look akin to respect. "Thought you were in Vienna."

"Your 'sources' are behind times, sir. I hope you haven't overpaid them. I've been back in England these three days."

To Tristan's surprise, Harcourt threw back his leonine head and roared with laughter. "Insolent pup. But you're right. My high-priced informants will find their pay packets a bit thin this quarter."

His attention turned to Garth. "And what have you to say, my lord? Or do you let your brother do your talking for you?"

Garth pulled himself up to his full height, which was still a head shorter than Tristan and shorter yet than the giant cit. "I speak for myself, sir, when I have something to say. At the moment, you have me at a disadvantage, all things considered."

Harcourt tapped a stack of papers on his desk with the tip of his index finger. "A considerable disadvantage, I'd say. But sit down and we'll talk about it." He indicated two chairs and promptly seated himself behind his desk. "No use trying to wrap it up pretty. Your father was the sorriest excuse for a man as ever God created. The only thing worse than a drunk and a womanizer is a card cheat—and he was all three. Left you in the suds, he did, and that's a fact."

Tristan exchanged a telling look with Garth at this cit's audacity, but there was no disputing the truth of his words.

Harcourt leaned across the desk. "Don't suppose you have any idea how you're going to take care of your mother and sister, not to mention the poor souls starving to death in those broken-down tenants' cottages on your estates."

The shocked silence in the small room was as thick and cold as a London fog.

"Just as I thought," Harcourt said, as if by remaining mute, Garth had as much as admitted he had no idea how to solve his financial problems himself. The big man sat back in his chair, a satisfied look on his weathered face. "Very well, my lord. Here's my proposition, plain and simple. I'll cancel out the mountain of debts you inherited and advance you enough blunt to put your estates on a paying basis . . . providing you agree to two things."

Tristan met Garth's look of astonishment with one of his own. They had discussed a dozen possible outcomes to this meeting during their long brandy-soaked night; an offer to put the Earl of Rand's affairs in order was not one of them. As one, they turned to face the man behind the desk. "What two things?" they asked in unison.

"First, my lord, I want your promise you'll work at restoring your estates yourself—not simply turn the task over to a bailiff. I've no use for a man, titled or not, who's afraid of work."

Garth swallowed hard, obviously choking on the pride he was forced to swallow. "I shall devote every waking hour to bringing things about if we come to an agreement." He swallowed again. "My interests are of a more sober mien than those of my father."

Tristan laid a supportive hand on his brother's arm. "And I'll help him."

"Not right off you won't," Harcourt declared. "I've a more important piece of work needs doing on the Continent and it just occurred to me you're the very one to do it, since my sources tell me you know France better than most Frenchies." He raised a hand to forestall Tristan's objections. "It won't take but a fortnight or so, and since this whole scheme with your brother hinges on it, I'd advise you to think twice before you turn it down."

Tristan gritted his teeth. He didn't like the implied threat in Harcourt's words, but he had no choice; for his family's sake, he had to listen.

Harcourt leaned his elbows on the desk and tented his fingers. "It's like this. My daughter, Madelaine, is living in Lyon with her maternal grandfather, a Frenchie count, but the old tartar sent word he's dying and he doesn't want Maddy left alone when he sticks his spoon in the wall. Well, neither do I, so I want you to go get her. I'll send you to Calais in one of my brigs, and my captain will wait there while you see Maddy safely from Lyon—a task that should be relatively easy for a man with your background."

Tristan gave a noncommittal grunt, deciding it prudent to hear the rest of this cit's demands before he made any promises.

Harcourt then turned to Garth. "Which brings us to the second term in our proposed contract, my lord. What I want from you in exchange for saving your bacon is a written promise that once Maddy gets here, you'll make her your countess."

The faint, hopeful color that had bloomed in Garth's face for a few moments receded like the tide vacating a beach, leaving him as pale and gray as a piece of sun-bleached driftwood. "You want me to mar-marry your daughter?" he gasped. "But, sir, how can I agree to such a thing? I have never met your daughter."

"Of course you haven't. Haven't seen her myself for fifteen years. Her mother went haring back to France, with Maddy in tow, once she found the titled biddies of the London *ton* wouldn't give a common merchant's wife the time of day. I'd but one ship then, which I captained myself, so I hadn't the wherewithal to do anything about it. The situation is different now. I'm a rich man and I'm determined no door in London, including that of Carlton House, will ever be closed in Maddy's face. And if spending a fortune to see a title tacked onto her name is what it takes to ensure that, then so be it."

Harcourt pounded his fist on the desk with such force his

inkwell skipped to within an inch of the edge. The sound drove through Tristan's aching head like a team and four. Only by sheer willpower did he keep from moaning aloud.

He could see Garth was beyond worrying about appearances. Eyes closed, he pressed his shaking fingers to his temples, as if the combination of Harcourt's bizarre proposition and the aftereffects of too much brandy had pushed him beyond his limits.

Harcourt waved the stack of vowels before Garth's nose. "Take my offer, my lord, or leave it and suffer the consequences. You may be the pick of the litter, but you're not the only impoverished nobleman in England."

Garth groaned.

"How many men in your situation get the chance to put their affairs in order and take on a fine strapping wife to boot?"

"Strapping?" Garth echoed faintly. His eyes were closed and his complexion had taken on an oddly bilious tinge.

Tristan eyed his whey-faced brother nervously, but Harcourt didn't appear to notice that anything was amiss. "So then, what do you say, lad?" he demanded in a hearty baritone that reverberated through the small room like a clanging gong. "Is it agreed then—a fortune for a leg shackle?"

Garth cast one pathetic glance in Tristan's direction. His eyes held the furtive look of a fox that, trapped by hounds, knows his fate is sealed. "Agreed," he said in a strangled voice and as Tristan watched in horror, the Fifth Earl of Rand fell forward onto his knees beside Caleb Harcourt's desk and, clutching his high-crowned beaver like a basin, cast up his accounts.

Madelaine Harcourt had no way of knowing if the person pounding on the door of her grandfather's small house was friend or foe—a fellow Royalist come to help care for the dying aristocrat or a Bonapartist bent on revenge toward the emperor's most outspoken critic.

Since the first rumor of the Corsican's escape from Elba reached Lyon five days earlier, bands of men sympathetic to the emperor had been gathering on the street corners talking excitedly of his return to power. Today, with the news that he and his loyal *grognards* had reached Grenoble, these same men had taken to roaming the streets, smashing the windows of shops and homes of known Royalists. Her grandfather's butler cum valet had already deserted his post, as had the sour old woman who had doubled as the housekeeper and Madelaine's chaperone for the past six years. She could scarcely blame them.

Silently, she crept to her chamber window, which overlooked the front entrance of the house, pushed aside the drape, and peered out. Darkness had fallen, but the man hammering on the door was clearly outlined in the bright light of the moon. He was tall—much too tall to be one of the French aristocrats who frequented the house.

For long, terrified minutes, she stood pressed against the wall until finally the pounding ceased and she released the breath she hadn't realized she was holding. With a sigh of relief, she hurried across the narrow hall to where her grandfather lay propped high on his pillows. His eyes were closed, his breathing horribly labored, his aquiline features waxy with the look of death.

She felt sick with grief. Grandpère had always been so fierce, so proud, so impossibly autocratic. She couldn't bear to see him like this, clinging hour after torturous hour to one small spark of life—stubbornly refusing to bow to the grim reaper until the moment he himself chose to die. Bending over him, she placed a tender kiss on his wrinkled forehead.

Without warning, the sound of breaking glass shattered the silence of the house. Madelaine's heart leapt in her breast. Dear God! The intruder had smashed the French window. Even now he must be reaching in to turn the knob and gain entry.

Desperately, she looked about her for a weapon to defend herself. Her gaze lighted on a marquetry chest standing against one wall and she remembered that, among other things, it contained the velvet-lined box in which her grandfather's dueling pistols were stored. They weren't loaded, but the intruder had no way of knowing that. Running over to the chest and opening it she lifted one of the lethal-looking firearms from the box and grasped it in both hands.

"Is anyone here? Answer me if you are." There was no menace in the intruder's voice, but his strong, guttural accent was that of the Paris streets. Madelaine's pulse quickened; she took a tighter grasp on her weapon.

Moments later, a man in a dusty riding jacket and buckskin pants loomed in the chamber doorway, his head just skimming the lintel. Unruly black hair framed his thin, brigand's face and his strange, pale eyes raked her with a look that nearly buckled her knees.

"*Arretez vous!* One step more and I will shoot." Madelaine heard the tremor in her own voice, but she managed to keep the pistol pointed at his chest, though it waved drunkenly in her trembling fingers.

"Mademoisele Harcourt?" The stranger eyed the pistol warily. "*Mon Dieu!* Watch where you're pointing that thing." He looked again and his mouth relaxed in a wolfish grin that raised the hair on the back of Madelaine's neck. "The next time you threaten to shoot someone, mademoiselle, you might consider cocking the pistol."

With a sudden movement that took her completely unawares, he whipped the weapon out of her grasp with his left hand and laid it down on the top of a nearby bureau. "Also, these things are generally more effective when loaded. Like this one is." He raised his right hand and Madelaine found herself staring at a small but lethal-looking pistol. "A word of advice. Never point an unloaded gun at a man. If I had meant you harm, you would already be dead."

Madelaine backed up until she was pressed against her grandfather's bedstead. "Who . . . who are you?" she stammered, her heart pounding. "What do you want?"

Tristan returned the pistol to the waistband of his trousers and studied the woman questioning him before he answered. His lips parted in an unconscious smile. If this dark-haired waif with the boyish figure and huge, frightened eyes was Caleb Harcourt's "fine, strapping daughter," she was a far cry from the lusty peasant he had expected to find. He looked again. Unless he was mistaken, she was also a good inch or two taller than her intended bridegroom.

He gave a cursory bow. "I am Tristan Thibault. I have come in answer to a request from le Comte de Navareil."

"What tale is this, monsieur? My grandfather maintains no correspondence with Paris these days."

"Paris?" The stranger raised a quizzical eyebrow. "Ah, my accent!" He shrugged. "Be assured, mademoiselle, I come not from Paris, but London."

Before Madelaine Harcourt could comment on this bit of information, the occupant of the bed behind her stirred. "Who is that with you, *ma petite fille*?" a voice asked weakly. "Was I dreaming or did I hear him say he comes from London?"

Tristan stared past the wild-eyed young woman to find a frail, silver-haired old man with a nose like an eagle's beak and deep-set eyes that searched him out in the shadowed room.

"You heard right, sir." He stepped to the foot of the bed. "I have been sent by Caleb Harcourt to find his daughter and take her back to London as you petitioned."

"*Dieu soit loué*, my prayers have been answered in time. Take her, monsieur. Take her to safety before the Corsican fiend reaches Lyon—before his evil minion, Fouché, takes revenge on the granddaughter of his old enemy."

"No, Grandpère! Do not speak so." Madelaine Harcourt grasped her grandfather's thin hand. "Do not ask me to leave you and go to a father who has never wanted me. You will only force me to disobey you—something I have never before done."

The old man's smile was tender and his rheumy eyes glistened with moisture. "It is not you who leave me, *ma petite fille*, but I who leave you—and where I go, you cannot follow."

He grimaced, obviously in pain, and his hawkish features took on an even more ghastly pallor. "The *Anglais* who is your father does want you. He always has. Have you never wondered who provided the funds that kept us in comfort all the years of Bonaparte's rule, when most Royalists were destitute?"

He gasped for breath. "Forgive me," he murmured, his voice fading to a whisper. "I deceived you about your father because I feared I would lose you if you knew the truth. It was your foolish mother who was at fault, not her English merchant."

Madelaine Harcourt raised his withered hand to her lips. "It does not matter. I would never have left you anyway."

Her words were lost on the crusty old aristocrat. As Tristan watched the fingers clutching his granddaughter's hand fell slack, his eyes drifted shut, and with a final heart-wrenching sigh, he relinquished his tenuous hold on life.

Two

Madelaine Harcourt threw herself across the inert form of her grandfather in a paroxysm of grief that totally unnerved Tristan. He crept silently from the room, leaving her to grieve in private, but the sound of her racking sobs haunted him long after he could no longer hear them. It was obvious she sincerely loved the old man and felt his death had brought her world tumbling down about her ears—much as his had tumbled some twenty years before when he'd witnessed the accident that had left his poor mother crushed beneath the wheels of a runaway carriage. Even now he could feel the bewildering emptiness, the searing pain that had scarred his young soul forever.

He stood at the window of the small first-floor salon and stared into the darkness of the winter night, wondering how he was supposed to handle this latest development in this supposedly simple assignment Caleb Harcourt had blackmailed him into taking.

So far, everything that could possibly go wrong had done so. First, that monumental fly in Europe's ointment, Napoleon Bonaparte, had had the ill grace to escape from Elba and land at Provence on the very day Harcourt's frigate put Tristan off at Calais. Word of the Corsican's return had spread like wildfire across the country and thousands of former soldiers had donned their war-stained uniforms and flocked to the emperor's cause. Over and over, as he rode the long miles south to Lyon, Tristan heard the cry, "Down with the hated Bourbons! *Vive l'empereur!*" Caleb Harcourt couldn't have picked a worse time to send a former British spy into France to retrieve his Royalist daughter. They would need the devil's own luck to make it safely back to England.

Then he'd scarcely finished introducing himself to Madelaine Harcourt's grandfather when the old fellow closed his eyes and breathed his last. Now he must convince a grief-stricken young woman to put her life in the hands of a complete stranger representing a father she had not seen in fifteen years.

"Monsieur Thibault?" Madelaine Harcourt's voice interrupted his musings, and he turned to find her in the doorway of the salon. She was deathly pale and her eyelids were red and swollen, but all things considered, she looked remarkably composed. The lady was obviously made of sterner stuff than her fragile appearance would lead one to suppose.

"I will need your help, monsieur." Her voice sounded flat, devoid of all expression. "I have wrapped my grandfather in his quilt, but he is too heavy for me to carry alone."

"Carry? Where are you planning to carry him, mademoiselle?"

"To the church of St. Bartholomew the Martyr. To the Navareil family crypt. He must have a proper catholique burial in a place consecrated by the church."

Tristan couldn't believe his ears. "You cannot be serious!" But he could see from the stubborn set of her chin that she was very serious indeed.

He consulted his newly acquired gold watch. "It is close on midnight, mademoiselle. Lyon is crawling with Bonapartists, and the mood of the streets is ugly. Can you imagine the kind of trouble we might well encounter if we tried to transport the body of a known Royalist through such a melee? Surely there are local officials who attend to such matters, even in times of political upheaval."

"The city officials are all Bonapartists and my grandfather's sworn enemies. They would not bury him in the family crypt, nor even in consecrated ground," she said flatly. "I have already failed him by not securing a priest to give him the last rites; I will not compound my sins by letting him be buried in ground from which *le bon Dieu* cannot claim his soul."

Tristan groaned. He had spent enough time in France to recognize the importance of such religious strictures to the papists. Ordinarily, he would gladly honor her wishes, but present circumstances were anything but ordinary; Lyon was a powder keg that could explode at any moment.

"I am sorry, mademoiselle," he said gently. "What you propose is not only dangerous; it is impossible without a conveyance. I have already searched the mews behind the house. Except for one small roan mare, your grandfather's stables are empty."

"There is the gardener's barrow." She shuddered, as if the thought of transporting her grandfather's body to its final resting place in such an undignified manner was too horrible to contemplate. "I do not ask that you risk your safety, monsieur. The church is not far; I can easily wheel the barrow there myself. I ask only that you help me carry him to the garden. If you will do this much, I promise that once I have seen him properly interred, I will go with you to England and my father." Her voice broke. "There is nothing left for me in France."

Tristan gritted his teeth. He couldn't help but applaud her loyalty to her grandfather . . . and her courage. Somewhere deep in his soul he even understood the pain she was suffering, but understanding it and acting upon it were two different things. He would not be a party to risking her life, as well as his own, for the sake of a burial ritual. Nothing on earth could make him change his mind on that score.

Nothing, that is, except her tears.

Hell and damnation! Before he could make his case, her wounded amber eyes turned into two pools of glistening liquid and a lone tear trailed down her pale cheek and splashed onto the somber gray fabric molding her breast. He had always been a fool where weeping women were concerned, and there was something about Madelaine Harcourt's tears that he found particularly unnerving. Another teardrop followed the first, and he felt his resolve crumble like a defenseless fortress put to the battering ram.

He wasted the next few minutes trying to convince her she must take what belongings she needed for the trip to England with her to the church. She flatly refused. "First things first," she declared stubbornly. "I will take care of my own concerns once I've completed my duty to Grandpère."

Tristan had two choices: acquiesce to her demands or drag

her kicking and screaming to Calais. Grimly, he carried the quilt-wrapped body of the old count to the garden, then trundled the wheelbarrow through the opening in the garden wall and onto the tree-lined street beyond.

A group of men, in the same ragged uniforms he'd seen earlier in other parts of the city, had gathered outside the gate. They fell silent as the bizarre little funeral cortege approached, but Tristan was alert to the ominous undercurrent rumbling through the crowd. He'd seen such gatherings as this in Paris; it had all the earmarks of a mob spoiling for trouble.

Madelaine Harcourt walked ahead of him, seemingly unaware of the danger she was in. The lantern she held aloft cast a bright circle of light, but her face was hidden beneath the cowl of her gray wool cloak.

A young soldier with one empty sleeve pinned to the shoulder of his blood-stained uniform leapt directly in front of her shouting, *"Vive l'empereur!"* Without pausing in her stride, she pushed back the cowl, letting it fall to her shoulders, and stared the soldier straight in the eye. With a curse, he fell back, and Tristan exhaled the breath he'd been holding.

The light of a pale three-quarter moon filtered through the bare tree branches above, lending an unearthly beauty to Madelaine Harcourt's lustrous dark hair and graceful gray-clad form. Head high and eyes straight ahead, she looked every inch a nineteenth-century Jeanne d'Arc leading her troops to battle. Miraculously, the sullen crowd parted before her. A few of the men even crossed themselves as she passed.

With a sigh of relief, Tristan followed her around the corner of the garden wall with his creaking, wooden-wheeled barrow, and onto a narrow cobblestone street that appeared to be empty of demonstrators. They had won the moment; only time would tell if they won the day. Even now he could hear shouting in the distance and what sounded like gunfire—and a reddish glow in the night sky bore testimony to the fact that somewhere in the city buildings were being torched.

"It is only a short way now, monsieur," Madelaine Harcourt said. "You can see the church steeple ahead." Tristan gave a noncommittal grunt. Tightening his grip on the barrow handles, he concentrated on following the bobbing light of her lantern.

Suddenly, out of the corner of his eye, he saw a shadow detach itself from the wall and fall in behind him. Every nerve in his body instantly sprang to attention. He looked down to make certain his pistol was safely tucked into the waistband of his trousers; then, glancing over his shoulder, he found a small man with stringy black hair and a face like a worried ferret trailing behind him.

He took another look. "Devil take it, is that you Forli?" he asked, recognizing one of the Allies' top agents—a man nicknamed the Oil Merchant because he had gained entry into Bonaparte's household on Elba by selling olive oil to his mother and sisters. Tristan had worked with him earlier when Forli and he had both infiltrated Fouché's Ministry of Police in Paris.

Madelaine Harcourt stopped dead in her tracks. Wheeling around, she stared at him with wide, startled eyes. "Monsieur?"

Tristan brought the barrow to a halt. "It is all right, mademoiselle. Monsieur Forli is a . . . friend."

"A friend?" Her eyes narrowed, but she turned back without question and resumed walking toward their destination.

Tristan picked up the handles of the barrow. "What in God's name are you doing in Lyon?" he quietly asked the little man who had fallen into step beside him.

"I rode up from Grenoble to send a message to Paris via the semaphore relay warning King Louis and his cabinet that Bonaparte intends to enter the capital by March 20, the birthday of his infant son, the King of Rome. But alas, I was too late; the semaphore is already in the hands of the *grognards* and by morning, the city itself will fall."

Tristan cursed under his breath. The bizarre situation he found himself in was worsening by the minute. "I had heard the Corsican was moving fast; I had no idea he was moving that fast—and gathering support as he goes, if the crowds I've seen in Lyon are any example. So what now? Will you ride northward to the semaphore relay at Roanne?"

"Not I, milord. The climate of France grows too unhealthy. I was on my way south to my parents' home in Tuscany when I saw you ride into the city I changed my plans and followed you here. My curiosity was piqued as to what would bring the infamous British Fox to Lyon at this particular time."

Forli's dark gaze slid to the barrow Tristan was wheeling. "Dare I ask why you have become so lost to discretion you have taken to carting the evidence of your political activities about in a wheelbarrow?"

"This is not one of *my* bodies, you fool. I am merely helping a lady bury her grandfather."

"Ah, the statuesque Mademoiselle Harcourt. My associate here in Lyon tells me she and her grandfather are well known in Royalist circles."

Forli's beady black eyes gleamed suggestively. "A lovely creature, to be sure. Still, are you not being a bit foolish? Fouché's power as Minister of Police was diminished when the Corsican was banished to Elba, but now that the tide has again turned against the Bourbons, he will be up to his old tricks. Should you be recognized by one of his minions, your days would be numbered. He has sworn to revive Madame la Guillotine in your honor, as well as mine."

Tristan scowled at the little man trotting beside him. "I have heard Fouché's threat; he will have to catch me first." His gaze slid to Madelaine Harcourt's rigid back. Something about the tilt of her head told him she was straining to hear their conversation. "Keep your voice down," he warned. "The lady believes me merely an employee of her father, which in this case I am."

Forli nodded. "The very rich British merchant, Caleb Harcourt."

"You know Harcourt?"

"I have never met him personally, but I have sometimes gathered information for him when I was not busy spying for Castlereagh." Forli's voice held a note of bitterness. "I will say one thing for him; *he* pays his debts. I have yet to be paid by the British war office for my stint on Elba and doubt I ever will be now that Bonaparte has escaped—though God knows I warned them often enough that to put Colonel Neil Campbell in charge of the Corsican was like setting a mouse to guard a lion."

Tristan nodded his commiseration. He, too, had back pay coming, which he fully intended to collect when he returned to

London. Adjusting his grip on his macabre load, he followed Madelaine Harcourt into the courtyard of St. Bartholomew's.

Forli stopped outside the gate. "So now you, too, are in Harcourt's employ, milord. May I ask in what capacity?"

Tristan considered his answer carefully. He was loath to discuss his plans concerning Madelaine Harcourt; but he might need Forli's help. "Harcourt has decided to call his little bird back to the nest and he sent me to fetch her," he said finally.

"How wise! Without the old count to protect her, she would be easy prey for every unscrupulous roué in Lyon." Forli's lips parted in a travesty of a smile. "Farewell then. I wish I could be of help. I owe you. I shudder to think what my fate would have been had you not come to my aid during that fiasco in Paris three years ago."

He raised his hand in a brief salute. "Good luck, Monsieur le Renard. You will need it if you plan to cross France in the company of the lovely mademoiselle during these troubled times. I suspect Fouché would enjoy laying hands on the granddaughter of the arch Royalist, Le Comet de Navareil, almost as much as on the infamous British Fox."

Père Bertrand, who headed the clergy of St. Bartholomew's, insisted on reading the brief burial service for the count himself, something for which Madelaine was deeply grateful. If her grandfather was looking down from heaven, he would be pleased; the two old men had been like brothers.

Many's the time she'd listened to the story of how the good father had hidden her grandparents from the murderous *sans-culotte* during the Reign of Terror. More than three thousand Lyonnais were sent to the guillotine during that bloody year, and the count and countess would surely have been among them had they not found refuge in the very vault in which they were now both entombed.

"Your duty to your grandfather is finished, Madelaine; there is no more you can do for him," the elderly priest declared as she and the man called Tristan Thibault helped him up the stone steps that led from the vault to the nave.

"Then I shall leave to join my father in *Angleterre* as soon as I collect the few things I need to take with me," Madelaine promised the portly, white-haired cleric who had been a second grandfather to her.

But even as she moved toward the great oak door that led to the courtyard, it was thrown open by the odd-looking little man who had followed them to the church half an hour earlier. "The home of le Compte de Navareil has been looted and burned and the crowd is heading this way," he cried. "You must flee Lyon instantly, milord. Both you and Mademoiselle Harcourt are in terrible danger."

Madelaine's heart leapt into her throat. It couldn't be true. Not her home—not everything in the world she owned. She swallowed her rising panic. Not the miniature of her grandfather that was all she had left to remember him by. Too late, she realized she should have listened to Monsieur Thibault when he warned her to gather her belongings before they left the house.

Hot, bitter anger penetrated the fog of grief numbing her brain. Many of the men who had waited outside her grandfather's gate were longtime neighbors—neighbors who had hovered like hungry vultures waiting for the hapless prey to die. The same men who just days before had wished her a cheery good morning had now ransacked and burned her home in the dark of night—even threatened her very life.

Sick with pain, she heard Monsieur Thibault question his friend about her mare and his own horse, which he'd left in her grandfather's stable. "I saw them being led away by two rough-looking fellows just before they torched the house," Forli stated.

"Well, that is it, then. If we must travel by foot, we had best get started." Tristan Thibault grasped Madelaine's arm in his strong fingers, as if to propel her toward the door.

Father Bertrand raised a restraining hand. "Hold, monsieur. You are safe here as long as you stay inside the church. The mob will not enter the house of God. Not even in the worst days of the Terror did they go that far."

Forli nodded. "The good father is correct. Bonaparte has issued a decree protecting all clerics from harm at the hands of his followers—an obvious bid for the support of the church in his efforts to regain his throne."

Madelaine stared at the ornate window over the cleric's

head, Even through the stained glass, she could see the flames leaping from the roof of what had been her home for so many years. She felt choked with grief and despair. "I will not stay in Lyon if I must go into hiding to do so," she said bitterly.

Tristan Thibault nodded. "I, too, am anxious to leave, and Bonaparte's decree could be our ticket to Calais—if you will help us, Father."

Father Bertrand leaned wearily against one of the marble pillars supporting the vast nave of the church. "I will do anything in my power to help the *petite fille* of my old friend," he said gravely. "Still, I cannot like the idea of an innocent young woman of gentle birth traveling without a chaperone."

"I am afraid the times are too desperate to worry about propriety," Tristan Thibault declared in a voice sharpened by impatience. "But if it is any comfort to you, I guarantee I will guard the honor of my employer's daughter with my life."

The priest sighed. "I can ask no more. Take this grandchild of my old friend then, monsieur. Help her to find a new life in a land where the soil is not saturated with the blood of Frenchmen killed by Frenchmen. Tell me how I may help you."

"I shall need a priest's cassock—a large one—and a razor, if possible. Mine is in my saddlebag. Thank God, I kept my papers and money on my person." Thibault glanced at Madelaine. "And a shirt and trousers such as a young *paysan* might wear."

Father Bertrand's eyes widened. "You plan to travel as a priest and his acolyte? But is that not risky? What if you are found out?"

"I think that is less a risk than the one we would face traveling without a disguise." Tristan Thibault ran his fingers through his unruly black hair. "Thank heavens the priests of your order are not tonsured."

His silver eyes swept Madelaine with an assessing look that made her feel as if he could see into her very soul. "But we shall need a pair of shears nevertheless. I believe mademoiselle will make a very handsome boy once we bob her hair."

"Bob my hair?" Madelaine heard the shock in her own voice. Instinctively, she reached up to touch her one vanity— the dark brown, waist-length tresses that were coiled in a neat chignon at her nape. She had lost everything else; now this insensitive lout, who rejoiced that he need not shave his own head, was insisting she must chop off her crowning glory.

Tristan smiled to himself. The lady's gesture and her look of abject horror when he suggested cutting her hair were so feminine, so vain, so sweetly vulnerable, that he felt the first glimmer of hope for the success of his thankless mission. He'd almost begun to think he was transporting a bloody saint back to London to become his brother's wife—a fate worse than death for any man, to his way of thinking. But she was just an ordinary woman after all.

With Forli's help, he finally convinced her of the logic of his plan. Then, with Father Bertrand in the lead, they trooped into the rectory to do the deed. In tight-lipped resignation, Madelaine seated herself on the stool provided, removed the kerchief she'd worn on her head when she'd knelt at the chancel rail and then one by one the pins from her hair.

Tristan felt his breath catch in his throat as the gleaming silken mantle spread down her back to graze the curve of her slender hips. Suddenly the shears the priest's housekeeper had pressed into his hands felt like instruments of torture. He stared at them, nonplussed, unable to bring himself to use them to mutilate such beauty.

"I will cut it if you wish, milord," Forli said with an eagerness that raised Tristan's hackles. "My father is a barber; I know something of the trade." Prying the shears from Tristan's rigid fingers, he proceeded to whack off the lustrous tresses just below the lady's ears with a few swift strokes.

Tristan stared at Madelaine Harcourt's white face and tightly closed eyes, then at the mound of dark brown silk curled around the base of the stool and felt a terrible urge to throttle the little man who was busily snipping away at what was left of her once glorious head of hair.

"C'est fini!" Forli stepped back to admire his work as Madelaine Harcourt's eyes opened and instantly sought Tristan's, asking his opinion of the results. Coward that he was, he turned away, loath to face her lest she read the truth—that with her butchered hair jutting out in every direction, she looked remarkably like a porcupine about to throw its quills.

"Perfect," Forli declared, reaching for the pan of warm water he'd demanded earlier. Wetting his fingers thoroughly, he ruffled them through the spikey hair, then toweled it briskly with the square of rough linen provided by the housekeeper. As if by magic, the ugly spikes softened into a becoming cap of silken curls.

Forli grinned. "Voilà, milord. Your handsome boy!"

Tristan felt a smile creep across his face that was echoed by the priest and the housekeeper, and even Madelaine Harcourt lost a touch of her grimness when Forli handed her a mirror.

She ran her fingers through the soft curls framing her face. "My head feels so light," she said wonderingly. Her gaze lingered for one brief moment on the tresses at her feet; then she squared her shoulders and raised her chin in the same haughty gesture that had intimidated her Bonapartist neighbors. "It looks much better than I had anticipated. Perhaps playing the part of a boy will not be so unpleasant after all. *Je vous remercie*, Monsieur Forli."

Forli's gargoyle grin widened until it spread from ear to ear. "You are welcome, mademoiselle. But I feel I must warn you that if you wish to successfully impersonate a *paysan*, you will have to relinquish the more formal speech of the aristocracy in favor of the simple *merci* of the lower classes.

"A point well taken, monsieur," Madelaine said gravely, and with a dignity Tristan could not help but admire, she gathered up the homespun shirt and sturdy pants and jacket the housekeeper had found for her and retired to the adjoining room. A few minutes later she emerged, the picture of a handsome young *paysan*.

Tristan donned the cassock provided him, and slipped the accompanying chain and cross over his head and his pistol into his pocket. He looked up to find Forli watching him, a thoughtful frown puckering his brow. "What is wrong?" he asked, raising a quizzical eyebrow.

"Nothing is wrong ... exactly. But I must admit to having second thoughts about this disguise of yours. You might fool some men, but I doubt any woman who views you will be taken in. Yours are not the eyes of a priest, milord."

"And yours is not the mouth of a prudent man," Tristan said dryly, leveling a look on the diminutive Italian that had been known to reduce men twice his size to quivering blobs of blancmange.

Forli merely shrugged it off. "Ah well, the church has survived the Spanish Inquisition and the excesses of a Borgia pope; it will undoubtedly survive a priest with the eyes of Lucifer."

Tristan gritted his teeth. The little Italian's raillery over his "devil's eyes" was no worse than what he'd encountered time and again in the years since he'd been old enough to be noticed by the opposite sex. He'd grown accustomed to the stares and the giggles and the lewd comments his odd-colored eyes evoked. He'd even managed to live up to the reputation they'd earned him in both Paris and Vienna.

But Forli's timing was unfortunate if Madelaine Harcourt had taken note of it. Spending days—and nights—alone with his brother's bride-to-be would be awkward enough; it could become a nightmare if the lady got it in her head he was a threat to her virtue. He dared a glance in her direction and, to his relief, found her at the far end of the room, busy packing a knapsack with bread and cheese.

He turned back to Forli. "The success or failure of my disguise remains to be seen. At the moment, my first concern is a means of transportation."

Forli nodded. "I have the cabriolet and horse I rode up from Grenoble hidden in a grove of trees beyond La Croix Rousse where the Saône and Rhône rivers converge. They are yours to use, but the streets between here and there teem with Bonapartists."

"It is too bad you are strangers to Lyon and do not know the *traboules*," Father Bertrand lamented. "They are little used at night, and since one of them connects with the church, you could reach La Croix Rousse without setting foot on the streets."

Tristan scowled. "The *traboules*? What are they?"

"The network of covered alleyways, built in the fourteenth and fifteenth centuries, which honeycomb Lyon. They are the quickest and safest way to cross the city in troubled times, as many Royalists discovered during the Terror. But they can be very confusing. Even knowledgeable Lyonnais have been known to become hopelessly lost in them on occasion."

Madelaine Harcourt looked up from her task. "Have you forgotten that I, too, am involved in this journey?" She bestowed a look on the assembled men that proclaimed, "If you cannot handle this, leave it to me."

Tristan groaned. If he'd ever had any doubts she was Caleb Harcourt's daughter, that look dispelled them.

"I am well acquainted with the *traboules*," she said with quiet authority. "My grandfather taught me how to find my way through them in case the need ever arose. We visited La Croix Rousse many times to buy silk fabric directly from the weavers. I am certain I can find it again."

"There is the answer then." Father Bertrand positively beamed. "God works in mysterious ways. Madelaine will leave St. Bartholomew's by the same door through which her grandparents sought its sanctuary during the Terror."

With Madelaine's help, he hoisted his considerable bulk from the chair on which he'd sat while Forli cut her hair. "Follow me," he said, and led them to a small room at the back of the church which housed the robes and vestments used by the St. Bartholomew clergy. In the center of one wall stood a massive oak door framed by a stone archway. The housekeeper turned the iron key in the lock and opened the door.

Tristan took a deep breath, strapped the knapsack to his back, and stepped through the opening. Raising his lantern, he found himself in a narrow, covered walkway walled in by huge, square stone blocks. A draft of damp, chilly air brushed his face, and the faint, sour smell of mold filled his nostrils.

A shiver crawled his spine. He had always had an irrational dread of enclosed areas, and though he knew full well how he came by it, no amount of reasoning with himself had managed to dispel it. These ancient passageways might be the only safe route out of Lyon, but traversing them would be a living hell. He hoped to God he didn't disgrace himself in the process. Even now he could feel his palms beginning to sweat and his knees tremble.

Behind him, the good cleric removed his own ornate chain and cross and slipped it over Madelaine's head. "I doubt we shall meet again in this earthly life, granddaughter of my heart," he said gently, "but I shall pray for you always. God bless you and keep you, dear child."

Eyes glistening with unshed tears, Madelaine hugged her old friend, then stepped past the tall Englishman into the *tra-*

boule that had played such an important part in her family's history.

Holding her lantern before her, she led her two traveling companions down what seemed an interminable dark corridor and finally up a flight of stone stairs into a wide alleyway. Here the covered sections were separated by long stretches open to the moonlit sky, and the half wall was topped by a grillwork which cast eerie shadows over the walkway.

She watched Tristan Thibault lean against the grillwork and stare up at the open sky. He was breathing heavily and beads of perspiration dotted his forehead. Even in the sparse light of the latern she could see he was deathly pale.

"Are you ill, monsieur?" she asked, anxiously searching his face. Thibault's muttered answer sounded suspiciously like a curse and he gave her a look so coldly angry, she felt the blood freeze in her veins. Acutely embarrassed, she quickly turned away. Grandpère had always claimed Englishmen were a nasty-tempered lot; Monsieur Thibault proved the story true.

"Stay close to me," she warned. "Many *traboules* converge near here. You could become lost if we are separated."

Tristan Thibault instantly moved forward to walk close behind her. Too close. The heat from his body warmed her back, and every inch of her skin tingled with the awareness of his presence. She found the sensation decidedly unnerving.

It was not as if she were a green girl unaccustomed to men. She had been flattered and courted by every young Royalist in Lyon who hoped to ingratiate himself with her grandfather. They were French; they were charming; they were romantic; one in particular was as handsome as any hero of any novel she'd ever read—but not one of them had made her skin tingle.

How could she have such a disturbing reaction to a man who snarled at her if she asked a simple question—a man who, in the best of moods, resembled a bear with a thorn in its paw. It simply was not logical . . . unless she was so weakened by grief and exhaustion she was no longer capable of reacting in a rational manner. Of course, that must be the explanation. Her grandfather had been ill for so long, she couldn't even remember when she'd last had the luxury of a full night's sleep.

She was still pondering her dilemma when she realized

they'd arrived at the spot she'd been dreading—an open court-yard onto which six separate arched passageways converged. She had not been entirely honest when she'd claimed she knew her way around the *traboules*. It had been years since she'd walked them with her grandfather, and the memory was vague, to say the least. But the alternative—hiding in the church, trapped and helpless—had been unthinkable.

Frantically, she surveyed the six identical arches, aware she hadn't a clue which one led to La Croix Rousse. One wrong turn and they could be lost for hours or, worse yet, end up in one of the notorious *traboules mystèrieuses*, where it was ru-mored the Black Mass was regularly celebrated. Then she would be in trouble—in the company of a "priest" whom Monsieur Forli had rightly claimed looked like a reincarnation of *le diable* himself.

"I must get my bearings," she said, halting so suddenly Tris-tan Thibault plowed into her and Forli into him.

"Whoa!" he said, catching her around the waist as the colli-sion sent her tumbling forward. He released her immediately, but not before she felt the incredible strength in his arms and in his lean, hard body.

There it was again. That tingling sensation. She shuddered, aware how foolish she'd been to put her life in the hands of this powerful stranger simply because he purported to repre-sent her English father—and equally aware it was too late to worry about it now. Good or bad, she'd been dealt a hand; she had no choice but to play it out. Crossing her fingers for luck, she made a quick decision and headed for the third arch on her right.

Forli followed her into the dark passageway and reluctantly Tristan brought up the rear, praying it would lead to another of these open areas before his traitorous nerves betrayed him. With grim determination, he forced himself to put one foot be-fore the other and concentrate on what she was saying.

"The rear entrances of the apartments of Lyon's wealthiest citizens open onto these *traboules*. When I find the door to the one that once belonged to my grandfather, I shall know we are in the alleyway that eventually leads to La Croix Rousse."

Tristan raised his lantern and stared at the series of identical doors lining the walls of the alleyway. "How can you tell one from another?" he asked. "They all look alike to me."

"The door I seek carries a double coat of arms, that of the Medicis, who first built the apartment when they came to Lyon in the fifteenth century, and"—her voice carried unmistakable pride—"that of the noble family of Navareil, the owners for the past three hundred years." She paused. "Now, of course, it is inhabited by the Prefect of Lyon, a Bonapartist who was a pig farmer before the Revolution."

Tristan heard the note of disdain in her voice and for the first time began to understand Caleb Harcourt's obsession with marrying his daughter to a member of the English nobility. Like her mother, Madelaine Harcourt would be satisfied with nothing less. From the connotation she gave the term "pig farmer," it was obvious she felt nothing but contempt for the lower classes.

He smiled to himself. How it must gall this descendant of the French nobility to have to impersonate a member of the peasant class . . . and wouldn't her blue blood freeze in her veins if she knew the man who would be her constant companion for the next fortnight was the son of a Rookeries prostitute.

Poor Garth! Spending the rest of his life leg-shackled to this French social climber was a high price to pay for the blunt to save his title and estates. For the first time, it occurred to Tristan there were certain advantages to being the old earl's by-blow.

It also occurred to him that he derived an inordinate degree of satisfaction from finding fault with his future sister-in-law.

It did not, at the moment, occur to him to wonder why.

Three

No more than five minutes down the chosen passageway, Madelaine began to have serious doubts that it was the one that led past her grandfather's former apartment. For one thing, the doors looked too small and too close together to be the apartments of the rich. For another, the farther they progressed, the shabbier and more disreputable the area looked. Finally they reached a spot where foul-smelling debris littered the walkway and charcoal scribbles, many of them embarrassingly obscene, littered the walls.

She raised her hand to signal a halt. "I am afraid I have taken a wrong turn," she admitted apologetically. "We shall have to retrace our steps." Absolute silence greeted her admission. She waited, expecting a show of frustration, even anger from her two companions. Instead, Tristan Thibault stood motionless, his head raised like a hound taking scent, while Forli studied him with anxious eyes.

"There are people ahead of us," Thibault said. "I cannot tell how many. They are still a long way off, but they are moving swiftly and in our direction."

Madelaine held her breath, listening. "Are you certain? I hear nothing."

"Believe him," Forli said. "I can tell you from experience, milord has the hearing and the instincts of . . . a fox."

"We cannot afford a confrontation." Thibault's expression was grim. "We need a place to hide and so far we haven't passed so much as an indentation in the wall." He handed his lantern to Forli and reached for the one Madelaine held aloft. "Our only hope is to make it back to the central courtyard in time to slip into one of the other passageways." So saying, he transferred the lantern to his left hand and grasping Madelaine's hand in his right, took off on a run.

Madelaine's legs were long, the Englishman's longer, and he had a death grip on her nerveless fingers. Desperately, she plowed down the narrow *traboule* after him in her clumsy peasant's boots, praying he wouldn't pull her off her feet. By the time they reached the courtyard, her heart was pounding and her lungs crying for air. Without a moment's hesitation, he dove through the closest archway and sprinted down the dark passageway just far enough to be out of sight of anyone in the courtyard.

"Give me your jacket so I can cover the lantern," he demanded. Madelaine slipped the canvas jacket from her shoulders and handed it to him. Instantly, they were plunged into darkness and her heart leapt into her throat. Normally she had no fear of the dark, but the combination of the ancient *traboules* and this mysterious stranger set her nerves on edge.

"Wouldn't we be safer farther down the passageway?" she asked when she caught her breath.

"Possibly so, but I prefer to stay here."

Madelaine's eyes had adjusted to the dark and she could see his gaze was riveted on the moonlit courtyard through which they'd just passed as if his very life depended on keeping it in view—a useless precaution to her way of thinking. She tried again. "Are we not too close to the courtyard to escape unnoticed if whoever was behind us chooses to travel this *traboule*?"

"If you have any influence in high places, pray they don't."

Madelaine sniffed. "If I had such influence, monsieur, I would not be cowering here in the dark."

"Cowering? You, mademoiselle?" He gave a derisive snort. "I would pit you against a cage of hungry lions and wager my last shilling on the outcome—and my money would not be on the lions."

"Am I to take that as a compliment?"

His gaze remained steadfastly fixed on the courtyard. "You may take it any way you wish."

Madelaine chose to ignore it. She changed the subject rather than give the rude oaf the impression she cared in the least what he thought of her. With anxious eyes, she made her own study of the courtyard. "I see no sign of Monsieur Forli's lantern. I fear we have lost him."

"Don't worry about Forli. He can take care of himself."

Madelaine shivered, filled with alarm for the odd little Italian who had befriended them, and certain this callous *Anglais* would show the same lack of compassion if she had been the one to fall behind during their mad dash. He struck her as a man complete unto himself—needing no one, caring for no one. She found herself wondering if it was this cold aloofness that had made Monsieur Forli label him "The Fox."

The object of her ruminations gripped her upper arm with fingers of steel, startling her to instant attention. "What in holy hell is that?" he asked in a hoarse whisper.

She looked up to find a host of black-hooded figures, each carrying a candle, filing into the courtyard. At that same moment, the moon disappeared behind a cloud, leaving only the pinpoints of candlelight to outline the unearthly procession.

In silent, orderly formation, the ten or more shadowy apparitions circled the open area. Then, as if defying the moon's rejection of their diabolic order, one of them began to chant in some ancient guttural language, the likes of which Madelaine had never before heard. One by one, the others joined in an unholy harmony that sent chills skittering down her back.

"Nom de Dieu!" she gasped. "The rumors of the Black Mass are true."

"The Black Mass?" Tristan Thibault swore softly in gutter French. "Just what we need to make this fascinating evening complete."

For the first time since he'd barged into her life, Madelaine found herself in complete accord with her irascible traveling companion. Crossing herself, she held her breath until she saw the last of the sinister-looking figures disappear through an archway on the opposite side of the courtyard from where the two of them were hidden.

Not a muscle in the Englishman's big body moved, but his grip on her arm tightened noticeably and his breathing sounded heavy and labored. She felt a brief moment of triumph. So, this seemingly imperturbable Englishman did know the meaning of fear after all.

Moments later, the moon broke through the clouds to once again flood the courtyard with silvery light. The Englishman relaxed his punishing grip, uncovered the lantern, and held it aloft, his eyes still riveted on the open courtyard as if the patch of moonlit sky drew him like a magnet.

"Well that's that," he said in a voice devoid of expression. "What now, lady guide? Have you any idea where we are?"

Taking her cue from him, Madelaine pulled herself together and gazed about her, determined to hide the fear that still threatened to buckle her knees. "It is hard to tell from the light of a single lantern, but there is something about this passage-way that looks familiar," she answered in the same flat tone in which he had posed his question.

"Good. The sooner we find our way out of here, the better. But if you have any doubts, for God's sake, express them now. One wild goose-chase through these curst *traboules* is more than enough."

Madelaine stiffened. "I shall do my best to keep from incon-veniencing you further, monsieur." Crossing her fingers once again, she moved ahead of him down the passage. This one was wider and cleaner than the one they had previously tra-versed, and the doors lining it were more ornate and spaced farther apart.

With a sigh of relief, she spotted an alcove containing an ancient stone well and beyond it a narrow passage branching off the main one. If memory served her, the apartment that had been her grandfather's lay but a few feet beyond this intersec-tion.

"Here is the door I seek," she said, stopping to run her fin-gers over the two coats of arms. Just so, she had traced these carved emblems on her fourteenth birthday when her grandfa-ther first brought her to this spot to hear the history of the noble family from which she'd sprung.

She remembered well the bitterness in his voice when he'd explained, "I dare not take you to the front entrance, *ma petite fille*; we must stand here like fishmongers at the tradesman's door, while a peasant occupies what has belonged to the Navareils for centuries." Even now, years later, she felt choked with sorrow for the old man who had wasted a lifetime grieving for the wealth and privilege that had once been his.

With one last look at her family's coat of arms, she closed the door on her noble past and opened another on the unknown future to which this stern-faced Englishman was taking her. It occurred to her he had been amazingly patient with her, considering the perversity of his nature. First he'd helped her give her grandfather a proper burial at great danger to himself; now he waited in this dark *traboule* while she bid her sad good-bye to her life in Lyon. Perhaps he was not so lacking in compassion as he appeared.

"I am finished now," she said, a tiny portion of her heart warming toward this enigmatic stranger her father had appointed her protector. "I promise I will detain you no longer."

"And I promise I will remind you of that promise if you do." His biting sarcasm made it all too apparent he was neither patient nor compassionate, but merely bent on completing the onerous task her father had assigned him with the least possible trouble. For some reason she could not fathom, this surly Englishman's disapproval cut her to the quick. She found herself wondering what the going price was these days for delivering long-lost daughters to wealthy London merchants.

"How much farther must we go?" he asked in an oddly breathless voice a few moments later.

"I am not certain, monsieur. It has been a long time since I last visited the *traboules*."

"If you could bring yourself to walk a little faster, I would appreciate it," he said through gritted teeth.

"Faster, monsieur?" Startled by the intensity in his voice, Madelaine glanced behind her. He had that look again—the black one that made him appear positively demonic—and his fists were tightly clenched as if he were exerting every ounce of control he possessed to keep from doing her bodily harm.

"Faster, mademoiselle. I would like to retrieve Forli's horse and carriage before it goes the same way as my horse."

So that was what was bothering him. Because of her, his valuable horse had been stolen, and the loss to his pocketbook infuriated him. "Never fear, monsieur," she said scathingly, "I will make certain my father reimburses you for your loss."

"Loss? What loss?" he muttered, mopping his streaming brow.

She stared at him in amazement. Was the man mad? Or was he running a fever that addled his brain? Why else would he be bathed in perspiration when the cold dampness of the *traboules* chilled her to the bone?

With the grim-faced Englishman hard on her heels, she forced herself to sprint the remaining quarter of a mile to the entrance of La Croix Rousse. "Here we are," she said breathlessly. "We have only to cross through this district and we will reach the confluence of the Saône and Rhône rivers where Monsieur Forli said his horse and carriage were hidden."

"Thank God," Tristan Thibault murmured, staring at the sky above him with a rapt expression in his strange, pale eyes. Here the walls of the buildings bordering the narrow alley were two stories high, but the passageway itself was uncovered. He leaned against the nearby wall, taking in great, gulping breaths of air, as if their short sprint had left his lungs totally depleted. For a man who appeared so strong, he was certainly in terrible condition.

Madelaine pressed her finger to her lips, cautioning him to silence. Once again she covered the lantern with her jacket, but this time the waning moon and the light pouring from the many open doors lining the alleyway dispelled the darkness. She took a deep breath. The air was heavy with the waxy smoke of dozens of guttering candles and an odd, musty smell she remembered her grandfather telling her emanated from the bolts of fabric waiting to be delivered to the shops of the silk merchants for which Lyon was famous.

Tristan Thibault touched her shoulder. "That noise? What is it?" he whispered.

Madelaine listened to the familiar click, clack, bang . . . click, clack bang. "The *canuts*—silk weavers—at work," she whispered back. "Every household in the district has its own *bistanclaque*. The family members take turns weaving and sleeping in the lofts above, so the looms are never silent."

She frowned. "Weaving is hot work. The doors of the *canuts'* apartments are rarely closed. We will have to pass dozens of open doorways to reach our destination. I pray we can do so without being seen."

"I take it these *canuts* are Bonapartists."

"To a man, though apparently not even the return of the emperor can lure them from their *bistanclaques*. Still, it is well known they hate the old aristocracy and anyone connected with it. They would turn us over to the *grognards* without a qualm if they suspected our true identities—or mine, any-way—and I cannot think how we would explain a priest and his acolyte wandering the *traboules* in the dead of night. We will not be safe until we put La Croix Rousse behind us."

Tristan paid but token heed to Madelaine Harcourt's dire warning. In truth, he felt almost giddy with relief that he'd managed to keep from turning into a babbling idiot back in those godawful *traboules*, and even more relieved that the bal-ance of their journey could be accomplished under the open sky.

Shifting the knapsack to a more comfortable position, he prepared to follow her down the shadowed alleyway, but not before he caught a glimpse of the first candlelit loom and the nocturnal weaver who labored at it.

Click, clack, bang . . . click, clack, bang. Over and over the white-haired *canut* threw his shuttle—as intent on his work as Rumpelstiltskin, the evil dwarf of the German folktale Tristan had learned as a child at Lady Ursula's knee. Never again would he wear a silk shirt without remembering the eerie sight.

Past one open doorway after another, his slender, boyish-looking guide slipped, as silent as the shadows that concealed her. Past one open doorway after another, Tristan followed her, careful to keep the flickering candle within the lantern hidden from view beneath her jacket.

He had just begun to congratulate himself on making it through this den of Bonapartists without mishap when they came to an area where two huge rolling carts laden with hun-dreds of ells of silk fabric blocked the passageway outside one of the apartments.

There was nothing for it but to move one of the carts enough to give them room to squeeze past the doorway. Hand-ing over the lantern, Tristan bent his shoulder to the task. For-tunately, the cart rolled easily despite its size; unfortunately, the ancient wooden wheels creaked loudly in protest.

The stocky, middle-aged *canut* instantly stilled his spindle and looked up from his loom, staring molelike into the dark-ened alley. Madelaine Harcourt flattened herself against the stone wall, her eyes wide with terror in the shifting shadows, and Tristan drew his pistol, fervently praying he wouldn't be forced to use it.

A terrible, waiting silence ensued. Tristan could see the horror etched on his young companion's face as she stared at the lethal weapon in his hand, could sense her quick intake of breath when he cocked it and raised it to the ready. Then, just when his nerves were stretched to the breaking point, the weaver gave a typical Gallic shrug and returned to his work—and the two fugitives slipped silently past his doorway and continued their flight to safety.

"One more potential disaster circumvented," Tristan whispered, returning the pepperbox pistol to the pocket of his cassock. Madelaine Harcourt didn't answer him—didn't so much as glance his way—and a new weariness engulfed Tristan, born of the knowledge that she now found him more fearful than the enemy they were trying to elude.

He was in no mood to pacify a squeamish female. He had been awake since dawn and it must be near that hour again. His head was pounding, his feet dragging, and the hellish trip through the *traboules* had sorely tested his belief in his own manhood.

To add to his dilemma, much as he hated to admit it, his admiration for the young woman in his care was growing by leaps and bounds. In the past few hours, she had lost everything in life she held dear. Any other female he knew would have been utterly devastated by the tragedies she had faced. Instead she seemed to gain in courage and stamina with every passing minute—two qualities he himself had been hard put to equal. In truth, he was beginning to wonder who was rescuing whom in this bizarre partnership they'd formed.

At long last they left the lofts of the silk weavers behind and found themselves standing on the bank of the Saône River just as the first pink-hued rays of the rising sun tinged the horizon. The acrid smell of smoke filled Tristan's nostrils. Behind him, the sky glowed red from the fires consuming the homes of Lyon's few remaining Royalists; before him lay the grove of trees, just as Forli had described it.

As he listened, a cheer rose from hundreds of throats. He heard snatches of the Marseillaise and the voices of men chanting names like Friedland, Marengo, Austerlitz, and other battles fought in the name of the emperor, and he knew that, as predicted, Lyon had fallen to General Cambronne's *grognards.*

Madelaine Harcourt covered her eyes in a gesture of despair. Instinctively, he reached out to her, offering the meager comfort of one stranger to another. "Unless my eyes deceive me, Forli's horse and carriage await us in the grove yonder," he said to divert her attention from the happenings in the city.

She lowered her hands and raised her head to gaze where he directed. At the same moment, a lone figure detached itself from a stand of trees across the river and waved in their direction. Tristan pointed him out to the woman beside him. "It's Forli, and devil take it, what is that he's leading? A donkey?"

"Stolen no doubt." Madelaine Harcourt managed a ghost of a smile. "You were right, monsieur. I need not have worried about your little friend. But how will he join us when he is on the other side of the river?"

"He won't. We are heading north to Paris and eventually Calais. He is going south to Tuscany."

"There will just be the two of us from now on?"

Tristan nodded. "Just the two of us."

She stared at him with wary, amber eyes that dominated her pale, exhausted face. As he watched, she swayed on her feet like a willow caught in a high wind.

"Hold on, Maddy," he exclaimed, slipping his arm around her waist. Half lifting, half dragging her, he strode forward into the trees to the waiting cabriolet.

"Maddy," she echoed, rubbing her eyes like a sleepy child. "You called me Maddy. No one has called me that in fifteen years. No one except my father has ever called me that."

Tristan smiled. "It is what I shall call you from now on. Since it is not a name any Frenchman would have heard, it could just as well be that of a boy as a girl." He busied himself blowing out the candle and stowing the lantern behind the seat. "And much as it may gall you, you'd best begin calling me Father Tristan if we're to carry off this disguise."

She leaned against the side of the carriage. "I should call you what?" Her voice slurred and her head dropped forward as if her neck was too fragile to hold it up.

Tristan caught her before she could fall. She felt boneless

and fragile in his arms and not at all like the young boy she was pretending to be.

"Father Tristan," he repeated, placing her gently on the seat of the cabriolet. He watched her curl her long legs beneath her and rest her pale cheek against the black leather seat cushion. "Did you hear me, Maddy?"

She didn't answer. Her eyes were closed, her mouth softly open, her breath slow and deep. His stalwart young traveling companion was sound asleep.

Maddy dreamed of running through endless dark *traboules*, chased by a black-haired man with strange, pale eyes who threatened her with a shining silver pistol . . . and woke to find herself curled up on the seat of a carriage which was lumbering along a country road. The top was down, the sun warm on her face, and, good heavens, her head was on the shoulder of the very man who had dominated her nightmare.

She sat up abruptly, planted her feet firmly on the floorboard, and looked about her. "*Nom de Dieu*, where are we?"

"On the road to Roanne. Well on the road, I might add. You have been sleeping for hours." The Englishman looked more than ever a minion of the devil with his unruly black hair tossed by the wind and a day's growth of beard darkening his lean face.

He turned his head and studied her with eyes that made a mockery of the priest's cassock covering his powerful body. "Tell me, Maddy, how are you as a whip?"

"A whip? I do not know the term, monsieur."

"Can you handle the reins? We are still too close to Lyon to risk stopping, but I am badly in need of sleep."

Madelaine stared at him, aghast. "I have never 'handled the reins,' monsieur. It is not a skill a lady of my station would be expected to learn."

"Maybe not in Lyon, but it's all the crack in London." He shrugged. "Well, no time like the present to learn. This old dobbin Forli provided us with is docile as a milk cow."

He passed her the reins. "It's simple really. Pull on the right rein if you want him to go right; pull on the left if you want him to go left. Pull on both and say 'whoa' if you want him to stop."

Without further ado, he slumped down in the seat beside her, closed his eyes, and promptly fell asleep.

Heart pounding, Maddy grasped the reins. Fortunately, the road ahead was straight as a lance, and the horse plodded forward down the center of it with little or no guidance from her.

By the end of the first mile, she'd come to the conclusion Monsieur Thibault had spoken the truth: handling the reins for the old dobbin required nothing more than a firm hand and a bit of common sense. By the end of the next mile, she even felt confident enough to relax her hold and let the blood flow back into her cramped fingers.

A serious mistake. A small brown hare chose that very instant to hop onto the road directly in the path of the dobbin's hooves. With a startled cry, Madelaine yanked on the reins. The old horse stopped dead in its tracks, and Monsieur le Lapin, having safely reached his destination, wriggled his nose indignantly, as if to say, "Did you think a strong, young hare could not outrun a plodding old dobbin?" Then, with a final twitch of his floppy ears, he disappeared into the hedgerow.

She could tell by the way the old dobbin snorted, he was not the least bit happy about the rough way she'd handled his reins. "I am sorry, Monsieur le Cheval," she said contritely. "I am new at this business. I did not mean to yank your teeth from your mouth, and I swear it will never happen again. You may proceed on your way now."

The horse stood rooted to the spot.

Madelaine tried coaxing in the sweetest voice she could manage, "S'il vous plaît, Monsieur le Cheval, it would be wise to keep moving with the Corsican so close behind us."

The horse snorted and flicked his ears, but his hooves remained firmly planted.

Though she felt certain the old dobbin was of French origin, she tried coaxing in English and Italian, even German, just in case.

Nothing happened.

It was obvious the stubborn nag would never move a muscle until she gave him the proper signal. But the stupid Englishman had only told her how to stop a horse, not how to make it start again.

Finally, in desperation, she shook the shoulder of the man

who dozed so peacefully beside her. "Wake up, monsieur," she cried. "I have need of you."

His eyes remained closed. But to her surprise, he reached up, caught her fingers and brought them to his lips, then turned her hand and flicked his tongue across the soft flesh of her palm, sending frissons of heat racing clear to her toes. "Go back to sleep, *chérie*," he purred deep in his throat. "I will satisfy your need in the morning."

Madelaine snatched her hand from his. He was dreaming about a woman. Undoubtedly his wife, since he thought they were sleeping together. Her face flamed. And even an innocent could guess what need it was he thought she was asking him to fill.

Unconsciously, she rubbed the spot on her palm, which still tingled from the touch of his tongue. It had never occurred to her that this Englishman with his devil eyes and temper to match might have a wife waiting for him back in London.

She wondered what kind of woman would put up with the miserable crosspatch.

She wondered what kind of woman such a care-for-nothing man would find so desirable, he would take her to wife.

She wondered what kind of magic that woman must know to turn the snarling tiger into a purring pussycat.

Four

With maddening persistence, the ceaseless clip-clop of the dobbin's hooves punctured Tristan's haze of exhaustion. Even half asleep, he could tell the carriage was moving much too slowly. What was the fool woman thinking of, meandering along this French country road at such a pace with Bonaparte and his *grognards* but a few miles behind?

He turned his head and tentatively opened one eye. The seat beside him was empty, the reins looped over the frame of the carriage. Then why was the carriage moving? Instantly alert, he shot upright and found himself staring at the back of Maddy's cropped curls as she walked beside the plodding horse, her hand on the bit.

"Hell and damnation, what are you doing?" he shouted.

She stopped in her tracks. "I should think that would be obvious," she said, her voice sharp with indignation. "I am leading this miserable beast because once he stopped, he refused to start again unless I gave him the magic signal—which you neglected to tell me."

"You couldn't figure out how to flick the reins and say 'giddyap'?" He raised a hand to forestall the angry reply he could see forming on her lips. "I know. I know. A woman of your station is not expected to learn the language of a coachman."

"Get back in the carriage," he ordered impatiently. "We need to put some distance between the Corsican and ourselves before this day grows any older." He watched her settle onto the seat and unconsciously smooth the rough fabric of her trousers over her knees as if it were the skirt she usually wore. It would take more than short hair and long trousers to conceal Madelaine Harcourt's femininity. When she was in a better mood, he would remind her of that fact.

"I don't suppose you'd care to explain why you issued the 'magic signal' that brought the horse to a stop in the first place?" He flicked the reins to start the old dobbin off at a brisk trot.

"No."

He could see she was embarrassed, and in spite of himself, he felt a smile crease his lips. "I thought not. It would be interesting, however, to learn why you considered walking preferable to waking me."

Two bright spots of color bloomed in her pale cheeks. "I tried, but you would not wake. You were dreaming." She glanced about as if to ascertain she could not be overheard. "Apparently about your wife."

"My wife?" Tristan's normal baritone voice rose to a stunned tenor. "What in God's name made you think I had a wife?"

Her color deepened until her cheeks positively flamed. "You were talking in your sleep. Naturally I assumed the woman you were addressing with such . . . such intimacy must be your wife."

Now it was Tristan's turn to be chagrined. He wondered what he'd been dreaming and of whom—and what he could have said that she found so shocking. With a sinking feeling, he recalled some of the erotic pillow talk that Minette, his longtime mistress in Paris, had found so stimulating. Surely he hadn't jabbered that sort of foolishness.

"I am not married," he said tersely, and let her draw her own conclusions—which he could see she did, from the stiff, disapproving set of her mouth. Devil take it, let the prissy creature make of it what she wished. He was used to dealing with women of experience, not innocent young females who took umbrage at everything a man said, even if he was asleep when he said it.

They rode in strained silence for the next hour, neither willing to be the first to speak, until Tristan belatedly realized the dobbin was long overdue for a rest. "This old fellow needs water and sustenance, and so do we," he said curtly. "I, for one, cannot remember my last meal."

He brought the carriage to a stop at the edge of a small apple orchard bordering a shallow stream. Quickly, he stepped down, adjusted the annoying cassock that had twisted around his long legs, and released the horse from its harness. "I'll lead him down to the water if you'll be good enough to carry the knapsack," he called over his shoulder.

Maddy didn't deign to answer him, but by the time he'd finished watering the horse, she had spread out the carriage blanket on the bank of the stream and laid out a loaf of bread and two wedges of cheese.

The warm spring sun was at its zenith and a gentle, blossom-scented breeze rippled the shallow, crystalline water of the stream. It was a perfect day for a picnic—a day that brought back to Tristan memories of similar outings at Winterhaven in years past. But then there had been laughter and chatter, sometimes even a song or two, with Lady Sarah accompanying them on her guitar.

He and Maddy ate in absolute silence, the only sound the whisper of the breeze through the branches above them and the scolding of a pair of robins diverted from the construction of their nest by the intruding humans. The peace of this lovely spot seemed so removed from the tumult and chaos of Lyon, Tristan had to remind himself they dared not dawdle any longer than the time it took the ancient dobbin to recuperate.

Replete, he stretched out on the damp, sweet-smelling grass, his hands behind his head. His companion remained as she was, her back ramrod-straight, her face averted, gazing across the open stretch of meadow.

Wearily, he studied her unyielding profile. "If there is something bothering you, Maddy, we'd best talk about it now when there's no one to hear a conversation ill-suited to a priest and his assistant. We have a long journey ahead of us. It will be difficult enough without the added problem of a misunderstanding based on something as silly as a dream I cannot even remember."

She turned her head and regarded him through narrowed eyes. "Your erotic dreams are of no consequence to me, *Father Tristan*, regardless of whom they may be about. They merely reinforce my opinion of men in general."

"Which apparently is rather low." Tristan plucked a blade of grass and chewed it thoughtfully. "How can I defend myself when I have no idea what I said that so offended your innocent ears? I can only say that while I have never purported to be a saint, neither am I the devil I've been told I so closely resemble. I pose no threat to your virtue, Maddy, if that is what worries you."

"What worries me, monsieur, is that all men are such devious creatures. The only thing I know for certain about them is that they are never what they appear to be." Her voice held an unmistakable bitterness. "How can I trust what you or any other man tells me when it turns out my own grandfather has been lying to me about my father for the past fifteen years!"

So that was what had started all this. Tristan felt a twinge of annoyance. Why was it women always circled an issue like hawks circling their prey before they finally got around to the crux of the problem. She had brushed off the old man's deathbed confession with such apparent ease, Tristan had been fooled into thinking it scarcely registered with her. He could see now her grandfather's perfidy had wounded her deeply.

"Even a total stranger could see le Comte de Navareil was a frightened old man who held on to the one person he loved in the only way he knew how," he said gently. "That does not make what he did right. But frightened men, and I dare say women, too, are often driven to do things they are not proud of."

She raised her chin in that arrogant manner he'd begun to suspect was her way of concealing her inner feelings. "So now, after fifteen years without a single word from him, I am to believe my father has cared about me all this time? That is asking a great deal, monsieur."

"I have met Caleb Harcourt but once, when my brother, the Fifth Earl of Rand, and I called on him at his office on the London docks. I can tell you little about him except that he appeared genuinely anxious to have you returned to him—so much so he was willing to go to unbelievable lengths to accomplish it." Tristan felt a stab of guilt at neglecting to mention the most important part of that fateful meeting, but a promise was a promise, and Harcourt had sworn him to secrecy about his plan to marry her to Garth as soon as she set foot in London.

"What unbelievable lengths, mon . . . Father Tristan?"

"Tristan will do when we're alone—and that is a question only your father can answer."

"Very well, then answer me this, if you will. Why would an English lord be willing to risk his life to return a merchant's daughter to him? My mother told me in what vast contempt the titled aristocrats of *Angleterre* hold the men of the merchant class."

He had not meant to divulge anything about himself or about why he had been sent to retrieve her. She would learn such truths soon enough once they reached London. But with those solemn amber eyes fixed on him, he couldn't bring himself to lie to her.

He pushed himself to a sitting position facing her. "To begin with, your father is not an ordinary merchant; he is one of the wealthiest men in all of England."

"My father is paying you then." She stared down her nose at him in that arrogant way of hers. "I hope, for your sake, he is paying you well"

"I am not being paid," Tristan said, barely managing to suppress his anger at her sarcasm. "I undertook the task of delivering you to your father because he helped my brother out of a difficult situation."

"Your brother, the Fifth Earl of Rand, I take it. He must have gotten himself into a very difficult situation indeed for an English lord to risk traveling across France in such troubled times as these simply to repay the debt owed a wealthy merchant."

Damn the woman. Why couldn't she leave well enough alone? "I am not a lord of the realm," he said in frozen accents. "I am merely the bastard son of the Fourth Earl of Rand. But the countess is a generous-hearted woman who raised me as her own, and my half brother and sister accepted me without question—a rare thing in the environs of the British *ton*. There is nothing I would not do for them. Does that answer your question?"

She shook her head. "Not entirely. You have told me your reasons for undertaking the mission, but you have not explained why my father felt you were qualified to do so."

The lady was too astute for comfort. She was not to be fobbed off with half truths. Hell and damnation! He might as well be honest with her. It was obvious she had no intention of giving up until she'd pestered it out of him. With a muttered curse, he threw caution to the winds. "Who better than an agent of the British Foreign Office who has lived the last six years in Paris posing as a Frenchman?"

"You spied against France during the war?"

"Not against France. Against the greedy Corsican who threatened to destroy all of Europe. Surely, as a loyal Royalist, you can see the difference."

"I fear the distinction would have been more apparent to my grandfather," she said coldly. "He could condone anything that furthered the cause of the Bourbons."

"But I take it you cannot." A hot spurt of anger surged through Tristan at being judged by this prissy French baggage. "I thought all you Royalists were loyal followers of the king," he sneered.

She shrugged. "I very much doubt that King Louis cares any less about his own welfare or any more about that of his subjects than does the emperor."

"Well, at least we agree on one thing." He found himself amazed that a young woman with her restrictive upbringing should be such an independent thinker.

Maddy leaned back against the trunk of the tree beneath which she sat and studied him with unnerving intensity. "Then why did you spy against Bonaparte?"

"Certainly not to put Louis the Eighteenth on the throne of France. I have great respect for both Wellington and Castlereagh, but we part company when it comes to who should govern France. After six years of living among ordinary hard-working Frenchmen, I am painfully aware of their deep and abiding hatred of the Bourbons."

"Which is all well and good, but you still have not answered my question. Why did you become a spy?"

Tristan fixed his gaze on the bank of dirty gray clouds gathering on the horizon and pondered how to answer her question without giving her an even greater disgust of him than she already had. He did, after all, have to spend the next fortnight as her traveling companion—and barring a miracle, the rest of his life as her brother-in-law.

"The fate of England was at stake," he said finally. "It was the only way I could use the brains God gave me to serve my country. My brother, Garth, bought his colors in the Fifth Northumberland Fusiliers. That option was closed to me; the British officer corps does not look kindly on bastards. Had I chosen the military, I would have been relegated to the ranks of the common foot soldier, and my patriotism did not extend to providing mindless fodder for French cannons."

Maddy sensed the barely leashed anger inside this dark, intense man—anger at the injustices heaped upon him because he was born on the wrong side of the blanket. Logic warned her that an angry man was a dangerous man. By the same logic, she should be trembling with fear at the thought of spending an hour alone with Tristan Thibault, much less twenty-four hours a day for the next fortnight. Instead, she felt a strange, inexplicable exhilaration.

She had never before met a man who admitted to being a spy, and she was bursting with questions she longed to ask him. She settled for, "So that is why Monsieur Forli called you the British Fox. It is your code name."

"*Was* my code name. I retired from my unsavory profession once Bonaparte was dispatched to Elba. This past year I have served on Lord Wellington's staff in Paris and as Lord Castlereagh's aide at the Congress of Vienna." He frowned. "And that is something, which at present I heartily regret. My face and reputation are known to too many Bonapartists in prominent places, including the infamous Citizen Fouché, who has sworn to have my head. I fear your father could have made a wiser choice of escorts for you."

Wiser perhaps, Maddy thought, but not nearly as exciting. Tristan Thibault might be moody and bad-tempered most of the time, but she doubted he would ever bore her—something every other man she had known had managed to do within half an hour of meeting him. She smiled. "It seems we have something else in common beside a distrust of the Bourbons. Fouché was a sworn enemy of my grandfather and I have probably inherited his hatred."

Tristan frowned. "All the more reason why we should put France behind us with all possible haste." Tossing aside his blade of grass, he rose to his feet. With a curse for the cassock that once again tangled about his legs, he strode the few steps to the grazing dobbin.

"Hurry up and get in the carriage," he demanded in a voice sharp with impatience as he slipped the harness over the horse's head. "We have tarried here far too long thanks to your everlasting questions. We need to put some miles behind us before we're forced to take shelter from that storm gathering in the north."

She could see he was regretting having confided so much about his colorful past and angry with himself for letting her nag him into doing so. His black brows drew together in a scowl fierce enough to send anyone in his path scampering in fright.

Anyone but her, that is. After fifteen years with her grandfather, she defied anyone, including this contentious Englishman, to try to intimidate her with a fit of temper.

At her own pace, she wrapped the remaining bread and cheese in the huckaback toweling Father Bertrand's housekeeper had provided. At her own pace, she walked to the carriage and settled herself beside her companion. "You may proceed now, Father Tristan," she said calmly and earned herself a muttered obscenity that could have curled the tail of a Paris gutter rat.

She merely folded her hands in her lap and ignored him. If she had learned anything while living with Grandpère, it was that one should always begin a new connection one meant to go on.

Tristan wasn't certain exactly how he had expected Maddy to react to his confessions of his illegitimacy and his former profession, but her calm acceptance caught him by surprise. She neither questioned him further nor commented on what he had already divulged. In truth, she said no more than a dozen words for the balance of the long afternoon. Still, the silence that stretched between them was oddly companionable, almost as if they were old friends rather than merely two strangers thrown together by a whim of fate.

For the first two hours after their stop they traveled through orchard country. Mile upon mile of glorious pink apple blossoms and snowy plum blossoms lined both sides of the narrow road, and with the rising wind whipping through the trees, the carriage was soon awash with their silken petals. He watched them settle onto Maddy's dark curls and smiled to himself at his fanciful turn of thought when he likened them to tiny pink and white butterflies.

Eventually, the orchards gave way to lush, green meadows dotted with grazing sheep that reminded him all too keenly of the small holding in Suffolk that Garth had once promised him. He doubted it would ever be his now. With Caleb Harcourt holding the purse strings, Garth would be in no position to be so generous to his illegitimate brother.

One of the fields was being plowed for spring planting, and the peasant farmer removed his hat and bowed as their carriage approached. "You must make the sign of the cross, Father," Maddy whispered. "He expects you to bless his planting." Tristan dutifully signed, relieved that his disguise seemed authentic enough to fool a believer, then crossed himself again for good measure. He was not a superstitious man, but he winged a silent apology to the papist God for his heresy just in case.

With each mile they traveled northward, the clouds grew darker and the wind stronger until at dusk Tristan felt the first drops of rain spatter against his cheeks. Night would soon be upon them. He was tired and hungry and though she made no complaint, Maddy looked near exhaustion. But search as he might, he could see no sign of an inn or posting house ahead.

Within moments, the rain started coming down in earnest and driven by the wind, pricked Tristan's face like hundreds of needles. Maddy's curls were soon plastered to her head and water dripped off her chin. Her coarse peasant's shirt clung to her in places that plainly revealed she was anything but the boy she pretended to be, and Tristan's reaction to the bewitching sight was most definitely not that of a priest. As much in self-defense as concern for her, he pulled her jacket from beneath the seat and wrapped it around her shoulders.

"We're going to have to find shelter," he said quickly to hide his frustration. Moments later he pointed to a group of farm buildings on the distant horizon. "It will be dark by the time we reach there. We should be able to sleep in the barn with no one the wiser if we rise before dawn."

"Sleep in the barn?" Maddy blinked. He expected her to spend the night alone with him in a hayloft? She doubted that even a parent as careless as her father would condone such sleeping arrangements. She gave him a quelling look. "For the sake of propriety, if nothing else, I believe we should find a respectable inn, monsieur."

"I can think of nothing I'd like better than a comfortable featherbed and a hot meal," he agreed. "If you can guarantee we shall find such accommodations within the next mile, which I gauge to be our trusty steed's limit of endurance, I shall gladly seek it out."

"You know very well I cannot."

He shrugged. "Then I am afraid you will have to be content with a pile of straw and another meal of bread and cheese."

As he'd predicted, darkness had fallen by the time they pulled into the barnyard of the neat little farm. A glimmer of candlelight shone through the narrow windows of the small stone farmhouse, but the sturdy stone and timber barn stood far enough from the house to ensure no one would be aware of their furtive arrival.

Tristan guided the old dobbin to a sheltered spot beneath the eaves of the barn, released it from the carriage and tied it to a handy hitching post. "Rest, old fellow; you've earned it," he said, and promising to return later with water and feed, opened the barn door and stepped aside to let Maddy enter ahead of him.

Closing the door behind them, he struck one of the flints Father Bertrand's housekeeper had provided and lit the lantern he'd carried in from the carriage. To his relief, the barn was as clean and tidy as the rest of the farm. Every tool was hung in place, every animal bedded down for the night; even the barn cat and her litter of kittens were settled in a basket just inside the door.

Bales of newly mown hay and burlap sacks filled with grain were stacked between the center posts, and two milk cows and a huge, gray draft horse that whinnied his annoyance at their entrance occupied three of the animal stalls. The fourth was empty, but fresh straw had been spread on the dirt floor.

Tristan breathed in the pungent odor of warm animal bodies and fresh manure, and memories surfaced of a long-ago night when Garth and he had stolen from their beds to watch the birth of a spring foal in the Winterhaven stables.

Long after the foal had stood on its wobbly legs and searched out its mother's tit, the two of them had lain side by side in the loft and told each other their dreams of the future. Even then Garth had dreamed of Sarah and the life they would one day share at Winterhaven.

What strange, unexpected twists their fates had taken, and how few of the dreams they had shared would ever come true. For now Maddy Harcourt, not Sarah Summerhill, would be Garth's wife and the mother of his children, and it was love of Winterhaven, not a woman, that would lead him to the altar.

Tristan lowered his gaze to the young woman who knelt beside the purring tabby, cuddling one of the kittens. Her teeth were chattering, but not a word of complaint did she utter. Whatever else she might be, Maddy Harcourt was a woman of spirit; she would not disgrace the title of Countess of Rand. To his surprise, he found himself hoping she would even find some happiness in the marriage her father had purchased for her.

But Maddy Harcourt's happiness was not *his* problem. It was Garth who was destined to wed her, and while he could not rejoice in the union, Tristan had vowed to carry out his part of the plan to save the Ramsdens' estates. It was the least he could do, considering all he owed them.

In the meantime, he intended to put the best possible face on a situation he could see was utterly bewildering to his young companion. "It's a fine barn," he said with a cheerfulness that sounded false even to his own ears. "We could do worse for a night's lodging."

He raised his eyes to search out the loft, and breathed a sigh of relief. There was plenty of room between it and the ceiling of the barn; he'd not feel dangerously confined. "It has been years since I've bedded down in fresh, clean straw," he continued on the same cheerful note. "No inn on earth can provide a finer bed than that." He eyed the row of covered buckets lining a sturdy shelf at the far end of the barn. "And there is no finer drink than milk fresh from a cow."

Maddy managed a smile, but she looked drawn and pale and her huge eyes seemed to swallow her fine-boned face. Tristan ruffled her damp curls, as if she truly were his young *paysan* companion. "Cheer up, *mon petit garçon*," he teased. "The gods have smiled on us. Tonight we shall live like kings."

Long after Tristan had extinguished the lantern, Maddy lay wide awake, clutching the heavy cross Father Bertrand had given her. The storm that had been threatening all afternoon had struck with a vengeance shortly before they'd climbed the ladder to bed down in the fragrant straw. Rain pelted the roof above her head with the steady rat-a-tat of a thousand pebbles plunging from the heavens and the wind howled around the corners of the snug little barn like a ravaging wolf. Never in her entire life had she felt so frighteningly lost and alone.

Not that the man sleeping beside her had been anything but gentlemanly. But there was something so impersonal about his treatment of her, she felt very much like the old dobbin he had led into the empty stall—just another creature he must tend to before he could eat his meager supper and retire for the night.

He had even rubbed them both down with the rough-textured grain sacks he'd found folded on a shelf. First the dobbin, then her, explaining as he briskly rubbed her back and shoulders that it was the best he could do since they couldn't remove their wet clothing.

Then he'd handed her a sack so she could do the same for him. He might have considered the procedure as impersonal as currying a horse. For her, it was the most personal thing she had ever done. She still trembled, remembering the feel of hard bone and rippling muscles beneath her hands. She had never really touched a man before, except Grandpère when she'd nursed him through his final illness. She hadn't realized how different a young man's strong, healthy body felt from that of a sick old man.

Grandpère. Just thinking about him brought a new wave of desolation. He had been selfish, irascible, demanding; he had even lied to her when it suited his purposes. But in his own way, he had loved her and needed her. Now there was no one in the world who either loved or needed her. Certainly not her father, who had managed very well without her for fifteen years.

A flood of loneliness and despair swept over her. Tears that had remained frozen drops of ice deep inside her heart through the long, exhausting day suddenly thawed and cascaded down her cheeks. She felt a sob rise in her throat and could no more contain it than she could hold back the flood of tears. Burying her face in her hands, she sobbed her heart out.

Tristan was not asleep. How could he be, with his fingers still tingling from the touch of Maddy's slender shoulders and rigid back? Hell and damnation! The truth was, every nerve in his body tingled with awareness of the woman lying beside him. What had begun as a practical way to warm her shivering body had ended up an excruciating experience that had left him shocked and aching and randy as a blasted billy goat.

He lay tense and wakeful, listening to the rustle of the straw as she tossed and turned, and fervently wishing they were at the end of their journey instead of the beginning. The last thing he needed was to start lusting after Garth's future bride.

He heard a sound. A strangled sob. Then another and another. Dear God, she was weeping again in that wild, soul-searing way of hers that sounded as if she were tearing the very heart from her breast. Overwhelmed by the frightening helplessness he always felt when faced with a woman's tears, he raised up on his elbow and stared into the inky blackness where he knew she lay.

"Maddy?" He wasn't certain what he was asking, and her only answer was another heart-wrenching sob. He reminded himself she was very young, scarcely older than Caro, and probably given to the same hysterics. It didn't fadge; the lie stuck in his throat. Neither Caro, nor any other woman he knew, could have weathered all she had gone through in the past twenty-four hours with the courage and resilience Maddy had shown. She was weeping because she had good reason, and his heart bled for her.

More than anything else, he longed to take her in his arms and comfort her, but he had an uneasy premonition that once he gave in to that impulse, his life would be forever changed.

Still, something about the pain etched on her face when she'd spoken of her grandfather's deception had touched him as nothing else had in a long, long time, and her vulnerability when she'd questioned him about the father she scarcely knew still haunted him. Premonition be damned! He reached over and drew her to him.

"Cry, Maddy. Cry it all out," he crooned, rocking her until at long last her rigid body relaxed and she released the startled breath she'd gasped when first he'd touched her. With a smothered moan, she burrowed her face in his shoulder and sobbed out her grief until his shirt was as soaked with her tears as it previously had been with raindrops.

Much later, when her sobs had subsided and her slow, deep breathing told him she had fallen into an exhausted sleep, he shifted his weight to arrange her more comfortably in his arms. For a long time, he lay listening to the storm raging outside, feeling the steady beat of her heart and the answering rhythm of his own.

The fierce thrust of desire that had gripped him earlier had mellowed, overshadowed by an aching tenderness for the slender waif sleeping so trustingly in his arms. The feeling was like nothing he had ever felt for any other women.

He stared into the darkness surrounding him, a man perplexed by the unexpected depths of his own emotions. With a sigh, he acknowledged that, as usual, his premonition had been right on the mark. From this moment forward, his life would be irrevocably changed, and he feared not for the better. For this time the ache that troubled him was of the heart, not the loins.

Five

"Wake up, Maddy. It's almost dawn."

The voice sounded clipped, impatient, and Maddy struggled to do what it demanded, but her eyes felt as if someone had rubbed sand in them during the night.

When she finally pried them open, she found Tristan bending over her, lantern in hand. With shocking clarity, she remembered she had wept all over the poor man before she'd finally fallen asleep.

Had she slept in his arms all night while the storm raged outside the cozy loft? The depression in the straw beside her would indicate she had, and the last thought she remembered before she'd dropped off to sleep had been how comforting a man's strong arms could be when one was badly in need of succor.

She wanted to thank him for his kindness and assure him he need not worry; she had cried her last tear. However, he gave her no opportunity to do so. Once again he had drawn back into that same impenetrable shell of cold indifference he'd assumed after their revealing conversation of the previous day. She wondered if he only tried to keep his human side hidden from her, or if his checkered past made him hold everyone at arm's length.

It was immediately obvious, once she climbed down the ladder from the loft, that she was back on a par with the dobbin when it came to claiming his attention. Lower, actually, since he completely ignored her, while he patiently coaxed the reluctant old horse from its comfortable stall with a promise of sugar when they reached a village where some could be procured.

To add insult to injury, he handed her a shovel and told her to muck out the stall while he harnessed the dobbin to the carriage. It was plain to see this moody *Anglais* needed to be put in his place and, she decided as she shoveled the old dobbin's foul-smelling droppings into the bucket Tristan had provided, she was just the woman to do it.

The first crow of the farmyard rooster greeted her as she stepped from the barn when her unpleasant task was completed, and the waiting horse and cabriolet were but a deeper shadow in the gray, predawn light. Before she had time to wonder where Tristan was, he bolted around the corner of the barn, swept her up, and dumped her on the carriage seat.

"Are you mad?" she gasped as he yanked the hem of his cassock up to his waist and crawled over her to take the reins. Then she heard it—an angry shout from the veranda of the farmhouse. Chickens scattered before the dobbin's pounding hooves, and she heard the unmistakable squeals of a mother sow and her piglets as the right side of the carriage careened against the post of their muddy pen.

Behind them, the farmer's threats grew fainter as they bumped along the muddy lane, but just before they turned onto the roadway, a bullet whizzed past Maddy's ear and imbedded itself in the trunk of an apple tree. "A near thing, that," Tristan declared grimly, glancing her way. "I'll not cut it so close again." Maddy swallowed the lump of terror choking her throat and nodded her heartfelt agreement. At that moment in time, she couldn't have managed a word if her life had depended on it.

A short distance down the road, they topped a small rise to find the eastern sky tinged a rosy pink and the first faint rim of a pumpkin-colored sun peeping over the horizon. "We're in luck," Tristan declared with a grin. "It appears the storm has blown over, and we should have a fine day for traveling." At least, Maddy thought it was a grin. With a two-day's growth of black beard masking his features, it was difficult to tell.

Slowing the panting dobbin to a steady trot, he settled back in his seat as calmly as if he were enjoying a pleasant country outing, and not escaping by the skin of his teeth from an irate farmer. Apparently this sort of hair-raising incident was nothing out of the ordinary to a man of his profession.

"I have every hope of reaching a particular village just this side of Roanne well before nightfall," Tristan said a few minutes later. "There is an excellent inn there which serves as fine a ragout as I've ever eaten, and the beds have eiderdown quilts as soft as a cloud."

He paused. "There's a marketplace as well, where I can do a bit of horse trading."

"Horse trading?"

He nodded. "We can't count on public conveyances. Thanks to Bonaparte's escape, most of them had already stopped functioning when I rode south. And our ancient steed has a stout heart, but his legs are ready to give out. It's time he was put out to pasture where he need do nothing more strenuous than father a few healthy colts."

Maddy glanced at the spavined old horse plodding down the road ahead of the small cabriolet. Though she hated to admit it, she could see Tristan's judgment of the animal was correct. He would never make it to Paris, much less Calais. It made her sad, as if she were somehow facing yet another painful loss to age and infirmity.

She blinked back her foolish tears. "I shall be sorry to see him go. I have grown quite fond of him, and I know you have too."

"Me?" Tristan gave a snort of disgust. "I never confuse sentiment with practicality. I have better uses for my brain than to muddle it up with such maudlin nonsense."

She felt as if he'd slapped her across the face. It was plain to see the conceited lout had more in mind than the ancient horse. He was, in fact, warning her she shouldn't attach any undue importance to his brief show of nocturnal compassion. As if she would! She might be many things, but a fool was not one of them.

She found herself wondering if all the men of his country were as boorish as he. If they were, she would certainly never make the mistake of becoming the wife of an Englishman.

They had had the road virtually to themselves the previous day; today, it grew increasingly crowded with each passing hour. Many of the travelers were heading north—Royalists fleeing before Bonaparte's encroaching army. Others, loyal to the emperor, were pushing south to join forces with him and General Cambronne's *grognards*.

Twice they were almost caught in brief, isolated clashes between the two factions, but in general the Royalists and Bonapartists passed each other with no more than shouted insults. Whatever their political persuasions, most Frenchmen were sick to death of bloodshed. Tristan suspected this general ennui would work in the emperor's favor. Unless some persuasive leader stepped forward to rally the Royalist troops, the Corsican might well make good his boast to reach Paris in twenty days.

Time and again, the travelers heading south stopped him to inquire if he had come from Lyon and if the rumors were true that the city had fallen to Bonaparte without a shot. At first he was wary of these eager inquisitors, but when no one challenged his and Maddy's disguises, he became more confident and answered their questions freely.

As luck would have it, when they finally reached the "excellent inn" he had touted, it was full to overflowing. All that was left was one small attic room usually reserved for the servants of wealthy travelers, and Tristan had to pay an exorbitant price for that. After thinking it over, he decided it would be prudent to wait until after they'd supped to apprise Maddy of the nature of their sleeping accommodations.

In the meantime, his stomach was rumbling with hunger and his mouth was watering for a trencher of the inn's delicious ragout. After seeing the horse and carriage delivered safely to the stable, he led Maddy in search of their supper.

The noise in the public room was deafening. Everyone seemed to be talking at once, and the stench of stale sweat and sour wine was so overpowering when they joined the other guests at the common table, it literally took his breath away. He determinedly ignored it; nothing could kill his appetite for a hot, tasty meal after another day of dry bread and hard cheese.

Beside him, Maddy ducked her head and hid her face. "I fear we must leave," she whispered in a voice hoarse with panic. "I recognize the two old men at the far end of the table, and they may recognize me if they see me. They are Royalists from Lyon and have visited my grandfather many times."

Hunger dulled Tristan's usual caution. "Nonsense! With your sunburned face and cropped hair, no one would take you for anything but the *paysan* you purport to be," he whispered back.

She accepted his judgment without demur, but the skepticism he read in her eyes said she was far from being convinced. In truth, though he pretended otherwise, he was more nervous than he led her to believe about the situation in which they found themselves.

He took another look at the men around the table, most of whom appeared to be shouting insults at those seated across from them. He groaned. To a man, those on one side of the table sported the white cockade of the Bourbons, those on the other the tricolor of the Bonapartists—and from the looks of things, they were on the verge of staging a reenactment of the French Revolution. If the old dobbin could take another step, he'd be tempted to demand his blunt back from the innkeeper and move on.

But the dobbin was on its last legs, and he could plainly see that Maddy was so exhausted she could scarcely hold her head up. In truth, he was not in much better shape himself. There was nothing for it but to hope for the best tonight and get an early start tomorrow.

But like a gambler whose luck has turned bad, Tristan's grew worse by the minute. The buxom black-haired serving maid who approached them with their ragout took one look at him and dropped the wooden bowl, sending chunks of meat and potato splattering in all directions.

"*Mon Dieu,*" she gasped. "It is you—the devil-eyed Parisian with the clever hands." She crossed herself fervently. "Mother of God, I have slept with a priest."

A deathly silence fell on the crowded room at her damning words. All eyes, Royalist and Bonapartist alike, turned accusingly in Tristan's direction.

He blinked, vaguely aware he remembered her as Babette— or was it Colette?—an obliging tavern wench from an inn a good day's ride to the north, where he'd spent an energetic night between the sheets on his way to Lyon. What cursed luck that she should have changed her place of employment at this particular time.

Out of the corner of his eye, he saw Maddy level a look at him that nearly singed his two-day growth of whiskers. He chose to ignore it for the moment and handle the more press-ing matter of the goggle-eyed serving girl.

"My good woman," he said in the same tone of voice he'd heard the priest use when delivering the old count's funeral mass, "I do not know who you think I am, but let me assure you, we have never before met."

"But your eyes, monsieur. No two men could have such eyes."

"Ah! "Tristan leaned back in his chair, with what he hoped was a beatific smile on his face. "That explains your confu-sion." He shook his head sadly. "I am sorry, nay ashamed, to admit, that you must have met up with my scapegrace twin brother. We are as alike as two hairs on a dog. But he, alas, has refused to enter the church as our good father ordained, but has chosen instead to follow the evil ways of Lucifer."

As one, the men at the table murmured their acceptance of his explanation. As one, they returned to their verbal jousting, if anything, more loudly than before. It was all too apparent that neither Royalists nor Bonapartists wished to be the first to cast the stone when it came to carnal sin.

"*Je ne connais pas* this Lucifer," the young maid said over the rapidly accelerating noise. "Never has he stopped by the inn of the Scarabee Noir. But this I say to you, Father. You need feel no shame for your handsome brother. There is no finer, more generous gentleman in all of France."

Dropping to her knees, she scooped the bulk of the ragout back into the bowl and wiped the remainder up with her al-ready soiled apron. Her task completed, she gazed up at Tris-tan with vacant brown eyes that gave her a distinctly bovine appearance. Lord help him, he must have been drunk as a brewer's horse to have consorted with such a dim-witted crea-ture.

The little maid rose to her feet, a dreamy expression on her plump face. "Left ten francs on my pillow, the gentleman did—just what I needed for coach fare to come join *mon cher ami,* who is the ostler at this inn."

Beside him, Maddy made an odd choking sound and Tristan groaned. Devil take it, he'd been hoisted by his own petard. "That is all very well, my child," he intoned in his most pious voice, "but fornication without the sanctity of marriage is still a sin, and I admonish you to confess your encounter with my reprehensible brother when next you visit your parish priest."

He cleared his throat. "In the meantime, would you be good enough to deliver our supper to our chambers as soon as possible. I fear the mood of the public room is about to become too violent for the tender sensitivities of my young assistant."

No sooner had he uttered the prophetic words than a young Royalist with glazed eyes and ruddy cheeks raised his glass and shouted, "*Vive le roi!*" An equally inebriated young Bonapartist immediately retaliated by tossing his wine in the face of the Royalist and shouting, "*Vive l'empereur!*"

Instantly, every man at the table was on his feet, sword drawn and murder in his eye. Tristan yanked Maddy from her chair and pushed her and the whimpering serving maid toward the door, keeping his body between them and the clashing swords behind him.

"Supper," he yelled at the maid, who scooted for the kitchen the minute she cleared the public room doorway. "And a basin of hot water for washing. If they are not delivered to my chamber within five minutes, I will come looking for you."

Maddy pulled her arm from Tristan's grasp with a muttered, "Keep your 'clever hands' to yourself." Her back was rigid as a post and her boots thudded ominously on the wooden treads as she made her way up the stairway. Stopping at the first landing, she waited for him to indicate which chamber was hers.

He pointed mutely to the stairs leading to the attic, and found himself thinking longingly of the melee going on in the public room below. That kind of male combat he understood and could handle with an aplomb gained from six years of surviving on the streets of Paris. But what man in his right mind would welcome confrontation with an irate female—especially one who thought she had him dead to rights? Grimly, he followed her up the stairwell and pushed open the door to the tiny attic room.

Maddy poked her head in the door and stared at the narrow bed and the wooden packing crate on which a single tallow candle dripped and sputtered. The anger already simmering inside her burst into a full-fledged conflagration and she wheeled around to face the man behind her. "What is this? Have you secured me a room in the maid's quarters?"

"Shhh, Maddy, lower your voice."

She lowered it to an icy tone only he could hear. "You are carrying our disguise a bit too far, *Father Tristan*. I agreed to pose as your assistant; I did not agree to lie on straw-filled ticking while you sleep in a feather bed."

Tristan gave her a gentle shove, followed her into the tiny room and closed the door behind him. "This was the only room available when we arrived." He consulted his watch. "And it is now half past the hour of ten. There is little likelihood another will become available tonight. You may rant and rave all you like; it will do you no good. It is either this or bed down in the stable with a dozen or more coachmen and stable boys, an arrangement in which I, myself, have no interest. But feel free to avail yourself of such accommodations if you wish."

He reached down and pulled a knife from his boot. "However, if you do, I would suggest you arm yourself with this. As you may have noticed when we arrived, they're a rough lot. God only knows what use they might find for a pretty young boy—and if they discovered he was, in fact, a female, it does not even bear thinking about."

"And how much safer am I here with a lecher who cannot even think of a plausible lie to cover his debauchery?"

Tristan's eyes chilled to two chips of silver ice, and anger thinned his mouth to a mere knife slash in his beard-darkened face. "Never fear, mademoiselle, you are as safe with me as if you were in one of your papist convents. Surely you realize that if I had found you the least bit tempting I could have ravaged you as easily in a hayloft as an attic—particularly when you draped yourself all over me in the middle of the night. The fact is, I only lust after warm-blooded, warm-hearted women; my lascivious urges do not extend to scrawny females with boyish figures and waspish tongues."

Maddy reeled as if he had struck her. She ached to lash back at him with something as vicious and insulting as his ugly denunciation of her. But before she could gather her wits, she heard a knock and a voice that declared, "Here is your supper, Father, and your hot water."

Instinctively, she stepped aside as Tristan reached for the door handle. The plump, little serving maid stood on the threshold, tray in hand, and behind her stood a pot boy with a basin of steaming water and two linen towels.

The maid smiled tentatively. "There's not a spoonful of ragout left in the kitchen. T'was the last of it that landed on the floor when you gave me such a start. Nor is there much else left to eat with those hotheads below filling their bellies like hogs at a trough.

"But never fear, Father, you and your young companion need not go to sleep hungry. For look what I managed to find you. She handed him the tray. "A nice bit of bread and cheese."

Morning, when it finally came, was as pale and chilly as a tax collector's smile. Through half-closed eyelids, Maddy watched the gray light filter through the narrow, dirt-encrusted window and seek out the shadowy corners of the tiny room. She had slept poorly, though she'd had the narrow bed to herself. After a silent meal, Tristan had wrapped himself in the blanket he'd brought in from the carriage, stretched out on the floor with his head on the knapsack and closed his eyes.

Long after the single, smoky candle had guttered out, she'd lain staring into the dark, remembering his disparaging description of her. "A scrawny female with a boyish figure and a waspish tongue."

She'd tried to convince herself the hateful words didn't hurt. He had, after all, spoken in anger—anger she admitted to triggering. But she suspected there had been more truth than temper in what he'd said. She had always been painfully aware of her small bosom. But a waspish tongue? If, indeed, she was guilty of that failing, then at least part of the blame could be laid at his door. There was something about the man that brought out the worst in her.

As she watched through half-open eyes, Tristan stirred, stretched his arms above his head, and yawned. A moment later, he rose stiffly from the floor and folded the blanket. Rummaging through the knapsack, he drew forth the razor the St. Bartholomew housekeeper had provided. With the remains of the wash water and a sliver of soap left from the night before, he proceeded to shave himself before the cracked mirror hanging on the wall above the packing crate.

Maddy had never before seen a man perform his daily ablutions. Her grandfather had been much too austere and formal a man to allow any female such a personal glimpse of him. Even when he had become so seriously ill, he had demanded she leave the room whenever his valet washed and shaved him.

Fascinated, she watched Tristan scrape away the black beard that had darkened his lean features for the past two days. Even in the dim light, she could see how handsome he was without it, and she found herself wondering how many women, like the little maid, had found him irresistible. The very thought made her ache in a way she was certain no lady was supposed to ache.

His task completed, he repacked the knapsack, picked up the blanket, and moved to stand over her at the side of the bed. Maddy pretended to be asleep, rather than meet his pale, knowing gaze and risk his detecting the embarrassment she felt over their enforced intimacy. A moment later, she heard him slip quietly from the room and close the door behind him.

She sat bolt upright. Where was he going? Too late, she wished she had had the courage to face him long enough to ask. Quickly, she shoved her feet into her boots, splashed water on her face, and finger-combed her short curly hair. He might be the most exasperating man she had ever met, but once he was out of her sight, she felt as if she were cut adrift from the only reality left in her life.

A peek in the doorway of the public room told her he was not there. Nor was anyone else except the little maid, who was busy cleaning up the debris from the previous night. She looked up from where she was scrubbing vigorously at a blood stain defacing the worn planking of the floor.

"Men!" she said disparagingly. "You are all alike. Drunken sods who rail at each other like raging bulls, then crawl away to sleep it off while we women clean up your mess. If I was you, lad, I'd follow in the good father's footsteps and steer clear of such was raising a ruckus here last night."

Maddy laughed. "Oh, I intend to follow in his footsteps all right," she said, lowering her voice sufficiently to preserve her disguise.

"Well, you'd best make tracks then," the maid said, obviously taking her literally. "For he come knocking at the scullery door a bit ago, bolted down a mug of coffee, and rode off in that little black carriage of his."

Maddy's heart dropped to her toes. "He left the inn?"

"*Oui.* Waved good-bye and threw me a kiss." The little maid sighed. "What a shame he had to be a priest."

Gripping the back of the nearest chair for support, Maddy recalled Tristan's fury when she'd called him a lecher, his cruel rejoinder that told her how unappealing he found her. The very air in the little attic room had crackled with his anger—but it had never occurred to her he would just walk out and leave her stranded without a sou to her name. What tale would the blackhearted devil weave to explain such infamy to her father? A clever one, she'd no doubt. He had already proven himself a cunning liar.

"I have to wonder why the good father left you here alone," the maid said, studying her curiously. "It seems an odd thing to do with the inn full of the kind of men who would use a pretty lad like you most cruelly if they thought you were without protection."

Maddy felt a chill slither down her spine, but she managed what she hoped was a confident smile. "My sister and her husband live nearby," she improvised hastily. "Father Tristan merely offered me a ride to where I could walk to their farm."

"Ah, so that's the way of it." The maid wiped her hands on her apron, which still bore the remains of the ill-fated ragout. "Well, come with me to the kitchen then. The father said I was to make certain you had a piece of bread and a mug of coffee when you woke."

"How kind of him."

"*Oui,* you'll not find many men in France as kind nowadays. They're all too busy fretting about who'll be sitting on the throne to worry about such as you and me, lad."

Half an hour later, her hunger satisfied, Maddy bid farewell to the little maid and stepped from the kitchen to find the courtyard strangely quiet and empty. The sounds of grooms and horses stirring about came from the stable and the smell of fresh hay filled the cool morning air, but apparently the inn's contentious guests were still sleeping off last night's debauchery—a blessing for which she was deeply grateful.

Blinking after the gloom inside the inn, she stood for a minute in the bright sunshine, collecting her wits. The first shock of finding herself abandoned had passed and a numbness born of sheer terror settled over her.

Grimly, she reviewed her options. There were only two that she could see. She could walk back to Lyon and hide in the church as Father Bertrand had suggested. If anyone questioned her en route, she could claim she was going south to join Bonaparte's army. It was by far the most sensible thing to do.

But if she could somehow make it to Calais . . . She remembered a remark Tristan had made in passing about her father's ship waiting there to carry them to England. All she needed was a ride. She could never walk that far—or even if she could, the ship would be long gone before she reached the seaport town. But with all the Royalists fleeing north, surely she could find someone with whom she might safely travel. A man and his wife perhaps, or a noblewoman traveling with her coachman and maid. If such a person still existed in southern France, she would surely be anxious to stay out of the Corsican's evil grasp.

She made her decision. Squaring her shoulders, she started walking . . . north. Her knees were still trembling, but the very act of making a decision lifted her flagging spirits.

The road was flat, bordered on both sides by peaceful green meadows, with sheep grazing on one side, cows on the other. A warm breeze carried the scent of newly turned earth and somewhere a lamb bleated for its mother. She found it difficult to believe this peaceful countryside might once again be the scene of a bloody battle over the throne of France.

Ahead, a narrow stone bridge spanned a small stream and beyond that she could see the village Tristan had mentioned, basking in the early morning sunshine. She had just started across the bridge when she heard the pounding of hooves behind her. Turning, she found a horse and rider bearing down upon her at breakneck speed. With a cry of alarm, she climbed atop the waist-high rock wall bordering the bridge just in time to keep from being crushed.

Swearing profusely, the rider reined in his horse at the end of the bridge and shook his fist at her. She recognized him, from his flame-colored hair, as the young Royalist who'd started the fracas in the inn the night before. He was hatless, and one eye was closed and surrounded by a purplish black bruise that gave him an odd, owlish look. A thin red line crossing his right cheek suggested he'd come out the worst in at least one contest of swordsmanship.

"*Sacre bleu*, you stupid *paysan*, my blooded stallion could have broken a leg if he'd stepped on you," he shouted, staring down his aristocratic nose at her.

Hot, angry blood throbbed in Maddy's temples. Her legs were still trembling so violently she dared not step down from her perch, and this idiot was accusing her of endangering the safety of his horse! "What of me, you clumsy *cochon*," she shouted back. "You'd have killed me if I hadn't been too quick for you."

"And good riddance. One less piece of riff raff to join the Corsican's band of cutthroats." Brandishing his sword, the young Royalist galloped back over the bridge toward her. She had no choice but to leap into the stream or be run through by his blade.

The water was cold, no doubt fed by mountain snows, and the rocks in the stream bed were slippery. No sooner had she landed than her feet went out from under her and she ended up sitting waist deep in the icy water. Frantically righting herself, she waded toward the nearest bank. But her tormenter would have none of that. Still waving his sword threateningly, he galloped toward her, forcing her back to the middle of the stream.

"Go on your way, you fool," she sputtered. "You've caused enough trouble for one day!"

"Fool? You dare call me, the Chevalier de Montrassat, a fool? It is time you learned respect for your betters, *paysan!*" Prancing back onto the bridge, he poised above her and swished his sword back and forth as if preparing for a duel. "We shall see how hot your peasant blood flows after you have cooled your heels in this stream for an hour or two."

"You c-c-cannot mean to l-l-leave me in this freezing water," Maddy stammered, though she could see from his expression of fiendish triumph he meant to do just that. But if the arrogant young *buffoon* thought she would docilely submit to

such barbarism, he had another think coming. Bending over,
she scooped up a handful of rocks and began winging them at
him, just as she caught sight of another rider astride a huge bay
gelding and leading a chestnut-colored mare approaching from
the direction of the village.

The sun was in Tristan's eyes, so it took him a minute to
register what was causing the commotion at the small stone
bridge that stood between him and the inn. He squinted. The
redheaded horseman was the young hotheaded Royalist from
the inn. It looked as if he had knocked someone off the
bridge—a Bonapartist, no doubt—and was heartily enjoying
his victim's discomfort.

He looked again, scarcely believing his eyes. My God! It
couldn't be! But it *was* Maddy standing knee-deep in the
stream!

He opened his mouth to call her name, but before he could
get a word out, she let fly a rock that struck her tormenter
squarely on the forehead. With a yelp, he dropped his reins.
His horse bucked and he catapulted backward out of his saddle
to land flat on his back in the middle of the bridge, where he
lay in a crumpled, moaning heap.

Tristan leapt from his horse and rushed to the bank of the
stream. "Devil take it, Maddy, are you all right?"

"Do I look all right, you fool?" she snarled, eyeing him with
a malevolence that suggested she would wing one of her mis-
siles at him if he posed another such question.

With a shrug, he left the shrew to fend for herself and made
a cursory examination of the loser in the bizarre battle. A welt
the size of an egg had already risen just above the young Royalist's one good eye and he was moaning pitifully.

Tristan looked up in time to see Maddy crawl up the slippery bank onto the far end of the bridge. She was dripping wet
from the waist down and shivering convulsively.

Eyes wide with horror, she stared at the prostrate form at
Tristan's feet. "Did I k-k-kill him?" she stammered through
chattering teeth.

Six

Tristan was tempted to tell her she had indeed done the fellow in. If ever a woman needed the fear of God drummed into her, that woman was Maddy Harcourt. Every time he took his eyes off her, she did some outrageous thing that was completely beyond his comprehension. But she looked so frightened and miserable, he couldn't bring himself to add to her distress.

He pressed his fingers to the pulse beating in the young Royalist's neck, a trick he'd learned from the Paris gendarmes who were frequently called upon to determine the chances of survival of one of the *canaille* after a street fight. The boy's pulse was strong and steady.

"I believe I can safely say he'll survive," he said dryly. "But, thanks to you, he is almost certain to have two black eyes instead of one, and twice the headache he already had."

The color returned to Maddy's pale cheeks at the welcome news. "Well, I'm glad I didn't kill him, for I'd not like to be responsible for terminating any man's life, no matter how much he deserved it." She tossed her head defiantly. "But as for a black eye and a headache, I cannot say I am sorry about that. The beast tried to run me down when I was walking across this bridge."

"Why?"

"For no other reason I could see than that he thought I was a peasant."

Tristan's scowl was so black it sent shivers down Maddy's spine that had nothing to do with being chilled to the bone. "I wasn't asking why the fellow tried to run you down, but rather why you were walking across this bridge."

Maddy almost said "to reach the other side," but resisted the temptation. Instinct told her it was a poor time to introduce humor into their conversation. She stared at the two horses tethered nearby and suddenly remembered Tristan had mentioned he meant to do some horse trading at the village market. So he hadn't abandoned her after all. The comforting thought kindled a spark of warmth somewhere in her chilled body, as well as a touch of chagrin. Her foolish fears had all been of her own making.

"I am waiting for an explanation, Maddy. Why were you walking across this bridge a good distance from the inn, instead of waiting for me to return as you should have?" Tristan's voice carried a note of sharpness, as if he was at the end of his patience, and Maddy knew he would be satisfied with nothing less than the truth.

She wrapped her arms around herself in an effort to stop shivering. "I was afraid," she said hesitantly. "I couldn't find you and the little maid said she'd seen you drive away."

"And naturally you thought I had abandoned you." Tristan rose to his feet to tower over her. "Why, Maddy? What is there about me that makes you think the worst of me? First you took me for a thief and murderer, then a ravager of innocent females, now a heartless blackguard who would leave you alone and penniless in a country torn apart by civil war."

Maddy hung her head, embarrassed that he had so easily guessed the insulting conclusion to which she had immediately jumped when she'd found him missing from the inn. In retrospect, it did look a little foolish. Whatever he might have been in his previous life, Tristan had been completely honorable where she was concerned. The only thing she could honestly accuse him of was a testy disposition.

"If it is my bastard status that worries you," he continued with a tough of bitterness, "let me assure you that I was raised by a woman who taught me how to act like a gentleman even if I could never actually become one."

"It has nothing to do with your . . . your unfortunate birth," she said contritely.

"I see. My profession then."

"As a spy? Heavens no. That just makes you all the more intriguing." Maddy felt her cheeks flame when she realized the slip she'd made.

Luckily, the young Royalist chose that moment to interrupt them with a groan and Tristan bent to once again place his fingertips at the spot in the lad's neck where his pulse throbbed. Maddy knew it was only a temporary interruption and her interrogator would still expect an answer to his probing question when he stood up.

But what to say? She could hardly admit the truth that had just moments before occurred to her—that she had unconsciously judged him far too harshly because it was more comfortable to find fault with him than to acknowledge the frightening effect he had on her.

She could just imagine the start she'd give him if she told him that every time he looked at her, her heart pounded and a queer kind of ache started in the most secret parts of her body. And when he touched her! *Nom de Dieu*, the feeling that engulfed her then defied description.

So, she simply said. "I apologize. I am not normally such a missish creature. But I have never before been cut adrift from everything familiar; nor have I ever before had to deal with an Englishman. The experience has been a bit bewildering."

She raised her eyes to meet his. "But I have regained my equilibrium. I promise I will never doubt you again. From this moment forward, I will trust you completely."

A rare smile brightened Tristan's lean features. "Do not go that far," he said gently, as he unrolled the carriage blanket which rested across the stallion's rump, wrapped it about her shivering shoulders, and secured it with a knot. "No man is completely trustworthy where a beautiful, desirable woman is concerned."

A beautiful, desirable woman. Because such a monstrous lie cut her to the quick after the bald truth he'd blurted out just hours before, Maddy resorted to a sharp retort to cover the stab of pain. "You have an odd taste in beauty for a man of the world, monsieur. A scrawny creature with the figure of a boy and the tongue of a wasp would not be the choice of many men."

"Hell and damnation, Maddy, you know very well those were simply words said in anger. What could you expect me to say when you'd just called me a lecher?" He sounded so sincere, she almost believed him. Almost, but not quite.

He held out his hand. "Shall we agree—no more angry exchanges for the duration of our time together? Surely we can manage that if we both try."

Maddy shook his hand solemnly, acutely aware of the note of finality in his voice when he'd said "the duration of our time together." It suddenly occurred to her that once Tristan had paid his brother's debt by delivering her to her father, he might well disappear from her life forever. The thought was oddly depressing.

She withdrew her hand from his. Strange as it seemed, she would miss him. The way one missed a toothache once the tooth was pulled, no doubt, she decided sourly.

She watched him prop the groggy young Royalist against the wall of the bridge . . . then chase down and tether his horse. "We cannot just leave him here like this surely," she protested.

Tristan raised an eyebrow. "What do you suggest we do with him?" he asked, laying the unconscious man's sword across his lap. "Tie him to his saddle and take him with us? His compatriots are sure to be along soon. They will see to him."

"But what if the Corsican's advance guard reaches him first?"

"Believe me, Maddy, if General Cambronne's *grognards* are that close, we should be worrying about our own necks, not his."

Tristan rose and walked to where the two horses he'd brought from the village were tethered. Beckoning Maddy forward, he cupped his hands to give her a leg up on the mare. But even with help, her effort to mount was clumsy, to say the least.

Tristan's brows came together in a scowl. "Devil take it, I didn't think to ask if you rode."

"Of course I ride," Maddy said haughtily. "I am an excellent horsewoman. I am just not accustomed to this kind of saddle."

Tristan slapped the palm of his hand against his forehead. "How could I be so stupid. Naturally, you ride sidesaddle. Well, that's out in your present disguise." He frowned. "Do you think you can manage?"

"I can manage. It is just a matter of adjustment, "Maddy declared, with a great deal more confidence than she felt. But she did manage—better than she'd expected, actually. Awkward as the saddle felt, it was still good to have a lively mount beneath her again, and the little mare was a sweet goer.

She watched Tristan wrestle with the narrow cassock, which was never designed for sitting astride a horse. It rode up his powerful thighs and bunched beneath his hips, until he finally yanked it impatiently up around his waist. "Our roles appear to be reversed, Father Tristan," she suggested, struggling to keep a straight face. "Perhaps we should procure a sidesaddle for you."

To her surprise, he merely grinned. "We shall see which of us is laughing at the end of the day, *paysan*."

He started off at a slow trot, but once Maddy began to relax in the saddle, he gradually increased their leisurely pace until they were heading northward at full gallop.

Instinctively, Maddy pressed her thighs against the little mare's flanks, dug in her heels, and kept up with Tristan the best she could. Despite the monumental effort it took, her spirits soared. The sun was bright, the air fresh, and the day already bidding fair to being unusually warm for early March. Gratefully, she soaked up the comforting heat, feeling it dry her soggy clothes and thaw the chill from her body.

After half an hour, she shed her blanket, tossing it across the saddle in front of her and with it the aura of fear and death that had haunted her during the long weeks of her grandfather's illness. Reveling in the feel of the warm breeze caressing her body and rippling through her cap of curls, she made a vow that from now on she would take each day of her adventure with this puzzling Englishman as it came and never again look back at what might have been.

They rode hard and fast for the next two hours, and Maddy soon learned what Tristan had been alluding to in his cryptic remark. Riding astride worked a completely different set of muscles than riding sidesaddle; in no time at all her thighs and buttocks began to ache abominably. With dogged determination, she ignored the discomfort and concentrated on the exhilaration of the ride. Pride dictated she neither ask any quarter of Tristan nor slow him down until he saw fit to rest the horses.

The sun was close to its zenith when they clattered across a covered wooden bridge and stopped beside a gurgling stream that wound through a grove of silver aspens. Maddy dismounted gingerly and hobbled to a spot upstream of the horses where she could drink deeply and splash water on her heated face.

Tristan stretched out on the grass at the stream's edge and watched her painful progress. He bit back a smile. What she needed was a good rubdown. But aside from the affront to her maidenly modesty, he would be subjecting himself to the worst kind of torture if he dared touch the intriguing little hellion in such an intimate manner. The thought was tempting, but Maddy would just have to live with her aches and pains.

Meanwhile, he had yet another problem to present her. "We're a bit short of money," he said casually as they sat on the bank of the stream while the horses drank their fill. "Your father gave me a generous amount to cover the trip, but he expected us to ride in public coaches, not purchase horses—three in all, counting the one I rode south."

He glanced anxiously at her face, trying to read her expression. "The few francs I got for the old dobbin and the carriage didn't begin to cover the cost of two fast horses. But I opted for them anyway. The sooner we quit France, the better."

Maddy nodded her agreement. "Do we have enough money for one good meal? I doubt I can choke down another bite of bread and cheese."

"We've enough for several good meals . . . providing we don't waste any money on sleeping accommodations."

"Does that mean we'll be sleeping in haylofts?" she asked, looking not the least bit disconcerted by the possibility.

"Haylofts, haystacks, horse stalls—who knows what will present itself for our use."

She leaned back on her elbows and stared up at the cloudless sky. "I vote for haystacks. I've always had a secret desire to sleep out under the stars. This may be my only chance."

Tristan couldn't help himself. As if of its own accord, his hand snaked out and ruffled her wind-tossed curls. "I'll say one thing for you, Maddy Harcourt. You're game as a pebble." For the first time, he found himself wondering if his very staid and proper brother would be capable of appreciating this plucky young original that fate had decreed he make his wife.

The rest of the day passed quickly. When the road became too dusty, Maddy moved up to ride beside Tristan. They spoke little, but there was a harmony in their silence that he found surprising. It had been his experience that most women were uncomfortable with silence, especially silence between them and a member of the opposite sex.

Dusk was falling when he spied a small slate-roofed inn set off the road next to an ancient stone gristmill. "This looks promising," he declared, reining in the stallion. "We'll take our meal here."

Maddy pulled to a stop beside him, her eyes twinkling with mischief. "To quote some long-forgotten poet, monsieur, 'Mine is the hunger of a hundred ravening wolves.' I warn you, I take no responsibility for my actions if my supper is lost to the clumsiness of some tavern wench who mistakes you for your generous-hearted twin brother."

Tristan felt an unfamiliar heat surge into his cheeks and swore softly under his breath. Not since his sixteenth birthday had any female made him blush like a callow greenling. "As I started to say," he continued, ignoring her jibe, "we will take our supper here, then look for a place to sleep. Though, I fear we shall have to opt for a hayloft or horse stall. This is the wrong time of year for haystacks."

Maddy didn't comment. Tristan could see her gaze was fixed on the giant waterwheel at the rear of the gristmill and the sparkling brook that tumbled down a rocky verge above it to turn the paddles in a slow, steady rhythm. Beyond the waterwheel stood a wooden platform on which a dozen or more sacks of grain were stacked.

"We can sleep there," she said, pointing to the platform. "We can bathe in the mill pond, and the sacks of grain will make a splendid bed." She searched the sky above her. "And there will surely be stars tonight for the sunset was spectacular."

She turned to Tristan, eyes sparkling with excitement. "Please say we may. Sleeping under the open sky on a night like this will be an experience I'll remember all the rest of my life."

Tristan felt certain he, too, would remember lying beneath a starlit sky with this bewitching minx who turned his blood to molten fire by simply laying her hand on his arm—and therein lay the problem. He neither needed nor wanted to spend the balance of his days haunted by such memories of his brother's wife.

"Please, Tristan. What could be more ideal?"

It was the first time she had ever called him by name without prefacing it with a sarcastic "Father." The effect was devastating, especially with her enchanting Gallic pronunciation.

"Treeston?" she pleaded again, and as if by magic the word "no" disappeared from his vocabulary.

A feather-soft breeze caressed Maddy's cheeks as she sat atop the mound of grain sacks, her back to the stone wall of the ancient mill. For the first time in days, she had eaten her fill. The *fricassée de poulet* served by the inn had been creditable, though lacking that particular zest that proclaimed it the creation of a master chef. She had taken the innkeeper's wife aside and suggested that in the future she use a white veal stock base and add a touch of thyme and a few juniper berries.

Later, she had bathed in the mill pond with the bar of soap Father Bertrand's housekeeper had slipped into the knapsack. Two such luxuries had made all life seem a great deal more pleasant.

Now, the sky above her was a black velvet cloak on which some celestial hand had sewn a thousand brilliant diamonds, and the full moon perched at its apex bathed the landscape in a bright, silvery light. Stretching out her legs, she wriggled her bare toes and breathed in the elusive scent of the honeysuckle climbing the wall beside her. She could hear the creaking of the waterwheel far below her and a splashing sound she knew to be Tristan bathing in the mill pond.

Eyes closed, she imagined the clear, crystal water flowing over his strong limbs—limbs whose masculine beauty she felt certain must rival the statue of a young Spartan warrior she had once admired in a Lyon museum. It was a deliciously wicked thought that had her blushing hotly when a few minutes later he climbed the stairs to the platform.

"That was probably the coldest bath I've ever taken," he grumbled, dropping onto the grain sack beside Maddy. Bracing his arms on his updrawn knees, he stared morosely at the dazzling moon. For some reason she couldn't fathom, he had been against sleeping outdoors. He still was, from the scowl that darkened his face.

"You'll soon warm up, as did I," Maddy promised. "Isn't it worth a few moments of discomfort to feel clean again?"

His answer was a noncommittal grunt.

Maddy tried again. "The breeze is so mild, my hair is already dry." Her gaze strayed to his hair. Jet black and glistening, it curled damply against his strong neck, making him look more than ever the brigand she had likened him to when first she'd glimpsed him.

She smiled to herself, imagining how shocked her despised former chaperone would be to find her alone with this enigmatic Englishman in such a romantic setting—indeed, with any man in any setting. But the old virago would never again make her life a misery.

All at once, she felt like a bird that had escaped its cage to savor its first taste of freedom. Something deep inside her stirred to life and she found herself longing to try her wings in the great, intriguing world that had heretofore been denied her. A night sleeping under the stars was a beginning. It probably didn't seem very exciting to a worldly fellow like Tristan; to her it was the most breathtaking of adventures.

Tristan watched the myriad emotions play across Maddy's lovely face and found himself wondering what thoughts were making her mouth tilt in an entrancing smile, her eyes dance with mischief. "What are you thinking?" he asked, though he wasn't certain he really wanted to know.

Bracing her hands at her sides, she tilted her head back to stare at the star-studded sky directly above her. "I am thinking there has never before been a night as glorious as this one. Nor will there ever be another. Everything about it is magical."

She turned to face him, and the glow in her amber eyes put the moonlight to shame. "Stop it," he ordered hoarsely. "Stop looking like that."

Her eyes widened. "Like what?"

"Like a woman yearning to be kissed."

Too late, he realized what an improper charge he'd made. He expected her to dress him down, at the very least deny it, as any woman with a proper sense of decorum would do. Instead, she merely studied him solemnly, as if pondering his statement. "I hadn't thought of it, for I've no experience in such things," she said gravely. "But now that you mention it . . . what could be more perfect than to experience my first kiss on this most perfect of nights."

She leaned toward him, an expectant look on her face which heated Tristan's blood far more effectively than the warm evening breeze. He drew back, cursing himself for every kind of fool known to man for making the provocative statement that had whetted Maddy's curiosity.

"The night may be perfect; the man is anything but," he stated flatly. "I am the last man on earth with whom you should share your first kiss, Maddy."

"Why?"

"Because I have done every despicable thing you've accused me of—and more. Hell and damnation, I have done things in the past six years that an innocent like you would not even be capable of imagining."

"Including kissing, I presume." The mischief was undeniable now, vying with the moonlight in her eyes. "I suspect you've become quite adept at that, which to my way of thinking would make you the ideal man to give a person her first kiss. Rather like establishing a standard of excellence one could use to judge all future kisses, don't you know."

She slid closer to him until they were sitting side by side. The clean scent of her hair filled his nostrils and the touch of her hand on his arm made him feel as if he'd drunk a flagon of wine instead of the two paltry glasses with which he'd washed down his supper.

"You are playing with fire, lady," he managed hoarsely, drawing away until his back pressed against the cool stone of the wall behind him.

Ignoring his warning, she eyed him curiously. "Am I supposed to close my eyes or leave them open when we kiss?"

"There are no hard and fast rules," Tristan murmured, staring at her soft, full mouth as if mesmerized. How had he, until this minute, failed to notice the tantalizing fact that her lower lip was slightly fuller than the upper, a phenomenon which somehow made her mouth appear indescribably kissable?

He moistened his own lips with a swipe of his tongue. This

was madness, he reminded himself. Maddy was slated to be his brother's wife. If he so much as touched her, he would be betraying Garth—in truth, betraying everything he himself held sacred.

"The eyes are a matter of personal preference, then," she said solemnly. "I think I shall close mine." She did so and leaned toward him. Instinctively, Tristan caught her before she tumbled forward. A mistake. The instant he touched her, he knew he was lost to all reason.

"Are you going to kiss me good night, Tristan?" she asked in a throaty voice, her eyes still tightly closed.

Tristan swallowed hard. "Yes, devil take it, I am. Though I suspect we may both live to regret it bitterly." Still, he no longer had a choice. The woman was driving him mad. It was either kiss her or strangle her, and how would he explain her murder to Caleb Harcourt—much less Garth, who depended on him to deliver the bride who would save Winterhaven for him?

With a groan, he lowered his head and covered her lips with his.

The kiss was everything Maddy had imagined it would be . . . and more. Hungry. Demanding. More angry than tender, but with an underlying loneliness so acute, it shattered her own solitary heart into a million jagged fragments.

It was as if she had been waiting for this man and this moment all her life, and recognizing him, she responded with every fiber of her being. Coiling her arms around the strong column of his neck, she abandoned herself to the sheer joy of the moment and to the magic of this most wondrous night of her life.

Then suddenly it was over. With a harsh, indistinguishable sound deep in his throat, Tristan thrust her from him. Bereft of the security of his arms, she fell backward until she was lying flat on her back across the grain sack on which she'd been sitting. "*Nom de Dieu*," she exclaimed, staring up at him, "I had no idea a kiss would be so . . . so astonishing."

He stared back, a stunned, almost haunted, look in his pale eyes. "Do not feel alone," he said, shaking his head as if to clear his mind of some puzzling confusion. "The astonishment is as much mine as yours."

Like a man in a trance, he rose to his feet and grasping the massive sack of grain next to the one on which Maddy lay, he stood it on its side, then positioned another beside it, creating a barricade around her. Maddy raised herself on one elbow and peeked over the top. "What in heaven's name are you doing?"

"Making certain necessary adjustments to our sleeping arrangements." Groaning from the effort, Tristan braced the two sacks with a third. "As I recall, the practice is called bundling, a term the early American colonists gave to the method they devised to keep inquisitive young innocents like you from getting into the kind of trouble you are courting with those flirtatious ways of yours."

"You think I have flirtatious ways? Maddy "asked, intrigued by the idea that he considered her a *femme fatale*.

His answer was merely another of his noncommittal grunts. He unrolled the carriage blanket and spread it over her. Then, pulling off his boots, he stretched out on the opposite side of the barricade and disappeared from Maddy's view.

"I have always felt a contempt for the Americans," he muttered, she suspected as much to himself as to her. "The few I've met appeared to be rather crude and unmannerly. I see now I have not given our former colonists the credit due them. While their backwoods customs may lack a certain refinement, they do give a fighting chance to some poor sod who's being tempted beyond his limits by an impossible female."

Seven

L ong after the moon had deserted the sky, Maddy lay awake lost in the wonder of the kiss she had shared with Tristan. Over and over, she relived the moment when his firm, warm lips had claimed hers with such hunger and passion she had found herself responding without thought or inhibition.

She tried to tell herself the experience had been so earth-shattering simply because it was her first kiss. But she had never been good at lying, especially to herself. The plain truth was, the earth had trembled beneath her because the lips that had claimed hers had been Tristan's.

He was obviously a worldly sophisticate who knew a great deal about kissing—and whatever else went on between a man and a woman. But his expertise was only a small part of the allure of this man; there was a inexplicable bond between them that transcended the physical. When he'd deepened the kiss with such unexpected intimacy, she'd felt as if their very souls had somehow touched each other.

He had warned her that they would both live to regret succumbing to the attraction they felt for each other. What a fool she'd been to ignore that warning. What a silly, childish fool to prattle on about "establishing a standard of excellence" for kissing. No wonder he had accused her of playing with fire.

Well, she'd live to pay the price for that bit of folly. For with that one brief, passionate caress, her eyes had been opened to the truth she had been trying so hard to ignore: She had been falling in love with this stubborn, bad-tempered Englishman from the very first moment she'd seen him.

And she couldn't even say why—except that he was the only man whose every glance made her heart beat faster, whose every touch made her feel wondrously, gloriously alive.

She sighed. But of all the men in the world to whom she could give her heart, he was probably the one most likely to break it.

Unless . . . he had appeared almost as startled as she when he'd thrust her from him after that heart-stopping kiss; he had even felt honor-bound to erect a barricade between them for the balance of the night because she "tempted him beyond his limits."

Maybe . . . just maybe he was not as jaded as he appeared. Maybe his heart was as vulnerable as hers.

She sighed again. And maybe indulging in that amazing flight of fancy was the most foolish thing of all.

The small, heartfelt sighs emanating from the other side of the barricade told Tristan that Maddy was having as much difficulty falling asleep as he. Probably for the same reason.

That blasted kiss.

What had possessed him to do such a thing? And why should kissing Maddy make him feel as wonder-struck as the greenest bantling who'd just discovered girls were different from boys? He'd chalk it up to "forbidden fruit," but that simply wouldn't fadge. He'd plundered that orchard too often in the past and walked away unperturbed by the experience.

He could deny it no longer. He wanted the woman who would soon be his brother's wife—wanted her passionately and with every fiber of his being. And the wanting went much deeper than the mere physical attraction he'd felt for far more voluptuous women in the past.

It had something to do with her guileless honesty and her courage and the fact that she constantly surprised him by doing the very thing he least expected her to do. In truth, if he believed in such a thing, he might almost think he was falling in love with her. And from her passionate response to his kiss, he could only surmise she felt the same about him. He would wager his last groat that someone as honest as Maddy would be incapable of responding with such ardor unless her affections were seriously engaged.

Which was why he must never again make the mistake of kissing her, or indeed touching her in any way. There must be no more sleeping beneath the stars or in haylofts, no more sharing of attics or secrets. He would push the horses to their absolute limits from dawn to dusk until they reached Calais, and if he had to sell both the pistol that had been a gift from Lord Castlereagh and the old earl's watch to do so, he would secure proper sleeping accommodations from now on.

Honor dictated that he keep his promises to Father Bertrand and to Garth, and return Maddy to her father as chaste as the day he'd found her.

With a sigh of relief that he had finally come to grips with the problem at hand, he silently slipped from his bed on the grain sacks, climbed down the ladder to the mill pond, and took his second icy bath of the evening.

Maddy woke at dawn, determined that from that moment forward she would show Tristan a mature and sober demeanor that would erase once and for all the image of foolish naïveté she had heretofore created. Long before the sun had slipped above the horizon, she lay shivering in the chill dawn, rehearsing what she would say to smooth over the embarrassment of facing him after their passionate embrace.

She could have saved herself the trouble. He gave her no opportunity to say anything whatsoever to him. In fact, he made such an obvious effort to keep her at a distance for the next three days, she could draw only one conclusion. He had taken her in complete disgust after—she blushed to even think of it—she had practically demanded he kiss her.

It was not enough that he remained unfailingly polite, but distant, during their daytime travels; he also made a point of securing them separate chambers at opposite ends of ramshackle coaching inns each night, despite his claim he had barely enough money left to pay for their meals. It wasn't until she innocently inquired the time of him that she learned he'd gone so far as to sell his ornate jeweled watch to pay for those accommodations.

She wanted to cry with vexation. Was the conceited lout so puffed up with his opinion of his own male charms he expected her to try to ravish him if he came close enough for her to get her hands on him? She couldn't remember when she'd been so angry or so humiliated.

By the morning of the fourth day she was so weary of his

boring politeness she abandoned her vow of decorum and racked her brain to think of something she could do that would irritate him enough to make him resort to his usual surly ways.

"Like it or not, you will have to help me into the saddle," she declared after they'd stopped to water the horses at a small, bubbling brook. "I am too stiff of joint from riding astride to mount by myself."

"I'll do no such thing," he grumbled, turning his back on her. But she stood her ground, and grim of face, he finally relented. Cupping his hands to give her a toehold, he literally catapulted her upward—a move for which Maddy was totally unprepared. She missed the saddle and, clutching at it wildly, fell back into his arms.

"I told you I felt stiff and clumsy," she said, laughing up at him.

Tristan wasn't laughing. For a long moment, he simply clasped her to his chest while his eyes darkened with some indefinable emotion. Maddy's heart leapt in her breast. "Tristan?" she asked in a voice soft with wonder.

His brows, black as crows' wings, drew together in a scowl. "Devil take it, Maddy, how many times must I warn you? Don't make the mistake of pushing me too far. I am doing my best to act the gentleman where you're concerned, but it doesn't come naturally—and believe me, you'd not like the beast you're so foolishly tempting." With those amazing words, he set her on her feet and strode to his horse, leaving her to mount her own as best she could.

For the next hour or two, Maddy followed him in a daze, her senses reeling. She hadn't misread his reaction to their kiss after all. He did feel the same magnetic attraction for her that she felt for him, but he was too honorable to declare himself while they were traveling alone and in such compromising circumstances.

Was he planning to court her once they reached London and he could do so properly? She shivered in anticipation. The thought of being courted by Tristan literally took her breath away.

With the bright spring sun beating down on their heads, they rode northward toward Paris through the lush vineyards of Bourgogne. Maddy scarcely noted the breathtaking beauty of the scenery around her. She was much too engrossed in her daydream of the moment when Tristan would, on bended knee, declare he had her father's permission to ask for her hand in marriage.

She frowned. But how could a man recently retired from the profession of spying hope to support a wife? She studied the proud set of his head, the strong line of his back and shoulders as he sat his horse. She doubted a man like Tristan would allow his father-in-law to support him, regardless of how wealthy that father-in-law might be.

Would his brother, the earl, deed him one of the family estates once he declared his intention to wed? Of course. That was the solution. They appeared to share a deep affection despite the fact that Tristan was born on the wrong side of the blanket. A noble family such as his must own any number of small holdings in the English countryside where one could raise sheep—and Tristan had a penchant for sheep. She'd seen the gleam in his eyes whenever they'd passed a flock grazing in a meadow.

Maddy felt suffused with a warm glow of happiness. She had found the man with whom she wanted to spend the rest of her days, and he felt the same about her. If the truth be known, she didn't really care where they lived. Life with Tristan would never be dull.

A raindrop splashed against her cheek . . . and another and another. She'd been so absorbed in her happy musings, she'd failed to notice the dark clouds gathering on the horizon. She could see now that a spring squall was about to burst upon them.

"We'll have to find shelter," Tristan shouted over the rising wind.

Shielding her eyes from the rain now lashing her face, Maddy searched for a barn or shed to wait out the storm. None were in sight. But off to her left, in the lee of a vine-planted hill, she spied one of the *cadoles* in which the vineyard workers slept during harvest. The tiny, stone, beehive-shaped structure might be dark and windowless and just barely large enough to hold two people—but it would protect them from the downpour.

"Over there," she directed, pointing to the barely discernible mound of fieldstones.

Tristan turned his head and his handsome features froze in horror. His face paled and he swiped at his brow as if beads of perspiration were mingling with the raindrops. "You cannot be serious," he choked. "It's scarcely large enough to hold a family of ground squirrels . . . and it has to be black as pitch inside."

Maddy smiled to herself as she urged her horse toward the *cadole*. Was Tristan afraid that if they holed up in such close quarters, he would be tempted to kiss her again? For a confirmed rake, he had certainly become a stickler for propriety. This latest revelation made her more certain than ever that he intended to court her once they reached London.

"This is no time to quibble over details," she declared, and promptly dismounted, tied the mare's reins to the nearest grape stake, and crawled through the narrow entrance into the *cadole*.

"It is roomier than it looks from the outside," she called over her shoulder.

Tristan gave no answer and she poked her head out to find him standing beside the hut in the pouring rain. "Don't be so foolish," she chided. "There is plenty of space for two people as long as you keep your head down."

Tristan groaned. Nothing in the world could induce him to crawl into that tiny stone hut and huddle in the dark until the storm passed. "I'll wait out here," he said tersely. "It is just a spring shower and will soon be over."

"Not soon enough to keep you from catching a case of lung fever." Maddy peered up at him, a frown puckering her brow. "Do not think I am unappreciative of your concern for my reputation. Your honorable conduct does you credit, but how do you think I will feel if in protecting my good name you make yourself seriously ill?"

Tristan stared at her, mouth agape. What was the fool woman prattling on about now? And what bearing did his fear of enclosed spaces have on her good name? Then he remembered she couldn't possibly know he turned into a craven coward at the very thought of being trapped in such a space.

Devil take it, he might as well confess his problem. He knew her well enough now to be certain she would never let up on him until he did—and what did it matter if she took him in disgust? Better that than the starry-eyed look she'd been giving him ever since he'd made the mistake of kissing her.

"My honor notwithstanding, I could not make myself crawl into that hut if my life depended on it," he said grimly. "I have had a terror of enclosed spaces since I was a small child—especially small, dark, enclosed spaces The *traboules* were hellish enough; I would turn into a raving lunatic if I crawled into this hut." There, he'd said it; let her scoff if she wished. Until now only Garth and Carolyn had been privy to his shame.

Maddy peered up at him from the entrance of the hut. "I have heard of such an affliction," she said matter-of-factly. "I do not believe it is terribly uncommon. But why in heaven's name didn't you mention this in the *traboules* instead of turning into a snarling beast every time we entered an enclosed space?"

She frowned. "Don't tell me. I already know. Your stupid masculine pride. I have to wonder what *le bon Dieu* had in mind when he made men the rulers of the world. They are such a silly, prideful lot."

In a matter of minutes Maddy had reduced the affliction that had haunted him since childhood to something she "didn't believe was terribly uncommon." One would think he'd confessed to having a hangnail, not a case of abject cowardice. But devil take it, this slip of a girl's calm acceptance of his debilitating weakness was almost as embarrassing as the weakness itself.

Shifting uncomfortably from one foot to the other, he watched her brush away the water that had dripped onto her forehead from the beam supporting the opening of the *cadole*. "Well, at least get the carriage blanket and cover your head," she said crossly. "I've no desire to be nursing you through a head cold for the balance of our trip."

Damn her eyes! First she'd made him out a fool; now she wanted to reduce him to some missish creature huddling beneath a blanket for fear of taking a chill. "I do not catch colds," he said stiffly. "I am impervious to such things. I have never been sick a day in my life."

Drawing the hood of his cassock over his head, he hunkered

down on the side of the *cadole* protected from the wind and prepared to wait out the storm.

"Do you remember what happened when you were a child to put this fear of confinement in your head?" Maddy asked, poking her head out of the hut when the wind died down sufficiently so they could carry on a conversation.

Tristan pulled the hood farther over his face. Of course he remembered. But that was one memory he had never divulged to anyone—not even his siblings.

"Sometimes putting such things into words is the first step toward conquering them," she said offhandedly, as if she had no idea she was asking him to bare the blackest secret of his soul.

Was she right? Would exposing his fears to the light take away the power they still held over him? He doubted it, but he knew from experience Maddy would wring the humiliating truth out of him sooner or later.

"My mother was a whore in one of the most notorious brothels in the London slums," he said finally, and heard Maddy gasp. *Let the nosy little busybody digest that bit of information if she could.* "The abbess let her keep me with her, but only if I didn't interfere with her professional duties. Hence, whenever she had a customer, which was nearly every night, she locked me in the clothes press. It was very dark and cramped and I was a mere tadpole with more imagination than sense. I used to stuff my fist in my mouth to keep from screaming in terror."

Maddy crawled from the hut to sit beside him in the rain, her eyes with wide horror. "But how could she do such a thing, knowing it frightened you so?"

"She didn't know," he said simply. "Why would I tell her? Even a six-year-old could see she had no other option."

Maddy felt as if her heart had been rent asunder. In her mind's eye she pictured Tristan as he must have been then— a little black-haired waif cowering, terrified, in his dark hidey-hole while his mother sold her body as a ten-penny whore.

He avoided her eyes, staring straight ahead to where, on the far horizon, the sun was breaking through the clouds. "As it turned out," he said softly, "the driver of a hackney coach solved my problem with the clothes press. He ran her down on a day much like this one. Though, in all fairness, with the rain and wind buffeting him, I doubt he ever knew she was beneath his wheels. She was such a little thing, he could easily have mistaken her for a pile of rags someone had tossed into the middle of Haymarket Street."

"Oh, Tristan, what a terrible experience for a young boy to suffer." Maddy slipped her hand into his. "And that's when the Countess of Rand took you in."

"Yes." He looked at her then—an odd, crooked smile twisting his lips. "The abbess knew who my father was, you see, and had one of her bully boys deliver me to the earl's town-house. He disclaimed me, of course, but the countess clasped me to her bosom, kissed away my tears, and made me as welcome as if I'd been one of her own. From that day forward, I was Lord Tristan, with nothing to remind me of my former life or my poor little mother except this blasted cowardly affliction which I'll probably carry to my grave."

Maddy gave his fingers a squeeze. "Don't ever call yourself cowardly again. I think you are the bravest person I've ever known. When I think of the torture you must have suffered in those dreadful, dark *traboules*, I could simply cry." And leaning her head against his shoulder, she proceeded to do just that.

Tristan shook his head in dismay. He'd been wrong in supposing he'd earn Maddy's disgust with his sordid tale. It appeared to make no difference whatsoever in her regard for him. If anything, her eyes held more stars than ever once she dried her tears—stars that spelled trouble ahead, unless he could dissuade her from this idiotic notion that he was some kind of tragic hero.

He was wrong about something else also. He was not immune to head colds. For the next two days and nights he alternated between burning with fever and shivering with ague. Maddy never actually said, "I told you so," but it was there in her eyes each time she looked at him.

Once she even went so far as to suggest he should spend a few days in bed at a small posting inn where they spent a night, but that only made him more determined than ever to push on toward Paris. By the time they entered the city late on the evening of March 19, he felt weak as a kitten. Furthermore, he'd developed a persistent hacking cough and a set of aching muscles that made sitting a horse constant agony.

Paris seemed strangely quiet—much too quiet to his way of thinking. One could scarcely credit that Napoleon and his legions were marching triumphantly toward the city—or that there was every likelihood that Parisians might go to bed this night under the king's rule and wake up tomorrow morning to find the emperor back on the throne.

"We must make our way to the Tuileries," Tristan said between coughing bouts. "Castlereagh will want a firsthand report on the fate of King Louis, and I may be the only one who can give it to him."

Remembering her grandfather's fanatic allegiance to the Bourbons, Maddy nodded her agreement, though more than anything else, she longed for a hot meal and a soft bed.

A crowd had gathered outside the gates of the royal palace. Tristan and Maddy dismounted and, keeping a tight rein on their horses, joined the people on the outskirts. "What is happening?" Tristan asked a grizzled old man leaning on a stout walking stick.

The fellow regarded Tristan through hooded eyes. "Nothing that should greatly concern you and the lad, Father. It is rumored the Little Corporal sleeps at Fontainebleau tonight, so Fat Louis flees to Ghent." He shrugged his narrow shoulders. "But it matters little who sits on the throne of France. Life will be no better or worse for the ordinary Frenchman."

He raised his head and peered toward the gate. "Ah, here is the king now," he said, doffing his narrow-billed cap.

As Maddy watched, two liveried footmen emerged, carrying an oversized chair in which sat a grossly obese man with thinning gray hair and a collection of chins which rested like great, white pudding bags on his purple satin waistcoat.

She stared at him in disbelief. "Never tell me that overstuffed toad is the king for whom my grandfather was willing to lay down his life?" she whispered to Tristan.

"That is the king," he said, stifling a cough.

A halfhearted cheer went up from the crowd and the perspiring footmen halted for a moment while the occupant of the chair raised a hand in greeting.

"My beloved countrymen," he said in a surprisingly strong, mellifluous voice, "I fear nothing for myself, but I fear for France. He who comes among us to light the torch of civil war brings us also the plague of foreign war. He comes to place our country once more under his iron yoke. He comes to destroy this constitutional charter I have given you."

A smattering of applause rippled throughout the crowd and one young soldier in a tattered Royalist uniform cried, *"Vive le roi!"*

The king mopped his brow with a lace-edged handkerchief and continued, "This is the charter which all Frenchmen cherish—may it be our sacred standard!"

Another cheer from the crowd, this time slightly more enthusiastic. Then, with the combined effort of half a dozen of his stalwart young guardsmen, Louis XVIII was hoisted aloft and stuffed into his ornate traveling coach. The last Maddy saw of him was a pudgy, ring-bedecked hand waving out the window as the carriage rumbled northward toward the Belgian border.

Her eyes prickled with tears. "I thank *le bon Dieu* my grandfather was not here to see his ridiculous travesty of a king fleeing before the Corsican," she said sadly. She looked about her. "At least he had some loyal supporters to cheer him as he left."

"Who will cheer Bonaparte with equal gusto when he enters the city tomorrow," Tristan said dryly. "The old man speaks for most Parisians. They are sick to death of strife and will settle for anyone who brings them peace. But that is not our problem."

He surveyed the crowd, which was scattering in all directions. "So far I have seen no familiar faces, but my luck can only hold so long. More than anything else, we need to leave Paris before someone recognizes me."

Mounting his horse, he made a careful survey of the broad avenue flanking the Tuileries. "But first we must find oats for the horses, as well as food for ourselves and beds on which to lay our heads for a few hours. We will make a dash for Calais at first light."

Wearily, Maddy mounted the little mare and followed him through the darkened streets of Paris. Once they'd passed the partially constructed Arc de Triomphe, which Napoleon had designed to celebrate his early military victories, the streets narrowed and the elegant buildings gave way to a rabbit warren of tenements and tiny, windowless shops.

The wind was rising sharply and the fetid air hanging over the city was soon thick with the dirt and debris that littered the ancient streets. Holding the reins with one hand and shielding her eyes from the flying grit with the other, Maddy struggled to keep up with Tristan as he urged his stallion down one narrow, twisting alleyway after another.

Twice he doubled back, passing through the same street they had traversed just moments before. But finally, just when she was certain he was hopelessly lost, he stopped before a recessed doorway at the end of a cobblestone street.

"My former abode," he explained in the gravelly voice he'd acquired with his head cold. He pounded on the door. "The landlady is an old friend who can be counted on for a decent meal and a clean bed."

He pounded again, and the door opened a crack, then was thrown wide by a small, dark-haired figure in a white nightrail. "Treeston, *mon ami*," she shrieked, winding her plump arms about his neck. "What are you, of all men, doing in the garb of a priest?"

Tristan chuckled, which started him coughing again. "It is a long story, Minette, and one better told over a glass of wine and a plate of your excellent food." He handed the reins of both horses to a ragged urchin lounging beside the open doorway and instructed him to lead them to the mews, then drew Maddy forward. "Can you put my young friend and me up for the night? We will want adjoining rooms with a connecting door."

Minette raised an expressive eyebrow as she stepped aside to let Tristan and Maddy enter. "So, *cheri*, you have not warmed my bed for ten months and now you wish such an arrangement with this . . . this creature!" She glared at Maddy.

Tristan glanced Maddy's way, as if to gauge her reaction to the risqué question, but by sheer force of will she managed to hide the shock she felt at the woman's frankness.

Furtively, she studied this "old friend" of his, who was apparently also an old lover. Even in the dim candlelight she could see the fine lines edging the woman's black, snapping eyes, which proclaimed her past the first blush of youth. Still, one could not deny her dark, sultry beauty, and her thin night-rail did little to hide her full breasts and rounded hips, two womanly attributes Maddy had always secretly envied in women more voluptuous than she.

Minette's lower lip protruded in a pout. "I have missed you, Treeston. It is my curse in life that my heart should never stop longing for such a cruel, uncaring man." She cast another venomous glance at Maddy. "And now, you insult me thus."

"I have missed you too, *cheri*," Tristan said, dropping a chaste kiss on the brow of the woman who had been his lover off and on for almost seven years.

He found himself strangely embarrassed by Minette's overt allusion to their former relationship. Her frankness had never bothered him before. In fact, there had been a time when he'd considered it amusing. But now that he was forced to view the situation through Maddy's eyes . . . Still, giving the little innocent a glimpse of his former life might be the best way to disillusion her about him.

In truth, he had no choice but to pacify Minette. She was a jealous little cat, and unless he buttered her up sufficiently, he would find himself with an empty belly and sleeping on the street. But honeyed words were all he intended to give her tonight. He had no desire whatsoever to share her bed—a rare phenomenon he felt certain must be attributed to his heavy head cold.

Gently he pried her clinging fingers from his arm. "What is this nonsense you've come up with?" he asked, chucking Minette under her softly rounded chin and giving her a brief kiss on her pouting red lips. "As I told you, the boy is merely a friend."

"This is true?"

"Have you ever known me to lie to you?"

"No, but I have often suspected you told me only half the truth." She shrugged. "Ah well, one cannot expect perfection, and"—her gaze roamed up and down his lean body—"there is much about you to admire." Within minutes, she had produced one of the delicious cold collations he remembered from when he was her tenant.

Maddy and he dined at the familiar round oak table in the ground floor parlor, and once she had laid out the food, Minette joined them. To be more precise, she joined him—at the hip. Despite his monumental efforts to control her, she literally crawled all over him while he struggled to consume his food.

"Behave yourself, Minette," he said finally, giving her a quick swat on the derriere. To no avail; her hands continued their suggestive exploration of his anatomy. He looked up to find Maddy's gaze riveted to her plate, her cheeks the color of the brightest apple in Minette's fruit basket.

Maddy's cheeks were still flaming when they repaired to their second floor chambers, probably because Minette's whispered, "My door will be unlocked as usual, *cheri*," echoed throughout the narrow hallway like a trumpet blown in a cave.

"Leave your candle lighted, as I shall mine, and the door opened between us," Tristan admonished Maddy as he stood in the doorway separating their two rooms. He removed his pistol from his belt and handed it to her. "I am usually a light sleeper, but I feel like the very devil tonight, so you'd best keep this beside you—and for God's sake remember to cock it if you feel the need to shoot."

Maddy studied the weapon in her hand with distaste. "Why would I need this? The only intruder we're apt to have is your former landlady, should you fail to take advantage of her unlocked door. Surely you don't want me to shoot such an 'old friend'!"

She turned away, lest he see how tempting she found the idea. She had never before been visited by the green-eyed monster, but the thought of Tristan's firm lips pressed to those of the Parisian Jezebel made her spitting mad.

"Minette will not come to my room. It is not her way. And since I have no intention of stirring from my bed once I'm in it, you should pass a restful night—but it is always wise to take precautions in times such as these."

He bent over, pulled his knife from the sheath strapped to his right boot, and placed it on his pillow. "Good night,

Maddy. Remember, we rise with the dawn." So saying, he removed his boots, crawled into bed fully clad, and promptly fell asleep.

Maddy retired to her own room, stripped off her dusty trousers and shirt, and pulled her boots from her aching feet. Attired only in her chemise, she splashed water from the bedside basin on her face and arms and crawled into bed. But exhausted as she was, sleep did not come easily. The mattress was uncomfortably lumpy and her mind was too full of the events of the day, indeed of the past fortnight, to allow for restful slumber.

For one thing, she had been profoundly shocked by Tristan's "old friend." She had never before met a mistress. It had been common knowledge that most of the former noblemen who frequented her grandfather's house kept such women, but they did so very discreetly.

She bit her lip in frustration. When Tristan got around to courting her, she intended to make it very plain that she would not countenance such liaisons once they were married. But then, he may have already mended his ways; he'd shown no interest in making a nocturnal visit to Minette, despite her provocative invitation.

Maddy could not begin to imagine how any man could find such vulgarity attractive. But she had to admit, it did give one pause for thought. There must be a happy medium somewhere between Minette's blatant sexuality and the chilly disinterest she'd seen most of the noblewomen in Lyon display toward their husbands.

A good hour later, she was still pondering the weighty question of how to remain a lady and still manage to keep one's husband out of the clutches of the demimonde when she heard the door to Tristan's chamber open and stealthy footsteps cross the tiny room toward his bed.

She gritted her teeth. Apparently he was wrong. Minette was not above visiting his room when he failed to show up at hers. As she listened, breath suspended, the footsteps ceased. There was a moment of silence, then a hoarse cry she recognized as Tristan's and a muttered obscenity in a voice that was most definitely not that of the landlady, nor indeed of any woman.

Maddy shot upright, reached for the pistol, cocked it, and sprinted to the connecting doorway. The dim candlelight revealed the intruder to be a massive black-haired man, dressed in a black jersey and tight black trousers that molded his powerful legs like a second skin.

He was grappling with Tristan atop the bed and as she watched, the two of them rolled over and over until they were jammed against the headboard with the intruder on top. He raised his arms, and Maddy's heart missed a beat when she saw a lethal-looking dager clutched in his beefy hand.

"Arretez vous!" she cried, raising the pistol with both hands. "Drop the knife or I will shoot!"

The assassin slowly lowered his arm and glanced over his shoulder with a pair of small, deep-set black eyes that sent chills skittering down Maddy's spine. She clutched the pistol frantically, her hands trembling like leaves in a windstorm. His evil gaze locked on the wildly weaving pistol, he cursed and raised his knife hand again.

"For God's sake, Maddy, shoot the bastard." Tristan's muffled shout came from where he lay crushed beneath his opponent's heavy body.

Maddy closed her eyes and pulled the trigger. Instantly the acrid smell of smoke filled her nostrils. She heard a thwack, a thud, then a muffled grunt as if someone had sustained a blow. She opened her eyes to see Tristan shove the inert body of the would-be assassin off him and struggle to his feet. She looked again. His hair and face were covered with some white, powdery substance that gave him a strange, almost ghostly appearance.

"Good shooting! You saved my life," he said, calmly dusting the same substance off the front of his cassock before he pried the pistol from her rigid fingers.

Maddy pressed her hand to her lips as bile rose in her throat. "Oh dear God! Is he . . . ? Did I . . . ?"

"He isn't and you didn't—but it was still a good night's work. As you will see, if you raise your eyes, your bullet struck one of the ceiling tiles, which fell on the blackguard's head just as he was about to plunge his knife in me."

He ran his fingers through his hair, sending flakes of powdery plaster swirling about his face, and his grin spread from ear to ear. "It would appear that head blows are your specialty, if the trail of cracked skulls you leave behind you as you quit France is any indication."

The figure on the bed groaned and Tristan promptly whacked him across the back of the head with the handle of the pistol. "I recognize this scoundrel," he said, slipping the pistol into the pocket of his cassock. "He is one of Fouché's hired assassins, and there's no one who deserves a headache more. In fact, I would be doing all France a favor if I disposed of the vermin here and now."

Maddy gasped.

"But out of deference to your tender feelings, I shall control my natural instincts and merely leave him sufficiently incapacitated to give us time to get safely out of Paris." Slashing the bedsheet into strips with his knife, he tied the fellow's ankles together and his hands behind his back.

"I am going to have a few words with Minette before we leave for Calais," he said grimly. "She has to have had a hand in this sorry matter; I made certain we weren't followed when we crossed Paris."

"But why would someone you considered a friend do such a thing?"

"Exactly what I mean to find out." He returned his knife to its sheath and moved toward the door. "Keep this locked while I'm gone. The tenants in this house usually mind their own business, but they had to have heard the gunshot. One of them might be tempted to do a little investigating if they see me leave the room."

He paused in the doorway. "In the meantime, I suggest you get back into your shirt and trousers. "You would have a hard time convincing anyone you were a boy attired as you are now."

Maddy followed the direction of his gaze and, to her horror, realized she was standing before him clad only in her thin chemise. Blushing hotly, she did an about-face and marched into her own room, slamming the connecting door behind her.

A cracked mirror hung on one wall of the tiny chamber and facing herself in it, she felt her spirits plummet to a new low. One thing was certain: if Tristan had ever had any doubts about the paucity of her womanly endowments, those doubts were now laid to rest, especially with the voluptuous Minette as a contrast. She frowned. Men were such strange creatures, and Englishmen the strangest of all. How could any woman know just how important such attributes were to a man when he chose the woman he wanted to grace his home and bear his children?

Eight

"W hy, Minette? Why did you do it? You have never had
any love for Citizen Fouché." Tristan fixed a chilly
stare on the woman occupying the bed he'd so often shared in
the past six years.

"Fouché? What does he have to do with the matter?"
Minette didn't bother to pretend she had not sent the assassin
after him, but she seemed genuinely surprised that he should
think the wily Minister of Police was involved. He half believed her; she had never been one to equivocate. Her lack of
pretense had always been the trait he most admired in her.

"You betrayed me," she declared, eyes blazing. "In my own
house. After all we have been to each other."

"How, may I ask, did I betray you?"

Tears welled in Minette's dark eyes. "Another woman I
might understand. We are neither of us the kind to limit ourselves to one lover. But a skinny young boy with the eyes of a
fawn! For that I shall never forgive you!"

"Maddy? You sent an assassin after me because you were
jealous of Maddy?"

"I did not send an assassin," she declared indignantly.
"What do you take me for? I merely asked my present *cher
ami*, who occupies the chamber that was once yours, to teach
you a lesson in manners."

"For your information, madame, this—*cher ami* of yours is
one of Fouché's most trusted minions, probably installed in
this house to spy on you since it is well known your sympa-
thies lie with the Royalists."

Minette stared at him with eyes blank with shock. "I swear I
did not know. And to think I have let the black-hearted devil
warm my bed for more than a month." She lowered her head

and peeped at Tristan from beneath her dark lashes. "Never think I would relish your death, Treeston. I could never be that angry at you."

She swiped at the tears spilling from her eyes. "But what kind of man have you become in that den of iniquity called Vienna? Did you think me some wide-eyed innocent raised in a convent that I would not know what you were up to when you demanded adjoining rooms with a connecting door?"

"Never that, Minette. I have always been aware you came from the gutters of Paris; I was just not aware your mind still dwelt there," Tristan said coldly. His fingers itched to throttle this jealous little French tart he had once found so amusing.

"So now, little gutter rat, you have not only put my life in danger; you have also endangered the life of the granddaughter of one of France's leading Royalists, whom I have been hired to transport safely to her father in England."

"The boy is really a girl?" Minette looked frankly skeptical. "But how could that be? Her figure is most certainly that of a slender boy."

"Not all women are as generously endowed as you, Minette. But I assure you, Maddy is a woman." *More woman than any other I have ever known.* "And just so you know how badly you have erred, she is not, nor ever will be, my lover."

Minette covered her face with her hands, the picture of contrition. "Mother of God, what have I done?" She raised her head and stared at Tristan beseechingly. "Tell me, *cheri*, what can I do to make amends?"

Tristan felt a twinge of satisfaction. This might work to his advantage after all. He leveled a look on his former mistress that had her cowering against the headboard. "Thanks to you, we dare not wait until dawn to leave for Calais," he said in his sternest voice. "But unfortunately, our horses are too spent to make the trip without sufficient rest."

Minette's countenance brightened perceptibly. "Say no more. My brother, Philippe, who is this very minute asleep in the next room, is the cleverest horse thief in all of Paris. I have but to ask and he will procure you two excellent steeds within the hour, even if he has to steal them from the stable of the royal palace."

With a sigh, she lounged back against the pillows, exposing

a generous amount of her remarkable cleavage. Her full, red lips formed the pout he had once found so provocative.

"So, *cheri*," she purred, "is there, by any chance, something else I can do for you before we wake Philippe?"

The storm that had chased Maddy and Tristan all the way from Paris abated as they neared Calais. They found the harbor crowded with ships and the docks swarming with anxious Royalists seeking transport to England before Napoleon Bonaparte once again claimed the throne of France.

"Your father's brig is riding at anchor out beyond the crush of vessels," Tristan said, shielding his eyes to scan the harbor from his vantage point at the far end of the southernmost pier. "We'll find an inn where we can wash off the dust of the road. Then I'll sell the nags. I need a pair of trousers and a shirt, and we must purchase you a proper dress and bonnet before we search out the longboat to row us aboard. You'll not want to arrive in England in the garb of a French peasant boy."

"*Merci*," Maddy said, grateful for his unexpected thoughtfulness. He really could be a love when he wanted to be, and thank heavens he'd finally shaken both his cold and the black mood he'd been in on their mad dash from Paris. He had been so glum and silent, she had come to the conclusion she must have somehow displeased him again.

She smiled. "What I mean to say is thank you. I must remember to speak English from now on."

"As must I." Tristan returned her smile, but it was a bleak smile that somehow stopped short of his eyes. He removed his riding glove and flicked it against his thigh, sending dust motes dancing around him. "So, Maddy, our epic journey is at an end at last. You must be greatly relieved."

Maddy nodded. "I shall not be sorry to leave France. It is a troubled land, and I feel no more allegiance to one faction than the other. All that I loved in this country died with my grandfather. But as to our journey, I could wish that would go on forever. It was a grand adventure and I shall have fond memories of it all the rest of my life."

"Indeed? Then you are truly unique, for I feel certain any other woman would gladly trade the hardships you have endured for the life of luxury awaiting you." He paused as if pondering how to proceed with what he had to say. "Your father is one of the wealthiest men in all of England and you are the sole heiress to his fortune, as well as the granddaughter of a French aristocrat. I predict the *ton* will welcome you with open arms."

Maddy laughed. "I sincerely doubt that. I was given to understand your British society makes a point of snubbing anyone with the slightest odor of commerce clinging to them."

"Times have changed, as have fortunes. Some of England's noblest families have suffered severe financial reverses in recent years, and it is not unusual to find them marrying their titled sons to the daughters of wealthy merchants. Not a bad arrangement, all told. The young lord saves his family estates from ruin and the lady in question gains the social acceptability that would otherwise be denied her."

"I have seen such arrangements in France also," Maddy said, "but I find them very sad. I should not like to be married simply for the money I can bring a husband." She leaned forward in the saddle to scratch behind the ear of her restless mare. "Wouldn't you find it distressing to know a woman married you only to get her hands on your father's money?"

"Obviously that is a problem with which I shall never have to deal," Tristan said dryly, "but if I did, I should endeavor to look at it realistically."

"I see, and what, in your opinion, is my reality?" she teased. "Should I seriously consider finding myself a titled husband so everyone of consequence in London society will overlook the fact that my father is in trade?"

"It is certainly something to consider," Tristan said, his expression so grave, Maddy felt as if a chill wind had suddenly whistled down her backbone.

She swallowed the lump that had risen in her throat. "But—speaking hypothetically, of course—what if I should decide I want a man who has no title . . . nor indeed even a surname that is considered respectable in proper social circles?"

"Then, Maddy, I would urge you to bestow your affections on some more worthy man, for if this hypothetical one of whom you speak was a man of honor, he would realize he had nothing to offer you—most certainly not marriage."

Maddy felt as if her heart had suspended its beating. "You

cannot be serious. Of course he would offer for me if he loved me . . . and if he knew I loved him. For nothing else really matters!"

"On the contrary, there are many other things that matter a great deal."

Maddy heard a quiet resignation in his voice that seemed totally alien to the vital man she had come to know and love over the past fortnight. What was he trying to convey with this frightening hypothesis?

She pressed her hand to her breast to still her thudding heart. "Tell me, if you please, what could possibly matter as much as the love two people feel for each other?"

"Loyalty, gratitude, responsibility . . . and most of all, honor." Tristan leaned forward in the saddle, his eyes fixed on the ship he had identified as her father's. "No one who calls himself a man can forswear such things as these—not even for love."

"But why would he have to forswear them?" she asked, gripped by a sudden premonition that without her knowledge, mysterious forces had been set into motion that would determine the course of her future life—forces over which she had not the slightest control.

"Because it is the way of things, Maddy," Tristan said, shrugging his powerful shoulders. "Because the ending of the drama in which your hypothetical man is a player was written long before the beginning—and there is nothing he can do to change it."

"I do not accept that." Maddy matched his grave expression with one of her own. "There is always something one can do if one cares enough. This I believe with all my heart."

Tristan could see he had hurt her, maybe even frightened her—a thing he would regret all the days of his life, almost as much as he would regret the weakness that had led him to kiss this innocent, trusting woman with such uncontrolled passion that he had ignited a flame that threatened to consume them both.

He could not undo the damage he'd done; but neither could he let her go on blindly believing in happiness ever after. At least now she would not be taken totally unawares when her father divulged his plan to make her a countess.

He told himself that her pain would be short-lived, that what she thought was love was only infatuation for the man who had given her the first glimpse of her own sensuality.

He told himself she would be better off in the long run because Garth would be a much better husband than he could ever hope to be.

Unfortunately, the one thing he could not tell himself was how to bear the pain of watching her become his brother's wife.

Tristan had purchased only the roughest of seaman's garb for himself—canvas pants, a jersey, duffel coat, and woolen seaman's cap. But he'd spared no expense on Maddy's new traveling dress, which was of French cambric, the rich amber color of an autumn maple leaf. It perfectly matched her eyes, as did her fur-trimmed pelisse of Utrecht velvet and the perky, high-crowned bonnet that covered her freshly washed hair.

It was without a doubt the most attractive outfit she had ever owned, and ordinarily she would have been over the moon. But thanks to the depressing conversation she'd had with Tristan, all the joy had gone out of the day for her.

He had made it all too plain that he would never offer for her—not because he didn't love her, but because his sense of honor forbade it. But what, she wanted to know, did honor have to do with it? As if he hadn't shown time and time again he was a man of honor despite his unfortunate birth.

Well, she simply would not accept his declaration—as she had already informed him—not unless he told her he didn't love her, and those words had never crossed his lips. No indeed, she was too much of an optimist to be defeated so easily, as he would soon see. Still, it was frightfully upsetting. And just when she'd been so certain all was going well! *Nom de Dieu*, what kind of weapons did a woman need to combat a man's misplaced sense of honor—especially a man as pigheaded as Tristan?

In a fog of misery, she climbed into the longboat and, with Tristan beside her, was rowed out to her father's ship, the masthead of which was a mermaid who bore a striking resemblance to Minette, both in face and torso. Needless to say, this did nothing to dispel Maddy's gloom.

The longboat circled the hull to where the rope ladder was hung and, raising her eyes, she saw the name emblazoned on the side of her father's brig—THE MADELAINE.

"He named his ship after me." Instinctively, she turned to Tristan, tears misting her eyes. "All those years when I was so certain my father cared nothing for me, this ship was sailing the oceans with my name on it." She choked back a sob and accepted the clean, folded handkerchief Tristan pressed into her fingers—one of the four he had purchased on their shopping tour of Calais. What with one thing and another, her emotions were very close to the surface at the moment, and this newest revelation touched her deeply.

What a wondrous, topsy-turvy carnival her quiet little world had become, and none of it would have happened if this stubborn, impossible, stiff-necked Englishman hadn't come seeking her in Lyon. She regarded him solemnly, her heart in her eyes.

"Damn it, Maddy, get that blasted puppy-dog look off your face." Tristan's voice was harsh, his mouth a thin slash of disapproval. "Now climb the ladder so we can get underway."

With one last swipe at her brimming eyes, Maddy folded his handkerchief and put it in her pocket. Nothing had really changed, but deep down inside her a tiny seed of hope germinated. "Methinks the fellow protests too much," she murmured to herself, happily misquoting the favorite bard of the English.

She reached for the rope ladder dangling at the side of the ship and placed her foot on the first rung. But no sooner had she attempted to move to the second rung than she realized that complying with Tristan's order in her new traveling costume was not all that simple. The skirt was too narrow to afford easy climbing, yet more than wide enough to allow the two sailors manning the longboat a view of her ankles that no lady could, in good conscience, allow—and however unconventional she might be in some respects, Maddy had been brought up to be a lady.

Cheeks flaming, she clung to the ladder, unable to move either up or down and thinking longingly of her rough peasant's breeches and the freedom of movement she had enjoyed as a boy.

"Look the other way or answer to me, you grinning apes,"

Tristan barked, and a moment later he moved to the rung below her, shielding her with his own body from any surreptitious ogling by the chastised seamen.

She sighed. Once again her hero had come to her rescue; how could he or anyone else question his sense of honor?

The crew was already unfurling the sails when Tristan and Maddy stepped onto the deck. The captain greeted them with obvious impatience and a searching perusal of Maddy when, to her surprise, Tristan introduced her as his friend, Miss Smythe. With a curt bow, the captain left them on their own and repaired to the bridge while the first mate supervised the hasty raising of the anchor.

"It was your father's wish that your identity be kept a secret until you reached England and he could make your existence known publicly himself," Tristan explained once the captain was out of earshot.

"Why?"

"That is something you will have to ask him." Something about the way Tristan avoided her eyes led Maddy to believe he knew a great deal more about her father and his wishes than he had heretofore let on. In fact, now that she thought about it, his answer as to why he had been the one chosen to return her to England had been much too glib to be entirely believable.

But why the mystery? What was he hiding? And why did she have a feeling that somehow her father and his wishes had a strong bearing on his refusal to offer for her? Maybe the answer to that was one of the weapons she needed to combat this mysterious code of honor he had chosen to live by.

Far above her, the sails caught the brisk salt breeze and the ship lurched forward; beside her, Tristan pulled the collar of his duffel coat up around his ears and jammed the seaman's cap on his head. Maddy's breath caught in her throat. More than ever, he looked the part of a buccaneer; she could almost imagine they were heading for the Spanish Main instead of the Straits of Dover.

The ship cleared the harbor and once in the open water, the wind freshened. She tied the ribbons of her bonnet more tightly beneath her chin to keep it from blowing off and her heartbeat quickened. They were well and truly on their way to England at last.

Curious, she stared about her at the ship that bore her name. The deck was immaculate, the brass gleaming, and the crew, though a rough-looking lot, appeared to be working with cheerful efficiency. Even the somewhat surly captain appeared in better spirits; quitting the bridge, he joined Tristan and Maddy on deck.

A short man, he was almost as broad as tall, but he was obviously all muscle without an ounce of fat on his square frame, and his face had the same weathered look as the teak planking beneath his feet. His uniform, if it could be called that, was a nondescript blue with tarnished brass buttons, and beneath his battered captain's hat, his iron-gray hair was tied at his nape with a narrow strip of frayed black leather. Apparently her father didn't demand the same look of perfection in his ship's officers as he did in the ship itself.

"I've been expecting you these past four days, milord, and I don't mind telling you I was getting mighty anxious," the captain said in explanation of their hurried departure. "If the Old Man hadn't issued orders to wait for you, I'd have weighed anchor long ago.

"My seamen have heard disturbing rumors in Calais that the Corsican is marching across France and gathering an army as he goes. If this is true, t'is no time to be caught lollygagging in a French harbor."

"No time indeed," Tristan agreed. "For the rumors are, in fact, all too true. Bonaparte is already in Paris and even after all he's put them through these past years, the soldiers who served under him are flocking to his standard by the thousands."

"Bloody hell! The man must be a bloomin' spellbinder." The captain flushed. "Beg pardon, ma'am. We don't often carry passengers—especially ladies. I'm not used to watching my language."

Raising his spyglass, he searched the horizon. "There's even talk of a French frigate lying in wait for any British merchantmen trying to cross the Channel, but I put little credence in that. We've seen little of the French navy in the ten years since Admiral Nelson put them to rout. Still, it never hurts to be on the alert."

He grinned sheepishly. "If the truth be known, I'd rather

face Bonaparte and all his legions than the Old Man if I let anything happen to *The Madelaine* while she's under my command. She's his flagship, you see, and his pride and joy. I doubt he'd have let her leave her home port if he'd had any suspicion Old Boney was about to cause more trouble."

Once again, he studied Maddy with undisguised curiosity. "Unless I miss my guess, he's cursing himself out this very minute for letting you talk him into putting the brig in harm's way. You must be a very persuasive fellow, milord, to have convinced him to let you use *The Madelaine* for your own purposes."

Maddy could see he was fishing for information, but Tristan merely smiled obliquely and sent him on his way none the wiser. She held her counsel, but more than ever, she felt certain the captain was not the only person from whom Tristan was withholding information. Minette had pegged him correctly. Tristan was very adept at divulging only what he wanted his listener to know—which, she supposed, was a very useful talent for a spy.

But damn the arrogant Englishman and his half truths. She had lived with half truths all her life and she was heartily sick of them. Her temper flared and with it an irresistible urge to do something so unbelievably outré it would shock Tristan out of his smug, self-righteous shell and wipe that infuriating look of cool indifference from his handsome face.

She curled her fingers around the smooth, polished wood of the ship's rail and breathed in the cold, salt spray thrown upward as the ship plowed through the choppy waters. "An idea just occurred to me," she said, raising her eyes to gaze at his stern, implacable profile. "You, sir, are rather deeply in my debt."

He turned toward her with a scowl. "How so?"

She smiled sweetly. "I saved your life, as you yourself admitted. Surely that warrants some compensation."

His eyes widened with surprise. "I cannot dispute the fact that I'd have had a knife between my ribs but for you, but I look askance at your lack of taste in demanding compensation for such a thing."

His scowl deepened. "But admitting a debt and paying it are not necessarily one and the same. You are the heiress, Maddy, not I. All I have in my pockets at the moment is what's left from the sale of the horses after outfitting us both with decent clothes—and I'll need every farthing to see us from Dover to London. I am afraid, my greedy little friend, you will have to wait for your compensation until I draw my last six month's pay from Whitehall."

Maddy watched the same wind that was billowing the sails whip a strand of Tristan's shoulder-length black hair across his face and smiled to herself. Just as she'd expected, he was falling nicely into her trap. She raised a querulous eyebrow. "But you do admit the debt?"

"Very well. I do admit the debt."

"Then it must follow, that you also admit it is my right to determine a just compensation."

Tristan leaned on the rail, his gaze riveted on the white-capped waves rolling back from the bow of the ship. The smallest of smiles curled the corner of his sensuous mouth as if, in spite of himself, he was enjoying their verbal sparring. "Ah," he sighed, "but what, pray, is a just compensation? Surely not the same thing to an heiress as to a man whose pockets are to let. I should not like to find myself in a debtors' cell at Newgate over this 'just compensation.'"

"On my oath!" Maddy raised her right hand. "The pittance I ask would not empty the pockets of the poorest chestnut vendor we passed just yesternight outside the Tuileries."

"Very well then." Tristan turned his back to the railing and, leaning his forearms on it, regarded Maddy with a speculative gaze. "Why do I have the feeling that something is amiss here—that you are not being entirely forthright?"

"Probably because, like all men, you tend to look at the world through your own devious eyes. So, let me see. How much will it be?" Maddy raised her left hand and counted off the fingers with her right. Forefinger, index finger, ring finger. "Three it is then."

"So I owe you three pounds for saving my life? That strikes me as more than fair."

"Three pounds? What are these 'pounds' of which you speak? I have not yet set foot in England and know nothing of your confusing currency."

"Three francs then? I believe I am insulted. Is that truly all you think my life is worth, mademoiselle?"

"But of course not. My life in France is behind me; I no longer deal in francs."

Tristan's expressive black brows drew together in a frown. "Three of what, then, Maddy? What is it you think I owe you?"

Maddy closed her gloved hand around the railing and braced herself against the rolling of the ship. Heart pounding with trepidation at her own daring, she raised her gaze to the heavens just as a pale sun burst through the bank of clouds blanketing the sky above the Channel. A good omen, she felt certain.

"Three of what?" Tristan asked again, a note of impatience sharpening his voice.

"Why the only currency in which you and I may deal equitably, of course. By my reckoning, monsieur, you owe me exactly three . . . kisses."

Nine

"**D**evil take it, Maddy, you go too far. You have always shown a penchant for the outrageous, but this is beyond the pale!" Tristan gritted his teeth in frustration. "How can you suffer such ladylike distress at showing a glimpse of ankle one minute, then act like the veriest hoyden the next?"

"It is not ladylike to enjoy being kissed?" Maddy looked positively dumbfounded. "But that simply does not compute. I have only been kissed once, but I could plainly see it was a most pleasurable pastime. If I must pretend I dislike it to project an appearance of propriety, I fear the cause is hopeless, for I have never had the least talent for dissembling."

Tristan groaned. That blasted kiss again! What kind of monster had he created with that one moment of moonlight madness? "I fault myself for your confusion," he said stiffly. "In an unguarded moment, I succumbed to my baser instincts—a transgression for which I am heartily sorry."

"You infer then that if I were truly a lady I should find kissing abhorrent?"

"Of course not." *Lord, how had he gotten himself into this bumblebroth?* "There is nothing wrong with enjoying a kiss, but a lady reserves such feelings for the man she plans to marry." Too late, he realized his blunder. Maddy had that starry-eyed look again.

He chose to ignore it rather than risk digging a deeper hole than the one he already found himself in. He hunched into his duffel coat and stared out to sea. "We will simply forget you ever broached the unfortunate subject."

"We will do no such thing!" Maddy's voice fairly crackled with indignation. "You were the one to make such a point about honor. What is honorable about refusing to pay one's debts?"

"This has nothing to do with paying debts. You wouldn't understand, but there are unwritten rules about such things. No man with even a modicum of ethics would poach another man's private preserve." *Another stupid slip of the tongue; he had almost given the game away with that one.*

Maddy drew herself up to her full height and stared him in the eye. "And what bearing does that have on the subject at hand, pray tell? I am no man's private preserve—and I'll tell you something else, Mr. Tristan Thibault. Neither am I some missish young schoolgirl whom you can wangle out of her due. I am a woman grown, and a merchant's daughter to boot. One way or another, I intend to collect what is owed me."

Tristan gnashed his teeth. He wasn't certain how or when he had lost control of the situation, but lost it he had, for he could plainly see that nothing he'd said had changed her mind one iota about the kisses she planned to collect from him. She was, without a doubt, the most stubborn, the most unreasonable, the most infuriating woman he had ever had the misfortune to meet.

Turning away from her, he leaned on the rail and stared at the churning water beneath him, his thoughts as turbulent as the white-capped waves rocking the ship. Hell and damnation! She had even gone so far as to blithely declare she would not collect the kisses all at once, choosing instead to keep them as special treats for when her spirits needed lifting. Like pieces of candy she could savor whenever the desire for a sweet struck her.

Though he racked his brain, he could find no logical reason for her bizarre behavior. She was not some trollop with the morals of an alley cat like Minette. But neither did she display the modesty and rectitude of a true lady. Rather, she was halfway between the two—a lady-hoyden, if there could be such a thing.

What kind of wife would this "lady-hoyden" make his staid, conventional brother? And what possible explanation could he give her father, and Garth, if she actually made good her threat to waylay him whenever she felt in the mood for a kiss!

As he saw it, his only hope lay in the possibility that once they reached London she would become so caught up in her new life, she would forget the whole silly idea. Or, failing that, he would find the will and the way to stay out of her sight until Garth and she were safely married.

It was late afternoon when they reached Dover. This closest of the English ports to the coast of France was shrouded in fog so thick, a ghostly pall hung over the docks. The other ships in the harbor loomed like dark shadows in the gray, swirling mist, and the dockmen who caught and secured *The Madelaine*'s mooring lines were merely half-seen specters with strangely disembodied voices.

Following the recommendation he'd secured from an innkeeper in Calais, Tristan searched out a moneychanger who converted the remaining francs from the sale of the horses into pound notes. The rate of exchange was ridiculous, but considering the times, no worse than he'd expected.

Next, with Maddy in tow, he stopped at the stable where, before sailing for Calais, he'd secured the pair of matched grays and the phaeton that were all that was left of the Earl of Rand's stable. "Have the horses fed and the rig made ready at dawn tomorrow, for we shall leave for London at first light," he directed the ostler.

That done, he searched out a clean but humble dockside inn and secured accommodations for the night. A tankard of ale and two plates of mutton and boiled potatoes depleted all but a few of his coins, but at least Maddy and he would go to their respective beds on the last night of their journey with full stomachs.

"I'll have my first kiss now, if you please," she said as he walked her to her chamber door an hour later.

Tristan's head whipped around. "You'll what?"

"I'll have my kiss," she repeated. "For if there was ever a time when my spirits were in need of elevating, that time is surely tonight. I cannot stop thinking about my grandfather and my home in Lyon . . . and I fear I find this England of yours a trifle depressing."

"Depressing? How so?"

Maddy frowned. "For one thing, the language is harsh to my Gallic ears; for another, the food is deplorable. *Nom de Dieu*, there was not even a hint of rosemary on the lamb, which I suspect was really mutton. Nor was there so much as a sprig of parsley on the potatoes." She shuddered. "And Dover is so cold . . . and gray."

"It's the fog," Tristan said, his heart aching at the sight of her woebegone face. He watched her finger the flowers on her new bonnet as if even the artificial blossoms reminded her of the sunnier clime of her home in southern France.

Gently, he brushed a tousled curl off her forehead. "The sun will probably shine tomorrow and everything will look brighter—and don't judge all English food by what is served in a dockside inn. There is nothing better than plain country cooking, to my way of thinking. Though admittedly our British cooks have not the skill with herbs and spices of their continental counterparts, which is why most of the peers of the realm staff their kitchens with French chefs."

He was prattling inanely, he knew, but he hoped such small talk would make her forget her homesickness. For that was the malady from which she suffered. He had dealt with it often enough himself in the past six years to recognize the symptoms. She was also close to exhaustion. Even in the dim light of the single wall sconce decorating the narrow hallway, he could see her extreme pallor and the dark smudges beneath her eyes.

She regarded him solemnly—waiting, he suspected, for him to comply with her highly improper request. As God was his witness, he had no intention of kissing her. Not now. Not ever again. He had learned his lesson on that score.

But devil take it, she looked so young, so vulnerable . . . so unspeakably lonely. A terrible, wrenching tenderness welled within him and he found he could no more refuse the comfort she asked than he could refuse to draw the breath of life into his lungs.

"Ah, Maddy," he murmured, and taking her in his arms, he kissed her with the same chaste compassion he'd often kissed away his sister Caro's childish hurts. Raising his head, he smiled down at her, congratulating himself that for once he had managed to maintain a tight control on his emotions where this perplexing lady-hoyden was concerned.

With a sigh, she snuggled deeper into his arms. Her eyes were closed, their amber light hidden beneath sooty lashes. "I didn't know," she said softly against his chest. "I am so ignorant about such things, I thought all kisses were the same. I see now they are not at all. This one was so . . . so different from the last. Very nice," she hastened to add, "but quite different."

Her eyes fluttered open and her gaze locked with his. "And how wise you are to know exactly what kind of kiss is apropos to the moment."

She cupped his cheek with her hand in a gesture of tender affection and instantly his heart started thudding heavily in his chest. "Maddy," he whispered hoarsely, and before his very eyes, lips that only moments before had trembled like those of a frightened child now curved in a seductive, womanly smile that sent tongues of flame licking along his veins. With a strangled sound deep in his throat, he again drank hungrily of her soft, open mouth.

"Oh my," she murmured a long time later, "I can see you really do know a great deal about kissing. All kinds of kissing. If I were not already . . ." She pressed her fingers to her lips. "Well, I certainly would be now."

Hell and damnation, she'd done it again! Driven him to lose the control he'd always prided himself was inviolable. How could a complete innocent be such a temptress? He dropped his arms to his sides and stepped back, determined to make her understand once and for all the folly of this attraction between them.

He took a deep breath. "Maddy—"

"Good night, Tristan, she said softly, interrupting him before he could phrase what he wanted to say. Opening the door, she quickly slipped into her chamber. "Dream sweetly, as I know I shall, for thanks to your lovely kisses, my flagging spirits have quite recovered."

She glanced over her shoulder, the same enigmatic smile on her face that had been his undoing just moments before. "But remember," she said softly, "I did not ask for the second one, so it was free. You still owe me two more."

As he'd predicted, they rose the next morning to a cloudless sky and a dawn bright with the promise of a sunny day. Maddy was obviously in a cheerful mood, and Tristan felt loath to risk upsetting her again with the lecture on propriety he had re-hearsed during his long, sleepless night. In truth, it scarcely seemed worthwhile. Once they reached London and Garth began to court her, she would forget all about those two kisses she claimed he owed her.

With dogged determination, he ignored the pain that such a picture of the future caused him and strove to make their last few hours together as pleasant as possible.

The grays were particularly lively after their long period of inactivity and Tristan pushed them to their limits, pausing only for the briefest of rests. For with every mile closer to London they drew, the greater his need became to end the torture of Maddy's presence. He could see now there was nothing for it but to request that Lord Castlereagh send him on an assignment as far away from London as possible.

Dusk was settling over London when they arrived—the daytime life of garrulous street peddlers and sober merchants, busy matrons and noisy children giving way to the painted prostitutes and wealthy pleasure-seekers that inhabited the ancient streets after dark.

Tristan guided the grays along Holborn Road to the busy crossroad leading to the section of the city in which Caleb Harcourt resided. "You can't miss Bloomsbury Square for it's that near the British Museum," the old man had said in the day he'd seen him off on his assignment. And indeed, he found it with an ease that he could see left Maddy thoroughly impressed with his knowledge of the vast city.

He had no idea what to expect of a residence so far removed from the genteel environs of Mayfair, where the townhouses of the Earl of Rand and other members of the *ton* were located. But the minute he saw the narrow, two-story, redbrick townhouse standing at the north end of Bloomsbury Square, he decided it suited Caleb Harcourt perfectly.

Neat, unpretentious, and unadorned by the Ionic columns and leering gargoyles that decorated the large mansions surrounding it, the small house had a symmetry and grace of line that somehow reminded him of Harcourt's trim flagship, *The Madelaine*.

"This lovely little house is where my father lives?" Maddy asked, her eyes looking more than ever like those of a startled fawn. "Are you certain?"

"I'm certain," Tristan replied. "He gave me explicit directions as to where I should deliver you, including the fact that I should look for the brass door knocker in the shape of a dolphin—and unless my eyes deceive me, there it is."

With the promise of a shilling, he tossed his reins to one of the ragged street urchins who obviously made his living tending the horses of the visitors to Bloomsbury Square, handed Maddy down from the carriage, and led her up the shallow steps to the door of the townhouse.

Scarcely had he raised the knocker than the door burst open, revealing an ancient fellow whose formal attire proclaimed him a butler, but whose scarred cheek and patch-covered eye more closely resembled those of a Barbary pirate.

"Come ye in, Miss Maddy, and ye too, young feller, and glad I am to see ye. The cap'n's been storming around like a sou'wester in the rigging this week past and I'm that weary of his evil temper," he declared with a familiarity no proper butler would presume to display. Remembering the old codger he'd met at Harcourt's office, Tristan decided the eccentric cit must make a habit of surrounding himself with colorful employees.

Stepping aside, the butler waved them through the door into a small entry hall, the walls of which were adorned by paintings of a dozen or more brigantines in full sail, all bearing the Harcourt flag and each with a brass nameplate at the base of its frame.

Tristan was so intrigued by the paintings and by the intricate ship's model displayed on an ebony pier table, he failed to see the old butler limp to the foot of the graceful staircase curving to the floor above. "She's ere, Cap'n. So ye can quit yer frettin' now," he hollered at the top of his lungs, then promptly disappeared behind the stairwell.

Moments later, Caleb Harcourt thundered down the stairs, sans both topcoat and waistcoat, and with his shirtsleeves rolled to the elbow. He stopped a few feet short of Tristan and surveyed him with a baleful eye. "So, you've arrived at last," he declared in the booming voice Tristan remembered all too well. "And high time too! I'd have thought with Boney at your heels, you'd have reached London sooner than my reckoning—not a full se'enight later."

Tristan felt his hackles rise at the injustice of this criticism.

"The circumstances did not permit setting a rigid timetable," he said coldly. "Indeed, with all that's transpired in France during the last month, we are lucky to have made it to London at all."

Harcourt looked taken aback by the vehemence of Tristan's reply. "Aye, I give you that now that I think on it," he conceded. "I wasn't complaining, lad, but merely giving vent to the frustration of the past seven days."

His gaze shifted to Maddy, traveling from the top of her head to the tips of her toes with a perusal so intense, Tristan saw the color blanch from her face. "Never say this woman grown is my daughter, Maddy," he said gruffly. "Hell's bells, girl, when last I saw you I could carry you on my shoulder. This day has been a long time coming. Much too long, to my way of thinking."

Maddy dropped into a graceful curtsy. "I am pleased to see you too, Papa," she said in a stilted little voice that told Tristan she'd been much more nervous about this meeting with her father than she had let on.

Harcourt raised his hand in dismissive gesture. "Here now, none of that bobbing up and down for me, girl. I'm a plain man and always will be. Save such folderol for the swells you'll be meeting once we've had a fancy modiste make you up some pretties."

He chuckled at Maddy's look of surprise. "Aye, that's right. I've plans for you, young lady. Plans I've been laying all these long years I've waited for you to remember who it was that fathered you."

Maddy felt her knees go weak, recalling her grandfather's surprising deathbed confession. "I believed *you* had forgotten me, Papa," she said, choking back the sob rising in her throat. "Only recently did I learn otherwise."

Harcourt's eyes blazed. "Forgotten you? How could you think such a thing when even with England and France at war, I managed to smuggle enough money to your grandfather each quarter to guarantee you were always well cared for?"

He studied Maddy with narrowed eyes. "That devious old Tartar never told you! And all the time I was thinking my own flesh and blood didn't care enough to write me a line once or twice a year." He pulled a handkerchief from his pocket, blew his nose, and wiped his eyes, which had grown suspiciously moist.

"Damn and blast! I should haver sent for you years ago." He shrugged his powerful shoulders as if divesting himself of a great burden. "Well, it's all water down the Thames now, and I'm not one to look back on yesterday when we've tomorrow ahead of us." He held out his arms. "Come here, girl. Give your old papa the hug he's not had these fifteen long years."

Maddy stepped into his embrace and instantly was deluged with memories of being swept up in the arms of this great bear of a man, of walking through Hyde Park, her hand safely clasped in his. And other memories of crying herself to sleep night after night in a strange bed not at all like her own little trundle bed, afraid to ask why her beloved papa had sent her away. She longed to tell him how much she had missed him. But she could see that with Tristan looking on he was already embarrassed by the emotion of their reunion, as was she, so she merely laid her head on his shoulder and gave way to her silent tears.

"But here now," he growled a moment later, "what are we doing standing around in this drafty entry hall like a bunch of gapeseeds fresh from the country?" He lifted her chin with his large, callused finger. "And you with circles as black as the soot from a London chimney beneath your pretty eyes."

His rugged face softened in a smile. "I think I should have old Griggins show you to your chamber so's you can have a lie-down while I trade a few words with the earl's brother here. Then we'll have a bite to eat and a nice, long gabble."

He'd called her a woman grown one minute, and was sending her to her chamber for a nap as if she were still a five-year-old, the next. She could see she would have to make him understand who and what she was. But not now. Not when every inch of her body ached from exhaustion.

She slipped out of his arms and as she watched, he reared back his head like a great bull elephant and bellowed, "Griggins, you blasted old swabber, where'd you get to now?"

"Hold your water, Cap'n. I just be finishing my supper." The voice came from behind the stairwell, and Maddy stifled the urge to chuckle as the old fellow emerged, evidently from the kitchen as he had a muffin in his hand and crumbs on his lip.

It was obvious her father was accustomed to his servant's lack of respect, for he made no comment about the fellow's cheeky reply, but merely ordered, "Take Miss Maddy up to her chamber while her legs'll still carry her."

Maddy turned to Tristan, and for one brief instant his eyes caressed her with tender concern. Then, as if he realized they had an audience, he donned his usual mask of cool indifference. Her gaze traveled to his strong, expressive mouth and she felt a sudden, overwhelming desire to collect another of the kisses owed her.

Nom de Dieu, she must have the instincts of a trollop to be constantly bedeviled by such unladylike thoughts. She only hoped Tristan made her an offer soon, before her feelings for him drove her to commit a serious impropriety.

Determinedly she pulled her wits together. "Thank you, Tristan," she said in the most proper of ladylike voices. "Ours was a great adventure and I shall treasure the memory forever. But Papa is right. Now that it is over, I find I am very tired. A nap sounds most welcome."

She followed Griggins to the foot of the stairs, where she hesitated, a wry smile on her face. "But I shall plan on seeing you later, Tristan."

"Not tonight, Maddy. My stepmother was not well when I left, and I am anxious to get home."

"Very well, tomorrow then." She held his gaze with her own, her lips curling in a mischievous smile. "Do not forget we have some unfinished business."

Caleb Harcourt poured two brandies, handed one to Tristan, and took a seat behind the Sheraton desk in his bookroom, where they'd adjourned after Maddy left them. With a wave of his hand, he indicated Tristan should occupy the chair facing him.

Like the entryway, this walnut-paneled room also had a nautical ambience. A ship's compass adorned the top of a small table, which on closer inspection appeared to be constructed of a brass hatch cover, and to the left of the desk stood a cluttered chart table.

Every wall was lined with books, and Tristan found himself wondering if Caleb Harcourt was actually an avid reader or if the hundreds of richly bound volumes were used merely to create the effect that this "plain man," as he termed himself, was really a learned scholar.

"Maddy favors her mother in looks, and that's a fact," Harcourt said, opening the conversation. "Except for her height, of course. Clarisse was a head shorter—prettiest little creature God ever created. I took one look at her and lost my head completely. It wasn't until after Maddy was born that I realized I'd married a woman who'd never had a sensible thought in her life. I'm trusting Maddy's inherited some of what's between her ears from me."

Tristan smiled, remembering how often she had outwitted him. "You need have no worry on that score, sir. She is highly intelligent and I'd stack her up against any man when it came to courage. We had some rather harrowing experiences on our trip across France, and she survived them all without a whimper."

"Got bottom, has she? Good. I'd expect nothing less of my daughter." Harcourt's shrewd old eyes studied Tristan closely. "What did Maddy mean when she said you had unfinished business?"

"Just a friendly bit of banter," Tristan said vaguely.

"Friendly, eh! I couldn't help but notice how friendly the two of you had gotten on the trip—enough so as to be calling each other by your given names."

He paused. "But not too friendly, I trust. Man for man, I'd take you over your half brother as a son-in-law any day, you understand. But he has the title, and I'll not settle for less where Maddy's concerned."

Tristan felt a sudden urge to plant the rag-mannered old tyrant a facer, even though he knew his anger was occasioned as much by his own sense of guilt as by Harcourt's insensitive remark. "Damn your eyes, Harcourt," he snarled. "Thanks to you, your daughter and I found ourselves in a very dangerous situation in France. We managed to survive it and, as a result, formed a fast friendship. I resent your implication that I abused that friendship in any way or that she is the kind of woman to inspire such base conduct on my part. For your information, sir, the fact that I am a bastard does not preclude my having principles."

Harcourt blinked. "Simmer down, lad. I meant no offense. I've nothing against bastards. Truth is, I'm one myself in every sense of the word, which is why I want something better for my daughter. I saw what being tarred by my brush did to her mother. I'll not have those biddies in the *ton* barring Maddy from their fancy doings like they did Clarisse."

"I can accept that. I'd probably feel the same if I had a daughter," Tristan said stiffly. "If there is nothing more you wish to discuss, sir, I shall take my leave of you. I've a good two-hour drive to Winterhaven, and both I and my nags are near exhaustion."

"You're not to go to Winterhaven."

"Sir?"

"Lady Ursula asked me to tell you the earl's London townhouse has been refurbished and the family will be staying there for the balance of the Season. She had your clothes and other belongings brought up from Winterhaven."

Tristan couldn't believe his ears. He had stayed at the townhouse the two nights prior to leaving for France and couldn't imagine the family in residence there. The staff had all been let go months before; furthermore, most of the furniture and all of the paintings and artifacts had been sold by the Fourth Earl to raise money for his gambling habit. He could only assume that Caleb Harcourt had already begun to replenish the empty Ramsden coffers in anticipation of his daughter's marriage into the family.

He had known all along this had to happen, had even convinced himself he accepted it. But this palpable proof that Maddy would soon be his brother's wife bore the terrible finality of a death blow.

Without further ado, he rose and prepared to take his leave before Maddy awoke from her nap and he had to face the agony of seeing her again.

Caleb Harcourt insisted on shaking his hand and offering his heartfelt thanks for delivering his daughter safely under such difficult circumstances. "Give us three or four days to get Maddy properly outfitted before you and your brother call on her," he said as he walked Tristan to the door.

Tristan's heart skipped a beat. "Call on her?"

"It was Lady Ursula's suggestion. Fine woman, that, with a keen sense of what's right and proper. She believes the best way to get Maddy and the earl together, natural like, is for you to introduce them, seeing as how you're the only one who knows them both."

Harcourt's smile was infuriatingly complacent. "I agree with her completely, for even though the deed is as good as done, I'd not want Maddy to think her marriage to the earl was anything but a love match. Women, especially young ones like Maddy, put great store in such things, if you take my meaning."

Tristan nodded stiffly and with a curt bow escaped to his waiting carriage before the cunning old man could guess that a gaping hole had just opened in his heart, and his lifeblood was seeping out drop by painful drop.

Maddy woke from a sleep so sound, she felt as if she had been drugged with laudanum. Disoriented, she lay perfectly still, trying to determine where she was and how she had gotten there. Then all at once she remembered. She was in her father's house, and this was the bedchamber to which his strange butler had led her.

"This be yer cuddy, Miss Maddy," the old fellow had said as he opened the door to the small chamber. "Though t'is not as grand as ye'd find in one of them Mayfair townhouses, I hopes ye find it to yer liking. Cap'n himself picked out the curtains and such."

Indeed, it was to her liking, Maddy decided as she looked about her. At least what she could see of it. Except for the pool of light cast by a fragrant beeswax taper on the bedside table, the room was in shadow. But she vaguely remembered noting earlier that the fireplace gracing one wall was of white Venetian marble, and the coverlet on which she lay, fully clothed except for her slippers, was a rich silk damask in pale, leafy green.

The clock on the mantlepiece chimed softly and Maddy gasped. She had slept more than two hours. Her father must have tired of waiting for her and dined without her. Her stomach growled, reminding her it was as empty as an almsman's larder, and she suddenly realized it had been a good twelve hours since she'd last eaten.

Swinging her feet to the floor, she pulled on her slippers and crossed to the small marble-topped commode to splash cool water on her face and finger-comb her curls into a semblance of order before she searched out her father for that long talk he had promised.

A nearby shelf caught her eye. A rag doll with scraggly yarn hair and black shoe-button eyes rested between a miniature sailboat and a dollhouse complete with tiny hand-carved furniture. Her toys, left behind in the hurried flight to France her mother and she had made fifteen years earlier. Her father had kept them all this time—displayed with the same care as the valuable ship's model in the entryway. A lump the size of a goose egg rose in her throat at the very thought.

The house was silent as a tomb when, with candle in hand, she made her way down the curved staircase to the floor below. Where was her father? Or Griggins? Or for that matter the rest of the servants needed to take care of the house?

Then she remembered Griggins emerging from behind the stairwell, muffin in hand. Servants or no servants, if she could find the kitchen, she could find something to eat—or better yet, something she could cook herself. She had little faith in English cuisine, and she prided herself on the culinary skills that, despite her grandfather's disapproval, she'd learned over the years from his excellent chef.

As she suspected, a narrow hallway stretched behind the curved stairwell in the entryway, and once she entered it, she could hear voices. Male voices.

She pushed open the door at the end of the hall and found herself in a kitchen much like the one in her grandfather's house in Lyon. A long pine worktable covered with an assortment of wooden bowls and spoons dominated the center of the room, an open range complete with drip pan, iron cauldron, and a huge copper teakettle was set in one wall, and on another hung a row of copper pots, most of which were stained green with verdigris.

"Maddy girl! So you've finally waked up!" Her father's booming voice filled the cozy room. She turned to find him, still in his shirtsleeves, seated at a round oak table with a plate of steaming food before him. Beside him, drinking a cup of tea, sat Griggins. She tried to picture her grandfather taking a meal in the kitchen with his servants, but the idea was too preposterous to be imagined.

Her father beamed at her, fork in hand. "I'd given you up for the night." He nodded toward an empty chair. "Sit down. Sit down. You must be famished and Cookie's had a pot of his tasty stew simmering for hours."

For the first time, Maddy noticed the third occupant of the kitchen. Startled, she looked closer. Two snapping black eyes regarded her from a swarthy face topped by a head of curly black hair, streaked with gray. Except for the stained white kitchen apron encasing his thin body, the small man removing a plate from the oven might well have been her benefactor in Lyon, Monsieur Forli.

"Guiseppi Pontizetti del Florino at your service, Princessa," the little man intoned in a heavy Italian accent.

Her father chuckled. "You can see why we call him Cookie. But the little toad is a genius when it comes to cooking, so Griggins and I put up with him." He paused while Cookie set a heaping plate before Maddy, the aroma of which made her mouth literally water.

"Well, this is it, my dear," her father continued as she picked up her fork. "My entire household."

"Just three people in a house this size?"

Her father nodded. "Oh, I've a housekeeper, two maids, a footman, and a pot boy who come in by the day. But I wouldn't have them for a minute if I could figure out how to get along without them. Never did like a lot of servants knowing my business."

He gestured toward the two men facing him on the opposite side of the table. "but I'm used to these two. Griggins was my first mate and Cookie manned the galley on my first ship more than a quarter of a century ago."

"That's right, Miss Maddy, and a rough old sea scow she was," Griggins said. "Nothing like the trim vessels as sails under the Harcourt flag nowadays. Cap'n retired her, and Cookie and me as well, when he come by this house. We've been doin' fer 'im ever since."

Maddy smiled to herself. It was plain to see these two men

who were "doing" for her father were his long-time comrades as well as his employees. What a strange household for a man who was counted one of the richest merchants in all of England. Yet somehow it fit the plain man he purported to be.

Her father finished off the last of his supper and placed his fork on his empty plate. His heavy brows drew together in a scowl and a flush darkened his weathered cheeks. "This is not a household that would suit any woman, and well I know it, daughter."

"It suits me just fine, Papa," Maddy said, wondering why he should think he need apologize for his beautiful little home.

"Never say so, Maddy. This house and its staff fit my simple needs, but it's much too small and much too far from Mayfair to be a proper residence for a young lady of marriageable age looking to make her connections in London society."

Maddy stared at him in amazement. "But, Papa, I do not care in the least about making such connections."

"Of course you do. All women care about such things, and I'll not be the cause of your missing out on them as I was with your mother."

He smiled smugly. "But things will be different this time. I've more money than a nabob, and by all that's holy, you'll make your connections if it takes every last farthing I own to see it done. I've a plan already set in place, and before another year is past, you'll have all the things a young girl dreams of: the balls and parties, the voucher to Almack's—even an invitation to Carlton House itself, I'll wager."

She wouldn't argue with him, not when he seemed to attach such importance to his plan to present her to London society. She could never be so cruel as to point out that if the stories she'd heard of the British *haut monde* were true, the chance of a merchant's daughter being accepted as a member of that exclusive body was almost as remote as the chance that men would someday fly like the birds.

Nor was she so foolish as to think that marrying an ex-spy who was the bastard son of an earl would add much to her social prestige. But she didn't care a fig for social prestige. Tristan was the man who held her heart in his hands, and marry him she would . . . as soon as the slow-top got around to making his offer.

Ten

Maddy rose late the following morning to find her father in the second floor salon in serious conversation with a thin, nervous-looking woman with lank brown hair and pale blue eyes. "Ah, Maddy girl," he said when she stepped through the doorway. "This is Madame Héloïse Blouseau, the French modiste Lady Ursula tells me is all the rage this season. I've instructed her to make you enough dresses to hold you over until Lady Ursula can plan an entire wardrobe for you."

Who this Lady Ursula was and why she should be put in charge of his daughter's wardrobe, he didn't say—and Maddy was loath to ask in front of the modiste in case the lady turned out to be his current mistress. She had made the mistake, just once, of alluding to the aging bird of paradise her grandfather visited every Wednesday afternoon between one o'clock and four. It was the one and only time he'd raised a hand to her, but the imprint of his fingers had remained on her cheek for hours. She would not make the same mistake with her father.

"Lady Ursula suggested two morning dresses, a carriage dress, and one simple evening dress that could be used either as a ball gown or a theater costume to begin with," Madame Héloïse said in an accent so atrocious, Maddy instantly knew the woman had never lived a day on the Continent. But though it was all she could do to keep from laughing out loud, she held her counsel. If she exposed this Madame Héloïse for the fraud she was, she would cast a slur on Lady Ursula's taste in modistes—and her father's taste in mistresses.

"From what part of France do you come?" she asked as soon as he left the room. "I have lived in Lyon since I was five years old and am familiar with the accents of most of the provinces, but I confess I have never heard one remotely resembling yours." She smiled to herself as she watched the bogus Frenchwoman turn brick red, then chalk white.

"Lord luv us," the modiste moaned, "my game's run out." She stared at Maddy through eyes wide with horror. "I suppose you're going to twig the old gentleman."

"If you mean I'm going to tell my father you're not French—of course not. Why should I? It's none of my concern, unless you plan to cheat him."

Madame Héloïse drew herself up proudly. "Never fear. He will get his money's worth. There is no modiste in London who can match my designs or my workmanship."

"Then why pretend you're French?"

The modiste gave a snort of disgust. "How long do you think I'd keep my fashionable customers if I was to admit I'm plain Mary Blodgett, born and raised above a gin shop in London's East End? About the time it takes my old mum to draw a pint of ale, that's how long."

"Ah, I begin to understand. A prophet is never revered in his own land."

"I don't know about prophets, but I know plenty about modistes and what makes them popular with the matrons of the *ton*," Madame Héloïse grumbled, nervously twisting her measuring tape around and around her fingers. "Ten long years I worked my fingers to the bone for a French tyrant name of Madame Adrianne. I designed and sewed all the gowns; she took all the credit. When the old harridan finally stuck her spoon in the wall, I come out of the back room and set up shop as her niece from Paris. I'd learnt enough French from her to get away with it too—until you come along."

"But your secret is safe with me, madame. I swear I will never tell a soul," Maddy promised.

The color slowly returned to the modiste's thin cheeks. "You'd do that for me? Why?"

"Because I think it is very enterprising of you to make such a fine career for yourself. I have recently come to realize I have great respect for people who rise above their humble origins." Maddy smiled. "Now, madame, shall we get on with the fitting? You would not want to disappoint your patroness, Lady Ursula."

Two hours later, after taking the necessary measurements and displaying the swatches of material she considered suitable for the planned dresses, Madame Héloïse took her leave of Maddy. Her last words were a promise to have one of the morning dresses completed the following day and the others shortly afterward, and at half the price she charged her titled customers.

True to her word, she sent a delivery boy around the following afternoon with a parcel containing a dainty yellow sprigged muslin dress, a chemise, a shift, and a pair of silk stockings, as well as a nightrail, dressing gown, and slippers.

Maddy immediately asked the day footman to carry a tub of hot water to her chamber so she could bathe and wash her hair. She brushed her curls dry—one of the advantages of her short hair; her long tresses had taken hours to dry.

Then dressing herself in her lovely silken undergarments and dress, she positioned herself in the window seat of the second-floor salon to wait for Tristan's arrival. She'd grown accustomed to his company on their trip and his absence left her feeling lost and lonely and anxious for his return.

He didn't come. Not that day, nor the next, nor even the next after that.

When five days had passed and he still hadn't called on her, she found herself tortured by the insidious thought that he might actually have been serious when he'd made that preposterous claim that honor forbade his ever offering for her.

But she managed to hide her fear behind a cheerful facade whenever her father was near. She was not so lost to pride that she could bear his knowing she had thrown herself at a man who had summarily rejected her . . . for whatever reason.

Each morning at half past eight her father left for his place of business, leaving Maddy to fend for herself during the long day ahead. The hours would have been interminable had it not been for Cookie. Once he learned of her passion for cooking, he welcomed her into his kitchen, a thing she suspected a few chefs would do. Under Griggins' watchful eyes, the two of them chopped vegetables and blended sauces and whipped up desserts that earned her father's lavish praise—never guessing his daughter had had a hand in the making of them.

She earned praise from Cookie as well. He even went so far

as to claim that if she were not Caleb Harcourt's daughter, she could earn her living as a chef in any of the finest houses in London.

She never told her father about her love of cooking, and swore Cookie and Griggins to secrecy as well. Instinct warned her that, like her grandfather, he would not consider it a proper avocation for the lady of the manor.

Instead, she dutifully donned her newest dress each evening before he arrived home and pirouetted before him, smiling at his admiration as if the only thing on her mind was the fit of a bodice or the swish of a skirt.

Then, one sunny afternoon when she was standing at the window watching for her father, Tristan came riding across Bloomsbury Square. She scarcely noticed the man beside him as she watched him dismount from a black horse whose flowing mane perfectly matched his own shoulder-length locks.

Gone was the rough-and-ready companion of her flight across France. He had obviously collected his long overdue pay, for this elegant new Tristan was dressed in a beautifully tailored topcoat in dark blue superfine, buff-colored buckskin breeches, and a jaunty high-crown beaver. In truth, he looked so breathtakingly handsome, she forgot to draw air into her lungs and soon found herself gasping for breath.

"Tristan," she cried, running to greet him at the door of the salon when Griggins showed him in, though she knew full well that was not what any well-bred lady would do. She smiled up at him, vaguely aware there was someone standing next to him—a small man whose head stood not much higher than Tristan's shoulder and whose pale hair and paler features seemed to disappear next to Tristan's dark brilliance.

"Good afternoon, Maddy." His cool, indifferent voice had a familiar ring; it was the voice of the man she had taken him to be before she'd glimpsed the fiery passion behind his icy mask. He drew his companion forward. "May I present my half brother, Garth Ramsden, the Fifth Earl of Rand."

Maddy extended her hand and the earl raised it to his lips. "Enchanted," he said, though he looked anything but. The line of his mouth was grim and his pale blue eyes held an expression of profound sadness. She wondered if this brother Tristan held in such high esteem had recently suffered a tragic loss.

Could this be the reason Tristan had been so slow to seek her out? Could his seeming indifference now be a mask to hide the grief he shared with his brother?

An uncomfortable silence settled over the three of them once they were seated, and Maddy gained the distinct impression she was being surreptitiously scrutinized by the earl, much as he might scrutinize a painting offered for sale.

It was all too apparent Tristan had decided he must have his brother's approval before he made an offer for her. The very thought of such ambivalence on the part of the man to whom she had unreservedly given her heart sent a twinge of anger skittering through her. She would never have expected a fellow as bold as Tristan to wave the white feather, and so she meant to tell him when next she had him alone.

Still, she was a lady and as such, rose to the occasion, racking her brain for some topic of conversation she could safely pursue with a peer of the realm. The weather came to mind and somehow that evolved into an incredibly boring discussion of the beauties of nature one could find in the English countryside. Maddy soon came to the conclusion that it was a lucky thing Tristan's brother had inherited a title, since he was obviously a dull fellow with little else to distinguish him.

Tristan added nothing to the conversation, but sat silent as a post, leaving the earl and Maddy to flounder in their tedium like two fish that had swallowed hooks they could neither digest nor disgorge. Maddy gritted her teeth and swore she'd make him pay for this transgression if it was the last thing she ever did. How dare he hang her out to dry in this manner. Was this some test of her ability to deal with his titled relatives?

She had literally reached the end of her wits and her temper when, to her relief, she heard her father's carriage pull up outside the open window. A moment later he strode into the room. "My lord Rand," he exclaimed, a grin spreading from ear to ear.

The earl rose instantly, as did Tristan. Standing between the two tall men, the diminutive earl looked as if he were lost in a forest—a thought she could see occurred to him as well, from the flush darkening his pale cheeks. For no reason she could explain, she found herself feeling sorry for the little man with the sad eyes and disgusted with the two men who towered over him.

Her father seemed blissfully unaware of the undercurrents in the small salon. "Well, now isn't this nice, Maddy. Your first visitors and to think one of them is an earl." He had the look of a hunter stalking his prey, and she was suddenly reminded of his plan to elevate her socially. She held her breath, hoping against hope he would stop toadying up to the earl before he made a complete fool of himself—and her. Of course, the hope was in vain.

"I've been wishing Maddy could meet someone who could help establish her in society," he purred, taking a seat and indicating the others should follow suit. Maddy cringed. The man was practically licking his chops over the poor earl.

"As a matter of fact . . ." The Earl of Rand cleared his throat. "I was just going to mention that Lord and Lady Faversham are giving a ball on Friday next. It will be a dreadful crush, as everyone who is anyone will be there, but an excellent introduction into the London social world nevertheless."

He cleared his throat again. "Faversham is a particular friend of mine. I have only to ask and an invitation will be extended to Miss Harcourt if she should fancy attending."

"What a grand idea and how kind of you to think of it, my lord. Of course she would love to attend, wouldn't you, Maddy?"

Maddy managed a strained smile. "I am sure it would be a delightful evening, my lord, and I thank you for the invitation, but I fear I must decline." She took a malicious satisfaction in the dumbfounded expressions she read in the three pairs of eyes turned in her direction. "It would be pointless to attend a ball, you see, because I don't dance."

"You don't dance!" the earl and her father exclaimed in unison. The identical looks of shock registered on both faces were comical in the extreme, and even Tristan looked baffled by her candid announcement.

"To what use did your grandfather put all the money I sent him, if not to teach you the necessary accomplishments of a lady?" her father demanded. "I suppose next you'll tell me you cannot play the pianoforte nor sing nor paint a watercolor."

Loyalty to her grandfather forbade her admitting she had

known nothing all those years of the money her father had provided. "I cannot account for every franc," she said quietly. "But I imagine most of the money was used for bribes to the local officials to keep them silent about the fact that a sworn enemy of the emperor, and Citizen Fouché, ran tame in Lyon. And no, I do not play the pianoforte, nor sing, nor paint. In short, I have acquired none of the talents required of your English ladies of fashion, so I am afraid your plan to bring me into vogue is doomed to failure."

Her father flushed—whether from embarrassment or anger Maddy couldn't tell. "Nonsense," he said gruffly. "Your deficiencies can be remedied. I'll hire the finest teachers in London."

"Mama will know who they are, sir," the earl said. "I will ask her to draw up a list this very night."

"Thank you, my lord. I would be most grateful. I trust Lady Ursula's judgment above all others in such matters."

The earl's mama—Tristan's beloved stepmama—and the mysterious Lady Ursula were one and the same? Maddy stared from one man to the other, her pulse pounding erratically in her temples as reality began to dawn. This insane plan of her father's—surely it didn't involve the Earl of Rand. Tristan had said he'd agreed to fetch her back to England because her father had "helped his brother out of a difficult situation." Dear God! Had the earl in turn been forced to agree to help launch her in London society?

Tristan shifted in his chair and crossed one leg over the other. "In the meantime, you can take Maddy to the theater, Garth. That would serve as a public announcement of your interest in her," he said, breaking his long silence to prove her worst suspicions true. "I understand that fellow Edmund Kean is opening in *Othello* tomorrow night."

He turned to Maddy with a smile that failed to warm the chilly glitter in his pale eyes. "*Othello* is a play by England's most famous bard," he explained.

"I am familiar with Mr. Shakespeare's work," Maddy said stiffly. "I may lack the prerequisite graces of your English ladies, but I am not illiterate. In fact, I enjoyed his plays so much, I translated a great many of them into French so my grandfather could read them as well."

"Then you should enjoy Mr. Kean's performance immensely."

And so she would, Maddy thought, if the circumstances were different. Though she felt certain that Tristan was promoting this theater engagement with his brother simply because he felt he had to help him erase the debt owed her father for whatever favor he had done him, it still hurt that he would do so. It was all so vulgar, so degrading, so unnecessary. She had no more desire to consort with the London *haut monde* than she'd had to join the tasteless romp at the court of the Emperor Napoleon.

She opened her mouth to say that very thing, but before she could get a word out, the earl interrupted her. "Of course," he said. "The theater is the obvious solution, and Kean is all the rage since he played Shylock last year. How clever of you to think of it, Tristan. And Miss Harcourt cannot possibly suffer any embarrassment there because of her lack of social training."

His shy smile completely negated the censorious sound of his words, and Maddy found herself thinking what a sweet-natured man he was—a little dull and not too bright, but sweet-natured just the same. No wonder Tristan was so fond of him. And because of her father, the poor little fellow was trapped in a miserable situation. Almost as miserable as her own.

"Drury Lane it is then, Miss Harcourt," the earl said as if it were a foregone conclusion. "Shall we say tomorrow evening?"

She would politely refuse him if she thought that would end the ordeal for them both, but she suspected the earl was every bit as stiff-necked about his honor as Tristan. The only way she could set him free was to allow him to fulfill his obligation.

She returned his smile with one of her own. "Very well, my lord, the theater it is then," she agreed. Then turning to Tristan she asked, "Will you be joining us? It was your idea, after all."

Eagerly she awaited his answer, as much for the earl's sake as her own. True, she wanted to share her first evening at the theater with Tristan, but she sensed the shy little earl would be much more at ease if he could have his brother along when he made a public appearance with her.

For some reason she could not fathom, her question disturbed Tristan. "No, Maddy, I will not," he said curtly, managing to avoid meeting her eyes. "I have a previous engagement, one I am obliged to honor since it pertains to my work with the British Foreign Service."

Honor. There was that word again. Maddy gritted her teeth in frustration. Did this *Anglais* think he had invented it? She might have known it would be Tristan's *honor* that prevented him from attending the theater with her, just as it had been his *honor* that forbade his offering for her and his *honor* that forced her to resort to trickery to get him to kiss her. Frenchmen took great stock in their honor too, but she had never known one who let it interfere with his affairs of the heart.

Nom de Dieu, what was she to do with such a man? Another woman she could compete against, but how was she supposed to know how to win the man of her choice when her rival was his *honor*?

He had hurt her with his rejection. The flash of pain and bewilderment he'd seen in her eyes had twisted the knife already embedded in his heart. Yet somehow he must find the will to hurt her even more. Only by disillusioning her could he set her free to find happiness with the man she was destined to marry.

Luckily the man in question had been content to ride in silence for the first half hour after they left the Harcourt townhouse. With his feelings as raw as an open wound, Tristan wasn't certain he could hide the fact that he had much more than a casual interest in Maddy.

Out of the corner of his eye, he saw Garth edge forward until their horses were neck and neck. "Miss Harcourt was something of a surprise," Garth said, gripping his reins so tightly, his knuckles shone white. "She may not be the 'strapping' French peasant her father's description led me to believe, but she is certainly tall for a woman."

Tristan nodded. "That she is."

"But she seems quite pleasant."

"I found her to be so during our travels together."

Garth stared straight ahead, a grim set to his chin. "However, she strikes me as outlandishly clever. I've never before met a woman who read Shakespeare, much less translated it into French!" He sighed. "Devil take it, I hope we shall manage to rub along together. I have always found clever women rather off-putting in the past.

Tristan didn't comment on his brother's observation. He could think of nothing he could say without implying that his sibling was a trifle slow-witted—which he was. But what Garth lacked in intellect, he more than made up for in heart.

A feeling of panic gripped him. He sincerely hoped the match between his gentle, sweet-natured brother and Caleb Harcourt's quick-witted, razor-tongued daughter did not turn out to be the complete disaster he envisioned. For there was nothing on God's green earth he could do to prevent the powerful cit's ill-conceived plan from coming to fruition.

He groaned as another wave of pain washed over him. It was enough to ask of a man to learn to live with his own heartbreak; he didn't need the added agony of knowing the two people he loved most were doomed to a life of misery as well.

The earl arrived at the Harcourt townhouse the following evening in an elegant closed carriage drawn by four matched chestnuts. His family crest was emblazoned on the door and both the groom and coachman were in full livery.

Maddy had felt very elegant when first she'd viewed herself in her new evening dress of rose silk gauze with tiny embroidered flowers scattered here and there. She had even decided she liked the effect of her short, curly hair with the diaphanous costume, but next to the earl, she felt almost dowdy.

He was turned out in full evening attire, including a cutaway coat in a shade of blue satin which complimented his fair coloring and a silver waistcoat draped with an impressive collection of seals as well as a quizzing glass. But strangely enough, despite his *soigné* appearance, he looked even more shy and miserable than on his previous visit.

"What a beautiful carriage this is," Maddy exclaimed as the groom handed her inside, hoping to put the earl at ease by complimenting him on what she could plainly tell from the smell of the red velvet squabs was a new acquisition. To her surprise, he blushed furiously, stammered something quite incoherent, and sat for the remainder of the ride to the theater staring bleakly out the window as if she had somehow insulted him.

Confused, she lapsed into silence and made no further attempt at conversation. Not for the first time, she concluded Englishmen were a baffling lot.

A short time later, they drew up before the entrance of the Theater Royal in Drury Lane. Maddy stepped from the carriage to find herself facing a magnificent structure with a series of impressive arched doorways and row upon row of windows ablaze with light. She took a closer look and decided it appeared surprisingly new compared to the structures around it—an observation she decided to keep to herself rather than risk offending the earl further.

"The theater is quite new. Only three years old, in fact," he said as if reading her mind. "Of course, there has been a theater on this location since 1663, but it burned to the ground for the third time in 1809 and this version was built in 1812," he continued in pedantic tones that made Maddy suspect he had memorized the monograph so as to have something to offer in the way of conversation besides another discourse on the weather. She was touched by his effort. In fact, she had an almost irresistible urge to pat him on the head and tell him, "Well done."

He offered his arm and Maddy placed her gloved fingers on it, conscious that he appeared taller than she had judged him to be. His eyes were on a level with hers, when she distinctly remembered looking down at him when they'd met the previous day.

He was also rather unsteady on his feet. Good Lord! Had he found the idea of escorting her to the theater so distasteful, he'd had to fortify himself with spirits? Embarrassed, she dropped her gaze and instantly discovered why he was teetering. The heels on his buckled evening shoes were at least three inches high.

Surreptitiously, she took a tighter grip on his arm. A wise move, as it turned out, for he stumbled twice before they managed to make their way to the box he'd reserved.

The theater was filled to capacity, and Maddy had to make an effort to keep from gaping like a country bumpkin at the impressive auditorium and equally impressive audience. It appeared that every wealthy theater patron in London had decided to attend Mr. Kean's premiere performance in his newest role, and the vast room sparkled with the jewels decorating both the men and women occupying the private boxes.

Maddy shivered with excitement. If only it were Tristan sitting next to her, this moment would be perfect. She literally ached with longing for him after their sadly disappointing encounter of the day before; so much so, her imagination was playing tricks on her. She could swear she saw him enter one of the first-tier boxes on the opposite side of the cavernous auditorium.

She looked again. There were two men and a woman in the box. The fair-haired man took his seat, while the dark-haired one who resembled Tristan removed the wrap from the shoulders of the woman. He was too far away to see his features clearly, but there was something so familiar about the tilt of his head, the breadth of his shoulders.

Beside her, the earl raised his opera glasses and studied a box in the tier above the one she'd been scrutinizing. "Someone you know?" Maddy asked without thinking.

"Viscount Tinsdale, his wife and daughter . . . Lady Sarah Summerhill. The viscount's country estate marches beside Winterhaven." He lowered his glasses and his eyes looked so glazed with pain, Maddy had to fold her hands tightly in her lap to keep from reaching out to him in sympathy. This grief he suffered must somehow be connected with his neighbor's family. Maybe the loss of a childhood friend through death or some unfortunate misunderstanding. She wished with all her heart she could think of something to say that would comfort the kindly little man.

But even as she acknowledged this was impossible without knowing the source of his grief, the babble of voices around her ceased and she realized the curtain was rising.

The opening set, complete with the Venetian army, was everything one could expect of London's premiere theater. Enthralled, Maddy settled back in her chair and prepared to suffer through the trials and tribulations of the Moor who commanded the colorfully costumed army.

Still, she couldn't help wishing she might have been treated to one of Mr. Shakespeare's charming comedies for the first theater experience of her life. She was not in the mood for a grim tragedy, particularly not Othello's. She had always thought him something of a fool to be so easily misled by a scoundrel like Iago. And as for Desdemona . . . what a silly fribble Shakespeare had made her out to be. No, *Othello* was definitely not one of her favorite plays.

But no sooner had Edmund Kean delivered his first line than she found herself hypnotized by the swarthy actor's performance. Small of stature and looking remarkably like one of the gypsies who had often camped outside Lyon, there was nothing about his physical person that was prepossessing. Yet, he projected an emotional intensity that held his audience spellbound. By sheer force of personality, he took command of the stage, relegating the other actors to mere shadows on the perimeter of his genius. Before Maddy's very eyes, he literally transformed himself into Iago, the jealousy-ridden Moor's evil tormentor.

She felt the earl press the opera glasses into her hand, and raising them found herself as fascinated by the myriad emotions twisting Kean's lean, vulpine face as she was by his magnificent voice. How, she wondered, could any man plumb the depths of his soul like this night after night and still manage to retain his sanity?

All too soon, the first act was over and the curtain descended for the intermission the playbill had announced. Maddy turned to the earl, her heart still pounding, her mind drained, to find his eyes closed and his head resting on his chest. She shook her head in disbelief. The man must have the sensitivity of a hedgehog to sleep through such a stirring performance.

Surely she wasn't the only one so deeply affected by Kean. Carefully, so as to not disturb the earl, she leaned forward to gauge the reaction of the audience on the floor below the box.

Most of them were out of their seats and stirring about. If they'd been moved by the great man, they'd recovered quickly. Or maybe, like her, they had found the performance so draining, they needed a respite before the next emotional act.

Many of them had opera glasses of their own trained on the private boxes—a surprising number on the very box in which the earl and she sat. Never say this dull little man sleeping in the chair beside her was of that much interest to the other members of London society. If so, they must indeed be desperate for diversion.

She raised the glasses the earl had given her and trained them on the box containing the man she had thought resembled Tristan . . . and gasped. It was Tristan, and he looked even more elegant in the stark black and white of his evening clothes than he had when he'd called at her father's townhouse.

He and the fair-haired man, who on closer observation looked to be much older than Tristan, were engaged in conversation with the woman she'd seen enter the box earlier. A statuesque blonde with a bosom that put Tristan's friend, Minette, to shame, she had rather coarse features and rosy cheeks Maddy felt certain were enhanced by Bloom of Ninon.

She was most definitely a mistress. Furthermore, the exquisite ruby silk gown that didn't quite cover her magnificent bosom and the matching rubies circling her throat and dangling from her ears proclaimed her the mistress of a very wealthy man. Maddy felt a stab of fear. Had Tristan's early years with his mother made him addicted to soiled doves? Would that addiction persist even after he married?

She adjusted the glasses to enhance the picture. The woman was laughing heartily at something either Tristan or the older man had said—her bosom heaving so mightily, Maddy feared it might lift right out of her scandalous neckline.

Now she was holding a jeweled fan in front of her face, as if she were whispering something first to one man, then the other. She was obviously playing them against each other and very successfully too, from the looks of it. For now both men were laughing as if the vulgar creature had just said the most fascinating thing either of them had ever heard.

Maddy made a mental note to practice the art of the fan in her spare time; it appeared to be a very effective adjunct to conversation. Still, she lowered the glasses. She had seen enough. What fools men were, even the best of them. Couldn't Tristan and his distinguished looking friend see they were making public spectacles of themselves?

The earl stirred and straightened in his chair. His eyes

popped open and he stared around him in obvious surprise. "Is the first act over?"

Maddy nodded. "Yes, my lord. Mr. Kean was superb."

"Excellent. I hope you enjoyed it, Miss Harcourt." He grinned sheepishly. "I can never stay awake. The theater has the same effect on me as my village vicar's sermons."

He eyed the opera glasses. "And have you been enjoying watching the *ton* at play as well?"

Maddy sniffed. "I have been watching your brother, Tristan, at play, my lord. He and his friend are in one of the boxes across the way."

The earl yawned. "Ah yes, he said he'd be here. With Foreign Secretary Castlereagh and the Grand Duchess Sophia."

"The woman is a grand duchess? Are you certain?" Maddy handed him the glasses. "She more closely resembles an expensive courtesan."

"Miss Harcourt!" The earl flushed with embarrassment. "I would not expect an innocent young woman to know either the name or the look of such a creature."

He adjusted the glasses and peered toward the box that Maddy indicated. "Hmmm. I see what you mean. She does rather give that appearance. But she is most definitely the grand duchess of some remote duchy in Austria, according to Tris. The two of them became fast friends when he was at the Congress of Vienna—though heaven only knows what he was doing there. To hear him tell it, he did nothing but waltz and drink and . . ."

The earl's flush deepened. "It is all beyond me, but Tris is very clever about such things. Apparently his friendship with the duchess has been of great help to Lord Castlereagh since she has the ear of Prince von Metternich."

"Who in turn has the ear of the Emperor of Austria," Maddy said, as relief flooded through her. Tristan wasn't dallying after all; he was merely protecting the interests of his country.

"And," she continued, "with Napoleon on the march again, it behooves Lord Castlereagh to keep Metternich as a friend since the Austrian emperor is biding his time, waiting to see who will rule France."

The earl's eyes widened. "How do you know that?"

"It is only logical, my lord. The emperor fears he may one

day have to defend Vienna against the Russian Cossacks, in which case he will need the support of the armies of France."

"The devil you say!" The earl's pale brows drew together in a disapproving frown. "Somehow that does not seem the sort of thing a proper lady should know. I hope, Miss Harcourt, you are not going to tell me you are some sort of bluestocking who fancies dabbling in politics."

Maddy couldn't help but laugh at the disgruntled earl. "But of course I am, my lord, if the term 'bluestocking' means what I think it does. I was raised on politics. It was the only subject that was ever discussed in my grandfather's salon."

The earl turned positively green—something Maddy scarcely noticed. She was too drunk with happiness to take note of anything as trivial as the Earl of Rand's complexion.

So, Tristan's natural milieu was international politics—not a sheep farm, as she'd surmised. Why had it never occurred to her before how logical the progression was from spy to diplomat?

But what lay ahead for the clever Englishman? Evidently the powerful Foreign Secretary didn't hold his illegitimate birth against him. Maybe, with Lord Castlereagh as his sponsor, he could become the British Ambassador to Vienna. Maybe even take a seat in the House of Commons if he played his cards right. What a coup that would be for a man who had started life as a bastard!

And who would make the ideal wife for a man with such ambitions? Why, a woman who had been the chatelaine of the most brilliant political salon in Lyon, of course.

Eleven

Lady Ursula Ramsden, Dowager Countess of Rand, selected a small frosted cake from the tea tray offered by her butler and added a spoonful of sugar to her tea. She waited until both her daughter, Lady Carolyn, and her guest had made their selections, then instructed the starchy retainer to leave them to enjoy their tea without further interruption.

"So, my dear Miss Harcourt," she said in her beautifully modulated voice, "it appears we have our work cut out for us if you are to be ready to make your debut this Season. Mr. Harcourt tells me that in addition to planning an appropriate wardrobe, we must rectify certain omissions in your social training as well."

She took a sip of tea before continuing. "But before we do anything else, we must secure you a suitable dresser. An older woman, I think, who can double as chaperone."

"A dresser? Whatever for?" Maddy scoffed. "I've been tending to my own needs since I was five years old."

"But your needs will not be so simple now, my dear. And your maid can accompany you shopping or visiting friends. A proper young lady never leaves her domicile without the company of a relative or servant. I hope you will remember that in the future."

Maddy stifled her urge to giggle. She had crossed France disguised as a boy, slept in a hayloft with her head on the shoulder of a rakish ex-spy, even shared a kiss with that same ex-spy on a moonlit evening—but now she dare not walk to the lending library without a proper chaperone.

"We can be thankful of one thing—Madame Héloïse has turned you out quite well," Lady Ursula said, pursing her pretty mouth and studying Maddy with the same judicial inten-

sity her son, the earl, had the first time he met her. "I would
not have thought of sarcenet for a carriage dress and in such an
unusual shade of green, too, but it is really most becoming."

"Thank you, my lady." Ordinarily, Maddy would have taken
umbrage at such scrutiny, but she found it impossible to do so
with either the countess or her son. Both had a kindness of nature that could not be mistaken. Especially the countess. For
hadn't she taken Tristan in to raise as her own when he was
abandoned on her doorstep as a child?

Furthermore, it was easy to see how the earl had come by
his diminutive size and his gentlemanly manners; Lady Ursula
was petite and blonde and so perfectly ladylike, Maddy felt
like a gauche country bumpkin in comparison. And Lady Carolyn was an exquisite copy of her mother. No wonder the
countess looked a bit bewildered at the prospect of trying to
turn Caleb Harcourt's oversized French daughter into one of
the delicate English china dolls admired by the *ton*.

"You must not take this 'plan' of my father's too seriously,
my lady," Maddy said, hoping to put her gentle hostess at
ease. "It is plain to see it is just a silly whim he's taken. But he
is an intelligent man. I feel certain he will soon see the idea is
hopeless and give it up."

"Oh, Miss Harcourt, never say such a thing!" Every drop of
color blanched from Lady Ursula's face, and Lady Carolyn's
teacup crashed into her saucer. Two sets of pale blue eyes
stared at Maddy with what she could only describe as absolute
horror. But why? She would have thought they would welcome any excuse to abandon "the plan."

"Of course it's not hopeless, my dear. It simply cannot be,"
Lady Ursula declared, pressing her hand to her heaving
bosom.

"Garth has committed himself. The 'plan' is already underway," Lady Carolyn added, her eyes as round and wide as the
teacup clattering in her saucer. She glanced fearfully around
the elegant salon of the Ramsden townhouse in which they sat,
as if the beautiful paintings, objets d'art, and exquisite furnishings somehow entered into the equation.

Honor again. This family seemed obsessed by it. The earl
apparently felt honor-bound to sponsor her entrance into London society to pay back the favor her father had done him, and

his mother and sister, God bless their loyal hearts, intended to back him all the way, no matter what it cost them.

Maddy sighed. It seemed she must agree to the preposterous scheme long enough to keep from offending them. "I am most appreciative of your efforts, my lady, and I do not mean to be difficult." She paused, pondering how to tactfully word what she had to say. "But I cannot help but believe we shall avoid a great deal of trouble later on if I begin by being perfectly honest about how I feel about the plan. It is my life that will be most drastically affected, after all, not my father's."

Now Lady Ursula's teacup was clattering in its saucer. "Of course, my dear," she said somewhat breathlessly. "Above all, we want you to be happy with the arrangements."

"We are hardly in a position to feel otherwise," Lady Carolyn said acidly, and earned herself a quelling look from her mother.

Maddy felt it best to ignore Lady Carolyn's brief but telling show of temper. Apparently she was not quite as honor-bound as the other members of the family.

"Tell us, my dear, exactly how *do* you feel about . . . everything," Lady Ursula asked gently.

Maddy looked down at the paper-thin teacup in her hand. "Well, for one thing, my lady, I really cannot abide tea. So your idea of introducing me to the ladies of the *ton* by giving a series of afternoon teas is not particularly appealing. It is not a popular drink in France, you see. I am accustomed to coffee. Strong, black coffee." She refrained from mentioning that the French had dubbed the Englishmen's favorite beverage *la pisse de chat*. She doubted a high stickler like the countess would see the humor in likening her precious tea to cat urine.

"Then there's the matter of all those lessons Papa and you discussed," Maddy continued. "I have nothing against learning to dance." She had, in fact, developed a passionate desire to do so the moment the earl mentioned that Tristan had waltzed his way through the Congress of Vienna.

She smiled at Lady Ursula. "I would be particularly interested in learning the waltz. I saw it executed once in Lyon and found it quite intriguing." In truth, the idea of waltzing in Tristan's arms sent shivers of excitement coursing through her.

"I have already arranged for dancing lessons with an unexceptionable tutor who numbers the waltz among his accomplishments," Lady Ursula said. "But, of course, you must obtain the permission of the patronesses of Almack's before performing that particular dance in public."

"Surely you jest, my lady. Why should these patronesses, whoever they may be, have anything to say about what I do?"

"My thought exactly," Lady Carolyn said. "The old dragons have yet to give me the nod, and I resent it bitterly."

Lady Ursula silenced her daughter with a scowl. "Lady Jersey and the other patronesses set the standards of decorum for the *ton*. Standards with which I heartily concur. You are barely eighteen, Carolyn. Much too young and innocent, in my opinion, to be dancing in the intimate manner required by that most scandalous of dances. I myself have never waltzed. Nor do I think I ever will."

"But you're hopelessly old-fashioned, Mama. It is precisely because I am young that I want to do all the exciting things I can think of while I am still able to enjoy them." Lady Carolyn gave an angry toss of her golden curls that led Maddy to believe this youngest of the Ramsdens was most definitely not blessed with as docile a nature as her mother and brother.

Lady Ursula fixed her daughter with a stare that plainly put an end to any further discussion of the waltz, and Maddy made a new assessment of the countess. Gentle and ladylike she might be, but Lady Ursula was obviously not a woman to be trifled with once she made up her mind.

"So, Miss Harcourt, we have the business of dancing lessons settled then," Lady Ursula said, ignoring her daughter's angry pout. She took another sip of her tea, then placed the cup and saucer on the small table on which the tea tray sat. "As to the other accomplishments you will need to acquire—"

"Now there's the rub, my lady." Maddy finished the last of her tea cake and set her plate aside. "I have no interest in painting with watercolors and I have the voice of a crow, so singing lessons would be a waste of time and money. And unless I'm willing to practice ten hours a day—which I'm not—the Season will be over before I progress beyond scales on the pianoforte."

Her gaze lighted on the tambour frame beside Lady Ursula's chair. "I'm afraid embroidery is out also. I'm much too impatient for that sort of thing. I tried it once and ended up throwing my efforts in the fireplace."

Lady Ursula's finely arched brows raised a fraction. "But my dear, what will you do with your days? You have eliminated virtually every occupation suitable to a well-bred young lady."

"Oh la, never worry about me, my lady. I shall be busy as a cat in a barn full of mice. I am the most avid of readers and Papa has a magnificent library which I am dying to sample." *And Cookie has an inexhaustible supply of recipes he is willing to teach me—but best I keep that to myself.*

"Ah yes, your reading." Lady Ursula's voice was noticeably lacking in enthusiasm. "My son mentioned that you were exceedingly clever. I understand you have not only read Mr. Shakespeare's plays, but translated them into French as well."

"Actually, I translated them into French, German and Italian." Maddy smiled reminiscently. "Just for fun, you know. I can't remember when I've enjoyed myself more."

Lady Ursula paled noticeably. "Oh dear, I do think it would be best to keep that our little family secret. It wouldn't do to have it bandied about that you were a bluestocking."

That word again. Maddy scowled thoughtfully. "You are saying, I take it, that the members of the *ton* do not approve of intelligent women."

"Let us rather say they do not approve of bookish women."

"Very well, my lady, I stand corrected. And since I am already aware they also do not approve of men of business, nor even any of their own kind who bolster their incomes using the wits *le bon Dieu* gave them, I have but one question left concerning that exclusive society."

"And what may that be, my dear?"

Maddy sighed deeply. "How in heaven's name do the silly twits manage to keep from boring each other to death?"

Tristan looked up from yesterday's issue of the London *Times* and watched his sister, Carolyn, lift the lids of the various chafing dishes on the sideboard and help herself to a generous breakfast of sausage and coddled eggs. The two of them were the only occupants of the cheerful morning room of the Ramsdens' refurbished townhouse on this bright morning in mid April; Lady Ursula was still abed and Garth had not yet returned from his early morning ride in Hyde Park.

"Lady Ursula tells me Garth and Maddy Harcourt have been inseparable while I've been in Belgium on Lord Castlereagh's business these past three weeks," he remarked offhandedly when Carolyn took her seat opposite him.

She speared one of the sausages on her plate, popped it in her mouth, and chewed thoughtfully before answering. "As usual, Mama exaggerates. He escorted her to two of Lady Faversham's Thursday musicales—the only place he's been able to take her in the evening until she learns to dance properly. But he has spent a number of days each week with her as well."

Carolyn chuckled. "I do believe the poor dear has seen more of London in the past three weeks than in all the previous twenty-seven years of his life. First Miss Harcourt talked him into taking her to the British Museum to see the Elgin marbles—"

Tristan laid the newspaper aside. "Garth viewed the Elgin marbles? And in the company of a woman? Good Lord!"

"Naturally, he was shocked to the core, especially since Miss Harcourt found them absolutely fascinating and insisted on examining them piece by piece. You should have seen his face when he described them to Mama. 'A few horses here and there, but in general nothing but a lot of disgusting nudes with half their arms and legs missing,' " she mimicked.

Despite himself, Tristan chuckled at the picture she conjured up with her perfect imitation of their staid brother.

"Then she dragged him to St. Paul's Cathedral," Carolyn continued, "which he promptly declared 'a gloomy old pile of stone,' and to the Tower of London, where he threatened to plant one of the keeper's a facer unless he bettered the living conditions of the poor beasts on display there."

She speared another sausage. "They even spent one entire afternoon in Hatchard's Bookstore. You can imagine how much Garth enjoyed that! The only time I've ever seen him open a book was to preserve the flower Lady Sarah wore in her hair at her come-out."

She pressed her fingers to her lips. "Oops! I must remember to be more careful what I say."

"Indeed you must!" Tristan scowled thoughtfully. "Lady Ursula mentioned that Maddy has taken tea with you here as well. How did the two of you get on?"

Carolyn cocked her head as if pondering his question. "Very well, actually. I was all prepared to hate her, as well you know. But now that I've met her I find I like her exceedingly. She'd terribly clever and funny and shockingly honest—and she has very definite opinions about what she will and will not do."

Carolyn's eyes twinkled. "She fairly curled Mama's hair when she flatly refused to take most of the lessons judged necessary to make her into a proper English lady. In short, she's nothing like the silly girls I met at Miss Highcliff's finishing school or the daughters of Mama's titled acquaintances. She is the first genuine original I have ever met, and I do believe we shall become fast friends."

His sister's candid description painted such a vivid picture of Maddy, Tristan felt a familiar ache start deep in his chest. "You approve of her as Garth's wife then, despite the differences in their interests?"

Carolyn's smile faded. "I didn't say that. In truth, I cannot think of any two people less suited to each other. She absolutely terrifies him, and I strongly suspect he bores her to flinders."

Devil take it, was it so obvious even an eighteen-year-old could see it? "I have wondered, myself, if they would be compatible."

"Compatible? You jest. They are like chalk and cheese, as anyone can plainly see. Except Mama, of course. As usual, she turns a blind eye to the truth when it is too painful to acknowledge."

Tristan pushed back his chair and rose, then strode to the window to stare with unseeing eyes into the street below. "I was hoping I just imagined their lack of commonality—for Maddy's sake as well as Garth's," he said bleakly. "But with each day I spent with her, I became more convinced Garth and she were totally mismatched. Can you imagine how I felt, knowing I was bringing her home to be trapped in an impossible marriage?"

"I'm sure you tortured yourself with guilt, as would any man of honor."

Tristan slammed his fist against the oak window frame. "Hell and damnation! It is enough to make a man take himself off to India or some such far-flung place!"

Carolyn's eyes widened. "Such as Belgium on an errand for Lord Castlereagh? I wondered why you volunteered to take an assignment on the Continent so soon after returning to England."

She stared at him, aghast. "Oh, Tris! Never say you've fallen in love with her." Carolyn leapt to her feet, and with a strangled cry flung herself into his arms. "You have! Don't bother to disclaim it. It is written all over your face."

Tristan didn't try to dissuade her. The pain inside him was too great to deny any longer.

"And the two of you would be so perfect together," she whispered against his chest. "Can't you make her father see that?"

"See that his precious daughter would be better off as the wife of a nameless bastard than as the Countess of Rand? I doubt any father would find much logic in that argument."

"But she's in love with you too. Now that I think of it, you were all she talked about for the hour the two of us were alone on the day she took tea with us. And she positively glowed every time your name was mentioned."

Carolyn raised her head to stare into Tristan's eyes. "But I'm not telling you anything you don't already know, am I?"

"I have suspected for some time that Maddy believes herself in love with me. But she is very strong and in her own peculiar way, amazingly practical. She'll recover from any heartbreak she may suffer and make the best of it."

"She is also very independent," Carolyn pointed out. "It occurs to me she may refuse to marry a man she doesn't love."

Tristan briefly considered the possibility, but shook his head in denial. "I don't doubt she'll balk at first," he said bitterly, "but she'll soon come around to her father's way of thinking. What choice does she have? Harcourt holds all the purse strings; the rest of us just dance at the end of them like so many puppets."

"If he forces her to marry against her will, he will earn nothing but her hatred, no matter how much money he pours into the Rand coffers," Carolyn declared. "Your Maddy doesn't strike me as a woman whose affections are capricious. Nor, I wager, do you love easily and often."

Her eyes glistened with unshed tears. "Is this cit so lacking in sensitivity, he thinks love is a malady that can be cured with a dose of Mrs. Peterman's honey and valerian? If it were, Garth would not still be looking like a whipped puppy and poor Sarah wouldn't be a pale wraith haunting the ballrooms where they used to dance together."

She slipped from Tristan's arms to pace back and forth across the room, the picture of frustration. "It is like the plot of one of Mrs. Radcliffe's novels; everyone is committed to marrying the wrong person. Only in her novels, one knows everyone will turn up happy at the end."

Stopping suddenly, she whirled around to face him. "Can't you just persuade Miss Harcourt to elope with you to Gretna Green? I'm certain she'd do it; she seems totally unconcerned about how she is viewed by polite society."

"Do not for a minute think I haven't considered whisking her over the anvil," Tristan said bitterly. "But only in the blackest hours of the night when I think with my heart, not my head. In the cold light of day, I know I couldn't live with myself if having her meant seeing her disowned by her father. She is, after all, the heiress to a vast fortune. I could not ask her to survive on the pittance I make at the Foreign Office."

He pressed his fingers to his aching temples. "Nor could I risk the chance that Harcourt's anger might drive him to have Garth thrown into debtor's prison when he couldn't pay the notes held against the estate. No, Caro, much as I might wish it so, that is not the answer."

"And it's all that horrible cit's fault," she wailed. "I don't care what Mama says about how grateful we should be for all he's done for us. I hate him and his stupid plan!"

"Caleb Harcourt is not the villain here, Caro," Tristan said, aware of the irony of defending the very man who was robbing him of the woman he loved. "It was not his fault our profligate father gambled away the family fortune and brought the house of Rand to the brink of destruction. He does what he does out of love for his daughter. He is firmly convinced that to ensure her ultimate happiness, he must secure her a titled husband."

"Even if that husband will make her miserably unhappy? How can the man be so blind?"

"It's a long story, one that goes back fifteen years." Tristan said. "Suffice it to say, his intentions are good, and Lady Ursula is right in feeling grateful toward him. Had someone other than he bought up the old earl's vowels and mortgages, Garth could be fleeing his creditors aboard a ship bound for the Americas at this very moment—or worse yet, be rotting in debtor's prison."

Anxiously, Carolyn searched his face. "So, what will you do, Tris? Flee to the Americas yourself? I cannot envision you spending the rest of your life watching the woman you love be wife to your brother."

"I am not certain where I will go, except that it will be somewhere far from England. Lord Castlereagh has offered me a post as an embassy attaché in either Paris or Vienna, but naturally that will not come to fruition until we have routed Bonaparte once and forever."

"But you think we will win out against the Corsican eventually?"

Tristan hesitated, weighing his words carefully. "We will win if those fools in Parliament give Wellington the command. Only in England is his leadership ability questioned. Europe's heads of state are well aware that he is all that stands between them and the power-hungry madman."

Returning to the table, he poured himself another cup of tea. "But whatever my future holds," he said, studying the leaves in the bottom of his cup as if he could somehow read that future, "I have promised Garth that while he is courting his heiress, I will spend my time at Winterhaven overseeing the workmen Harcourt has hired to bring the old place up to snuff. I think he fears the meddlesome old cit will try to change it to suit his taste."

He leaned his elbows on the table for support and just for a moment held his aching head in his hands. "The arrangement suits me fine. It matters not to me if I am at Winterhaven or the Court of Vienna, just so long as I stay out of Maddy's sight."

Tears coursed down Carolyn's face. "Oh, Tris, my heart

breaks for you, and for Garth too. Would that I could do something to help you both."

"You can, Caro, by promising me you will never divulge what you have learned about my feelings, or Maddy's, to either Garth or Lady Ursula."

"I promise," Carolyn said solemnly. "Garth is burdened enough with his own heartbreak; I think it would kill him to know that by marrying Miss Harcourt, he robs you of your happiness as well. And Mama would simply refuse to let herself believe that the people she loves would not live happily ever after."

"Then I have but one more chore I must tend to before I can leave England with a clear conscience."

Carolyn nodded, the sorrow etched on her face making her appear far older than her tender years. "Garth's wedding."

"Exactly, my wise little sister. I must see him through that ordeal," he said wearily. "I can do no less, considering all he is sacrificing to perpetuate the House of Rand. But devil take it, since there is no way out of this coil, I wish he would make his offer and be done with it."

Maddy listened with half an ear to the conversation swirling around her at the dinner Lady Ursula and the earl were hosting to introduce her to a few of their influential friends. She scarcely noticed the elegantly appointed candlelit table nor the equally elegantly dressed guests who surrounded it.

In truth, she was beside herself. First Tristan had gone haring off to Brussels on an errand for Lord Castlereagh; now she had learned, just minutes before taking her seat at the table, that he had again left London, this time to oversee the renovations to Winterhaven.

One could almost believe he was avoiding her. But why? Did he think the stigma of his illegitimacy would rub off on her if they were seen together in public? Couldn't the stubborn fool see how little she cared for anyone's regard but his?

Her cogitations were interrupted by the aging Viscount Haliburton, seated on her right, and she was forced to carry on a few moments of desultory conversation with the obese old man on the merits of breeding one's own dogs for the hunt—a sport that made her blood run cold.

Then the pimply-faced young Baron Fitzhugh, seated on her left, proceeded to relate the latest *on-dit* about the scandalous affair between his hero, Lord Byron, and Lady Caroline Lamb. Maddy had heard the same tale before dinner from the Dowager Countess of Wylde, and the second telling held no more interest for her than the first.

Nom de Dieu, this ridiculous campaign of her father's to bring her into vogue with the *ton* was becoming more annoying by the minute. She had nothing in common with these people. If she had not been convinced before, she would certainly have become so during the three weeks she had spent in the company of the Earl of Rand.

How she would have enjoyed viewing the majesty of St. Paul's Cathedral with Tristan; her only regret in leaving Paris had been that they had not had time to visit Notre Dame together.

And she felt certain he would have loved the wondrous Elgin marbles as much as she had; the earl could do nothing but cluck about their disgraceful nakedness.

Furthermore, the poor fellow had been so bored during the afternoon she explored Hatchard's incredible bookstore, he'd actually fallen asleep leaning against one of the bookshelves.

Still, she couldn't help but like him. His was the kindest of hearts, and he had done his level best to see that she had a proper introduction into London society. But enough was enough. She had spent ample time in his company to see and be seen by the members of the *ton*, and her patience was wearing thin. It was high time Lady Ursula and her father realized she was a square peg who would never fit into the round hole they had chosen for her.

Then maybe they would leave her to her own pursuits—namely to convince Tristan she would be the ideal wife for a man whose ambitions lay in the diplomatic field. But how could she convince the stubborn man of anything if she never saw him?

The evening progressed at a snail's pace through a mediocre dinner—she could have given Lady Ursula's high-priced French chef a lesson or two on how to prepare *la mousseline de faison*. He had shown such a heavy hand with the nutmeg, the delicate flavor of the pheasant was nearly lost.

And as for his *noisette de porc* that these *bourgeois Anglais* raved about, she could scarcely bring herself to think about that. With the first bite, she had ascertained the lazy fellow had never bothered to inquire what the pig had been fed prior to butchering. Any chef worth his salt knew that only pigs fed with plums or apples dressed out suitably for such a dish; this pig had obviously been fattened on garbage scraps. She could scarcely wait to get back to Bloomsbury Square to discuss her deplorable dining experience with Cookie.

"I think the evening went very well," Lady Ursula said when the three Ramsdens and Maddy gathered in the first-floor salon after watching the last of the guests depart in their carriages. "I was particularly proud of you, Madelaine," she said, sinking gracefully onto one of the room's ornate Hepplewhite chairs. "Your deportment was unexceptionable."

"Thank you, my lady," Maddy replied. Restless, she had elected to stand just inside the door until she realized that the earl would not take a seat until she did. With a sigh, she plopped down on the empty chair beside the countess.

"I couldn't help but notice you scarcely touched your dinner, my dear," the countess remarked as soon as Maddy was seated. "A case of nerves, I imagine. Meeting so many exalted peers of the realm all at once can be rather intimidating."

"Indeed it can, my lady."

"Then, I'm certain the cuisine was a great deal more exotic than that served in your father's house."

Maddy smiled. "It was indeed different from that to which I've become accustomed, my lady."

"I shall have the chef's assistant prepare something more suited to your simple palate before you leave. I cannot bear to think of you driving all the way to Bloomsbury Square on an empty stomach."

Maddy cringed at the very thought of what that simple something might be. "You are too kind, my lady. But I believe I shall wait until I reach home. Cookie is sure to be awake, and I am accustomed to his cooking."

"Whatever you think best, my dear. But you will have to learn to appreciate *haute cuisine* sooner or later, you know. All he great houses of London are staffed with chefs of Monsieur Berthier's caliber."

Maddy smiled obliquely. "I don't doubt they are, my lady, out I shall try to make the best of the situation anyway."

The countess's eyes widened a fraction. "Yes, of course you will, my dear." She folded her hands in her lap. "Now as to the agenda for tomorrow, my son tells me you've expressed a de-sire to see the waxworks."

"It was only a remark in passing," Maddy said, casting a glance across the room to where the silent, sad-eyed earl sat on a Sheraton loveseat beside his equally silent, sad-eyed sister.

"Nevertheless, tomorrow morning would be an excellent ime for such a pleasant excursion," the countess continued. Then you can return here in time for luncheon, after which Garth and Carolyn can help you practice the country dances ou've learned. For I've the most splendid news. Lady Jersey ent your voucher for Almack's around this afternoon, so it is ime you tried your wings, so to speak."

Maddy felt a twinge of anger. She was tired of having her ime arranged for her, even by someone as well-meaning as Lady Ursula. "That sounds like a lovely idea, my lady, and I m certain I would enjoy it immensely, but unfortunately I ave made other plans."

"Other plans?" three incredulous voices asked in unison.

"Yes, I find I grow weary of the city," Maddy improvised. The noise and dirt, you know," she added, warming to her ubject. "I long for a brief sojourn in the country, where the air s clean and pure and the only sound is the occasional bleating f a sheep." She smiled beatifically at the three other occu-ants of the small salon. "I have decided to ask my father to ease a cottage for a month or two in some rural area."

"You plan to leave London at the height of the Season?" Lady Ursula looked positively horrified. "But, my dear, it sim-ly isn't done. What will Lady Jersey think if you fail to use e voucher she has so kindly provided you?"

Another twinge of anger assailed Maddy. She had met the enowned Lady Jersey on one of her rides in Hyde Park with e earl, and the woman had spent the entire ten minutes look-ng down her nose at her. "I neither know nor care, my lady.

The truth is, my spirit is badly in need of renewing and th
source of that renewal is only to be found in the country."

"Then perhaps in lieu of some rented cottage, you woul
care to visit my country estate, Winterhaven," the earl sug
gested. "I would be most happy to escort you, and your fathe
there if you so desire. It is but a two-hour drive from the city."

Maddy could scarcely believe her luck. The earl had take
her bait as easily as a mouse lured into a trap by a piece c
cheese. "I cannot imagine anything I would enjoy more, m
lord," she declared, favoring him with a radiant smile.

"But you can't go to Winterhaven!" Lady Carolyn's voic
held a note of panic.

"Why ever not? I think Garth has come up with a brillian
suggestion." Lady Ursula frowned at her daughter. "I can'
imagine why I failed to realize that returning to Winterhave
is just what he needs to spur him on to . . . to make certain th
workmen are provided with whatever it takes to complete th
necessary renovations."

"But Tris is doing that," Lady Carolyn said, "and you kno
how ill-tempered he can get if he's interrupted when he'
working."

The countess looked positively flabbergasted. "I know n
such thing—and furthermore I'll not hear another word agains
the dear boy."

"But surely you must realize how inconvenient it will be i
we all traipse down there when the house is still crawling wit
carpenters." Lady Carolyn laid her hand on her brother's arr
and looked pleadingly into his eyes. "Please, Garth, don't d
it. Please believe me, it is not a good idea."

"Cut line, Caro," the earl said somewhat impatiently. "Wha
are you thinking of? The renovations are finished, except fo
the south wing, and there is plenty of room to put up ou
guests without using that part of the house."

Maddy held her breath, hoping the earl would not let his sis
ter convince him to change his plans about opening Winter
haven. It was her only hope of seeing Tristan away fron
London and the prying eyes of the *ton*. Surely in the peace an
seclusion of the English countryside, she could bring hin
around to making her the offer she so fervently desired.

She couldn't imagine why Lady Carolyn was so opposed t

the idea of the house party, but she felt like throttling her for interfering. As it turned out, Lady Ursula did some verbal throttling of her own. "Carolyn, go up to my chamber and fetch my paisley shawl. I feel a chill coming on," she said in a voice that brooked no refusal.

"But Mama—"

"My shawl, Carolyn. Now."

With a last pleading look at her brother, Carolyn burst into tears and ran from the room. Maddy could hear her sobs long after she disappeared from sight.

Lady Ursula stared after her daughter, a puzzled look on her face. "I do believe Carolyn must be sickening with something. For no apparent reason, she has turned into a complete watering pot these past few days. Now this display of emotion. She is not at all herself."

"She is eighteen, Mama," the earl said dryly.

"Perhaps you are right." With a shrug, the countess returned to the business at hand. "So, it is all settled then, my dears. We'll leave for Winterhaven in . . . shall we say three days' time?"

"Three days sounds just fine, my lady." Maddy would have preferred to leave on the morrow, but she made herself curb her impatience. It would never do to let Garth and Lady Ursula know her real reason for wanting to adjourn to the country.

"Then I'll pen a brief note of invitation for you to carry to your father," the countess said, and crossing to the small escritoire standing beneath the window, proceeded to do so.

Half an hour later the earl handed Maddy and her elderly dresser into her father's town coach. She settled back against the squabs, a smile on her face, Lady Ursula's note in her reticule, and the worthy lady's parting words ringing in her ears.

"Won't our darling Tristan be surprised to see us! The dear boy must be desperately lonely off there all by himself."

Twelve

Tristan was indeed surprised by the unannounced arrival of Garth and his houseguests at Winterhaven—in much the same manner that Napoleon was surprised by the outcome of the battle of Trafalgar.

He was supervising the repair to the stone exedra circling the south terrace at the time and literally could not believe his eyes when he saw the caravan of travel carriages and baggage vans approaching up the long tree-lined drive.

Carolyn was the first to reach him. She leapt from the lead carriage before the groom had a chance to hand her down, sprinted up the shallow stairs, and crossed the terrace to stand breathlessly before him. "I tried to stop them, Tris, I really did. But Mama would not be deterred. She has this idea that seeing the renovations at Winterhaven will give Garth the impetus to make his offer, you see. Mr. Harcourt has been grumbling about how long it's taking him to get around to it."

"I understand," Tristan said, numbly acknowledging he could scarcely blame the powerful cit for being impatient. The man had already invested a fortune in his plan to make his daughter a countess; he must be champing at the bit to place the announcement of her engagement in the London *Times*.

In truth, Tristan was nearly as impatient as Harcourt to get the deed over and done with. He had almost convinced himself that once the commitment was made, he would find it easier to resign himself to losing her.

Until she stepped from the carriage and looked his way.

Her joyful smile was like a knife plunged in his heart; the sound of her voice calling his name a cruel twist of the blade. She approached him with outstretched hands. "Oh, Tristan, it is good to see you again. It has been so long!"

The touch of her gloved fingers on his sent such a jolt of desire coursing through him, he felt as if his knees must surely buckle beneath him. "Maddy," he said, and for one brief bitter sweet moment, the joy of seeing her and touching her swept every other thought from his mind. Their gazes locked, her beautiful amber eyes devouring him with the same ravenous hunger that had been gnawing at his soul this past three weeks away from her.

"Here's Mama, Tris. And Garth. And Mr. Harcourt." Caro's voice, sharp and anxious, penetrated his hazy euphoria, and instantly he dropped Maddy's hands as if their touch scorched his flesh.

"My lady!" he said, and collecting his scattered wits, clasped Lady Ursula in his arms. Tenderly, he kissed her first on one cheek, then the other in the fashion he'd become accustomed to in France.

He had scarcely released her when Caro demanded her share of hugs. Then Garth started pumping his hand as if it had been years, not days, since he'd seen him, and Harcourt began issuing orders to the footmen to unload the baggage vans, as if Winterhaven were his estate not Garth's. Then suddenly everyone was laughing and talking at once, one voice louder than the next.

Everyone except Maddy, who stood silent and alone, watching him with her heart in her eyes.

It had been a long afternoon and a busy one for Maddy—most of it spent on a tour of Winterhaven conducted solely for her benefit by the earl. She could not imagine why he had singled her out for this honor; she would have thought he would want to share it with her father as well.

But, whatever his reason, there was no disputing he had miraculously come to life as soon as he began showing her his beloved home. Once or twice he had looked positively animated while recounting in boring detail every change that had ever been made to the sprawling building by each of his long line of ancestors.

"So, Miss Harcourt, now you have seen Winterhaven, the principal residence of the Earls of Rand for almost two centuries," he said when, with the tour finished, they stood together on the sunny north terrace.

"Indeed I have, my lord—from one end to the other, and a lovely structure it is, as is the park surrounding it."

"Thank you, Miss Harcourt." The earl surveyed the rolling meadows and graceful stands of the trees stretched out before them with obvious pride. "The park was designed by the great Capability Brown at the behest of my grandfather, the Third Earl. Luckily, the formalized naturalism for which Mr. Brown was famous requires little care, since the gardening staff has been somewhat reduced in the last few years."

He turned his head and smiled at her, the first genuine smile she had seen on his face in all the weeks she had known him. "As you have probably already surmised, my home means more to me than anything on earth—except my family, of course."

"Home and family are very important, my lord. My heart still aches whenever I think of my grandfather and my home in Lyon."

"Then you will understand why I am compelled to do whatever is necessary to see that the house of Rand survives. The family holdings include five lesser estates, for which I am also responsible, two of which are unentailed." He hesitated. "I have promised the estate in Suffolk to my half brother, Tristan, and would very much like to keep that promise, unless there are serious objections to the idea."

"I can't imagine why anyone would object, my lord. A promise is a sacred pledge of honor, after all, and I know how important honor is to the members of your family." *So Tristan was to have his sheep farm after all. It was probably a good thing. Even an international diplomat needed a place to call home.*

Vaguely, she wondered to what remote part of the estate said future international diplomat had disappeared. Not once on the entire tour had she caught a glimpse of him, though she'd constantly been on the lookout for his tall figure. Not that she needed to see Tristan in person to maintain the happy glow that had sustained her during the tedious afternoon. She could survive for days on the memory of the passionate look the two of them had exchanged during the few moments they'd been together.

"I believe it is time to dress for dinner now, Miss Harcourt. We keep country hours at Winterhaven." The earl's pleasant voice jolted her back to reality. Accepting his proffered arm, she walked with him through the bay of French windows lining the terrace and thence into the house.

At the foot of the staircase leading to the upper floors, he made a graceful bow and once again smiled at her. "I am heartened by our discussion, Miss Harcourt," he said gravely. "I do believe we are of like enough minds that we may manage to rub along together quite satisfactorily."

"Thank you, my lord," Maddy said automatically, although she hadn't the slightest notion why it would be necessary that the earl and she "rub along together." Unless—her heart leapt in her breast—he knew Tristan meant to offer for her and wanted to make certain she fit into their closely knit family.

Maddy was still puzzled by the earl's odd statement when, more than an hour later, she seated herself at the dressing table in her chamber while her maid brushed her wayward curls into some semblance of order. But with a shrug, she finally abandoned her fruitless pondering, deciding it was not worth worrying about.

She stood up and surveyed herself critically in the cheval glass which stood next to the armoire. Not normally given to fussing unduly about her attire, tonight she had chosen and discarded one gown after another, until she found the one she felt certain would most appeal to Tristan. A pale primrose creped silk, simple of line but trimmed in a lustrous satin of an equally pale green, it could not have been more perfect a costume for a warm spring evening.

Even her cap of curls, which Lady Carolyn had assured her was all the vogue in London at the moment, seemed an appropriate *coiffure du printemps*. Turning this way and that to gain a better view, she decided that, for once, she was entirely pleased with her appearance.

Her pulse quickened at the thought that it was not inconceivable that Tristan and she might manage to slip away from the others long enough for her to collect another of the two kisses he still owed her. She might not even have to squander one of her precious hoard if the hunger she'd seen in his eyes had been a portent of things to come. She smiled to herself. The long, lonely month without him had been worthwhile after all; he had obviously missed her every bit as much as she'd missed him.

But with so many people in residence, where could they rendezvous with the assurance of privacy? The orangery, she decided as she dismissed her maid and prepared to join the others for dinner. What a romantic spot that would be with its lush foliage, and with the April moon shining through the glass dome overhead.

She felt a flush heat her cheeks, remembering how she'd listened with half an ear while the earl held forth on the virtues of raising one's own fruits and vegetables under glass in the winter months—and all the while picturing herself in Tristan's arms, with Tristan's lips pressed to hers.

A young, red-haired footman in full livery waited at the foot of the stairs when she descended. "I've been instructed to show you to the salon adjoining the dining room, Miss Harcourt," he said in a lilting accent that proclaimed him a native of Ireland.

Maddy thanked him politely and moments later stepped through the door he opened and gazed about her at one of the few rooms she had missed on her tour. To her surprise, the earl was the only other person in the small salon.

Once again, his formal attire was blue satin, but a paler blue than what he had worn the night they'd attended the theater. It was, in fact, the exact shade of the delicate wallpaper covering the wall of the salon, and his gold waistcoat perfectly matched the gleaming metallic stripe in the dark blue draperies at the window.

Maddy chuckled to herself. What a funny, vain little man this brother of Tristan's was. She found herself wondering if he'd dressed to match the salon or had the salon decorated to match his attire.

Surreptitiously, she studied his somber face. Something was definitely troubling him. The animation that had brightened his countenance earlier in the day had disappeared; in its place was a deathly pallor, and the hand in which he held a glass of sherry shook noticeably. "Ah, so here you are, Miss Harcourt," he said, clearing his throat self-consciously. Maddy instantly glanced over her shoulder, thinking he must have expected someone else.

He cleared his throat again. "Your father has graciously given me permission to speak to you." His voice cracked and the sherry sloshed over the edge of the glass and splashed onto the blue and gold Axminster carpet on which they stood.

"He has?" Maddy surveyed the little earl with a puzzled frown, wondering if her bombastic father had somehow intimidated him. "But why should you feel you need his permission to talk to a guest in your own home—especially a person to whom you've been chattering all afternoon?"

Like drops of blood on a parchment, two bright dots of color flamed in the earl's pale cheeks. "But the 'chatter,' as you put it, was not of the personal nature I have in mind at this moment."

Personal nature? Maddy felt a frisson of uneasiness.

"We have been acquainted just under one month," he continued, "but in that time, I have come to sincerely admire and respect you."

"Why thank you, my lord. What a nice thing to say. I like you too." Maddy beamed at the kindly little fellow with genuine affection. "In fact, I do believe I should like you even if you were not Tristan's brother."

"I am gratified to hear that. I had hoped to find favor in your eyes, but one can never be certain, can one?" The earl fixed his gaze on a spot just above Maddy's head, his brow knitted like that of a schoolboy trying to recall the text he'd memorized to recite to his tutor. He swallowed hard. "Will you do me the honor, Miss Harcourt"—he swallowed again—"of consenting to become my wife and the next Countess of Rand?"

"Will I what?" Maddy gaped at him as if he had gone mad, as indeed she felt certain he must have.

"Will you marry me, Miss Harcourt?"

"No, my lord, I most certainly will not," she said emphatically. "Though you do me great honor in asking, I have to believe you are as aware as I that we would not suit at all."

"But Miss Harcourt," he stammered. "You . . . you cannot refuse me. What will your father say?"

"I neither know nor care. It is my life, not my father's, we are discussing here." She peered at the earl through narrowed eyes. "Is this proposal something my father has pressured you into doing?"

"He . . . he has expressed a hope that . . . that is to say, he did go so far as to . . ."

"Ha! Just as I thought!" Maddy frowned. "It is most certainly not your own idea. For heavens sake, just look at you, my lord. I have never seen a fellow more down in the mouth. Hardly the demeanor one would expect in a man who has found the woman with whom he wishes to spend the rest of his life."

"But you don't understand, Miss Harcourt. It is essential that we marry; your father expects it."

The poor earl looked so miserable, Maddy's heart bled for him. She put an arm around his narrow shoulders and gave him a friendly squeeze. "Nonsense, my lord, we don't have to do anything we don't want to do, no matter who expects it— and plainly, neither of us wants this marriage. Just leave my father to me. I have a lifetime of experience dealing with tyrants."

With her arm still encircling the earl's shoulders, she looked up as the door of the salon burst open, revealing none other than the "tyrant" himself, looking like the cat who had not only swallowed, but thoroughly digested a particularly fat mouse.

"So, Maddy, my lord, may I be the first to wish you happy? I've a groom standing by ready to ride to London with the notice for tomorrow's *Times*. I shall dispatch him forthwith." Her father's booming voice bounced off the walls of the small salon, and his triumphant grin spread from ear to ear.

Maddy felt the earl cringe as if he'd been dealt a severe blow. She had no idea what hold her father had over him, but the very thought of anyone terrorizing the dear little fellow made her hackles rise.

"No, Papa, you may not wish us happy," she said with icy disdain. "The earl has made his offer, urged on by you, I've no doubt, and I have refused him. We simply would not suit, as anyone with no more perception than a barn owl in broad daylight could readily see."

"Not suit? The man is an earl without a feather to fly with;

you are an heiress without a title. Where could you find a better match than that?"

Money. So that was what this was all about. Maddy gave the earl another friendly squeeze. The poor fellow's pockets were to let and to save his beloved Winterhaven, he had put himself on the auction block. Apparently her father was high bidder. Maddy felt choked with anger and disgust. "I like the earl very much," she said coldly, "but I do not love him, and he certainly does not love me."

She glanced at the earl, standing mute as a stone beside her. "In fact, now that I think on it, I feel certain his heart is already engaged." The sudden flush suffusing his pale cheeks confirmed her suspicion that she had read the sadness in his eyes correctly. "He may be trapped by his circumstances, but I am not. I will never embark upon a marriage founded on anything other than true love."

"True love!" her father sputtered. "Hell's bells, girl, you're well past the age when you should be believing in such romantic nonsense. I can tell you from personal experience that unless a marriage is a practical arrangement meeting the needs of both parties, it is doomed to failure."

"I will believe in true love until the moment I draw my last breath on earth—and beyond that if there is a heaven," Maddy declared stubbornly.

"Damn it, Maddy, I've let you ride roughshod over my plans to turn you into a proper lady because Lady Ursula begged me to humor you. But I'll not humor you in this. I have looked the field over and the Earl of Rand is the man who most perfectly fits the requirements I set for a proper husband for you."

"Requirements *you* set?" Maddy clenched her fists in frustration. "What about *my* requirements? Don't they count for anything with you?"

Her father turned his baleful gaze on the trembling earl. "Leave us, my lord. I would have a word alone with my daughter."

"You sorely disappoint me, miss," he said as the door closed behind the hurriedly departing earl. "I had thought you had a few brains in your head. I see now you're the same witless kind of creature as your mother."

"And you likewise disappoint me, sir. I had foolishly believed you cared about me."

"Of course I care about you. Why do you think I've spent thrice what I pay all my sea captains for a year before the mast on refurbishing Rand's dilapidated townhouse and country manor if not because I intended you to be mistress of them? Think of it, Maddy. with my money and Rand's title, you'll be the darling of London society. Not one of those stiff-necked society matrons will ever dare snub you the way they did your mother—and your firstborn son will be a bona-fide earl with a seat in the House of Lords."

Maddy eyed her father, shocked to realize for the first time how deeply wounded he had been by her foolish mother's defection. She shook her head sadly. "How ironic that a man who has accomplished all that you have with your life should consider an inherited title so important in the measurement of a man's worth."

"Don't you see, girl—it is the one thing my money can't buy. Oh, I've arranged to obtain myself a second-rate baronetcy by paying off Prinny's debts, but that's small potatoes compared to an earlship. My plan will ensure that you and your children will have the kind of prestige I can never hope for."

"Well, I am sorry to disappoint you, Papa, and sorrier yet that you have wasted so many of your precious guineas, because I can see you are truly convinced you are doing what is right for me. But it is not right. I should be absolutely miserable in a marriage such as you suggest."

"Nonsense. The earl is a fine fellow. A little shy maybe, but you've spirit enough for both of you. I'll not be thwarted in this, Maddy, for I do know what is best for you."

Maddy shook her head sadly. "No, Papa. Only I can determine what is best for me, and much as I care for you, I cannot let you rob me of the right to make my own decisions about the course my life should take. I shall be one and twenty in a fortnight and free to follow my own dictates, which I fully intend to do."

"Humpf! Free to starve in the streets is more like it. You forget I hold the purse strings—a fact that sharply curtails this freedom you appear to think you have."

Maddy raised her chin defiantly. "And you, sir, forget I am not one of your milk-and-water English misses. If a French-woman like Madame Héloïse"—she crossed her fingers behind her back—"can make her own way in London, so can I."

"So now you're telling me you can sew a fine seam," her father's heavy brows veered upward. "Don't try to bamboozle me, daughter. I have already heard from Lady Ursula that the simplest embroidery is beyond you."

"True, but I have never aspired to be a seamstress. My talents lie in a different field."

"And what, pray, may that be?"

"I am an excellent cook, Papa. A master chef, as a matter of fact. Who do you think has cooked all those superb French dishes that have graced your dinner table for the past three weeks?" She tossed her head defiantly. "Even Cookie admits I could easily earn my living managing the kitchen in any great house in London."

"Cookie! By God, I'll skin that traitorous little weasel alive and feed his carcass to the wharf rats."

"For merely stating the truth? Don't be ridiculous, Papa."

"And what of you, miss? Would it not be ridiculous to choose to cook in another woman's house rather than be mistress of your own?"

"Of course. Contrary to your opinion, I am not a fool simply because I disagree with you as to whom I should marry. I can think of nothing I would rather have than my own kitchen in my own house—but only if I can share it with the man who has won my heart."

"Some prissy French Royalist your grandfather picked out for you, no doubt. You know no man in England other than the earl." His eyes narrowed. "Except his devil-eyed half brother. By God, I knew I smelled something rotten in that quarter. If that slippery son of Satan has defiled my daughter, I'll see him swinging from a yard arm."

"Tristan has not defiled me. Nor has he done anything else of which he need be ashamed," Maddy declared indignantly. "He is the most honorable of men."

"He's a penniless bastard, and one of Castlereagh's spies to boot—the last man on earth I would allow my daughter to marry. Why, you'd be a social pariah married to such as that."

Maddy faced her father squarely. "Please, Papa, let us be done with this pointless squabbling. We have spent too many years apart; let's not allow a difference of opinion to separate us further. I know what I want in a husband, and the earl is not it. I am determined to marry the man I love. He may not meet your standards, but to me he is everything that is honorable."

"But will this honorable bastard of yours choose to marry you if you force me to send his brother to debtor's prison and turn his stepmother and sister into the street? I doubt it. From what I've seen, he's mighty fond of the lot of them, as well he should be, considering all they've done for him."

Maddy stared at her father in horror. "You cannot mean you would do such a terrible thing just because you didn't get your own way."

"This has nothing to do with getting my own way," he said grimly. "You may not believe it, but I love you dearly, Maddy, and I'll do whatever it takes to keep you from making a mistake that would deny you everything I have worked so hard to provide you."

Maddy felt consumed with a helpless, smoldering rage. "If you force me into a marriage that is abhorrent to me, I shall hate you, Papa," she said coldly.

"That is a chance I will just have to take. Better that than see my only daughter ruin her life." The ruthless set to his jaw warned her he meant every word he said.

"If you doubt I've the will or the way to destroy your honorable bastard and his precious family, try me," he added grimly. "But think long and hard on it before you do. And you might think on this while you're at it as well: Tristan Thibault has been part and parcel of the plan to save his brother's bacon from the very beginning. All the while this 'most honorable of men' was winning your heart, as you so quaintly put it, he knew full well you were slated to be his brother's wife."

Like a condemned man heading for Tyburn's gallows tree, Tristan wound his way through the labyrinthine halls of Winterhaven to the salon where Caleb Harcourt had told him Maddy was waiting to talk to him.

He had no doubt what was ahead of him; his ears were still

burning from Harcourt's version of what had transpired to abort his daughter's long-awaited engagement announcement.

Now Garth was in a panic, Lady Ursula had taken to her bed with a migraine, and Caro was holed up in the library, weeping copiously. All had agreed with Harcourt that since Tristan was the "fly in the ointment," so to speak, it was up to him to make Maddy see reason. But no one offered the slightest clue as to how he was to bring this about. Nor did anyone except Caro appear to realize that he must accomplish this miracle while nursing his own aching heart.

He took a deep breath, knocked on the door of the blue salon, and entered to find Maddy seated on a fiddle-back chair, her eyes downcast, her hands folded in her lap. She raised her head, but instead of the anger he expected to see sparking in her eyes, there was only a dull resignation and the same, terrible sadness that had wrapped its stifling tentacles around his heart.

She searched his face. "Papa said you have known all along he intended me to be your brother's wife. Is that true?" she asked, getting straight to the point as he'd known she would.

"Yes."

"Why didn't you tell me?"

Tristan reached back and closed the door. Propriety be damned. This was between Maddy and him and what he had to say was for her ears alone. "Your father had sworn me to secrecy before I ever left London. Had I known then what I do now, I would never have given my word to keep the knowledge from you."

"As I thought. I could not believe you would willingly lie to me, even by omission. Now I know what you meant when you said honor forbade you from poaching another man's preserves." Her sad little smile widened the fissure in his wounded heart in a way anger never could have—even as her unquestioning belief in him fell like warm rain on his parched spirit. Once again she had surprised him with her brave and loyal heart.

"Was I terribly foolish and naive to fall in love with you?" she asked, in a sad little voice that was nearly his undoing.

"No, Maddy, never think that." He would give her up because he had no choice, but nothing—not even his loyalty to

Garth—could make him lie to her. "If love is foolish, my love, then we are foolish together," he said softly.

A single tear coursed down her cheek and dropped onto her hands, still clasped tightly together. "We have that, then, if nothing else. It will make the loneliness a little more bearable."

She searched his face as if memorizing every feature. "I don't suppose you had any more success dissuading my father from his course than I did?"

"I knew better than to try. He has a fetish against bastards, especially penniless ones. I could cheerfully kill the man if I were not so certain he believes he is acting in your best interest."

"Papa is a fool," Maddy said, "but a well-meaning one who holds all the winning cards in this particular hand—and I know him well enough to believe he will play those cards if I refuse to marry the earl."

She shook her head, as if unable to believe all that had transpired. "Unfortunately, such well-meaning fools often create more havoc in the lives of those around them than men of a truly evil nature."

Absentmindedly, she pleated a fold in her skirt. "I am fond of your brother," she said. "Who could not be fond of such a kind and gentle person. I could no more be the instrument of his destruction than you could. But I shall make him a terrible wife, which is very sad since he deserves to be deeply loved, not merely tolerated."

She smiled. "And I would have made such an excellent wife for you. I do not even think my waspish tongue would have bothered you overmuch, since I feel quite certain you would never have felt the need to take a mistress once we were married."

She watched the knowing smile play about his sensuous lips, and knew he, too, was remembering the fiery kisses they had shared. "And therein lies the saddest truth of all," she said with a sigh. "By the time my father realizes how wrong he has been, it will be too late to undo the damage he has wrought."

For a long, silent moment she studied the face of the man she had come to love so dearly—as much for his unmistakable courage and honor as for the passion he had awakened in her.

He looked tired and gaunt and his eyes held a haunted look that made her want to clasp him to her breast and comfort him as the countess had when he was a little boy.

"I love you, Tristan," she said shyly. "Just once, I wanted to know the pleasure of saying the words."

"I love you too, Maddy." He held his body rigid, never moving from the spot where he'd stood since he'd entered the room, as if the tight control he'd imposed on himself would snap with the slightest variation of stance.

Maddy rose and walked toward him. "I would have my second kiss now, please."

He stepped back, his fists clenched at his sides. "Do not ask it of me, my little love. It would be like tearing my very heart from my chest to kiss you, knowing it must be for the last time."

"But I do ask it of you," Maddy said, "For the joy of remembering it will far outweigh the pain in the empty years to come."

"Ah, Maddy," he moaned, "what am I do with you . . . and whatever shall I do without you?" Without another word, he took her in his arms and covered her lips with his in a kiss so fraught with tenderness and longing, she felt as if he had lighted a candle deep in her soul that would burn hot and pure and bright all the days of her life.

The kiss ended, and gently she touched her fingers to his cheek. "Go now, Tristan," she said, "before I am disposed to collect my last kiss. For I am a merchant's daughter and would keep you in my debt. That way, wherever you are, some small part of you will always belong to me."

Thirteen

The engagement of Garth Ramsden, Fifth Earl of Rand, to Miss Madelaine Harcourt was the main topic of discussion in every fashionable drawing room in London on the afternoon following the announcement in the *Times*.

The Ramsdens were not the first noble family to bail out their sinking ship by bestowing a title on the daughter of a wealthy industrialist. With times so hard, a number of others had been forced to do the same in recent years. But the earldom of Rand was by far the most distinguished house to go such a route—and Caleb Harcourt the richest of the merchant princes. In the eyes of other indigent noblemen, this particular alliance gave the solution an air of respectability it had heretofore lacked.

As Beau Brummel laughingly remarked to his fellow diners at Watiers, "It appears the stench of commerce becomes palatable to even the most noble of nostrils once they feel the pinch of poverty."

At Lady Ursula's urging, the visit to Winterhaven was cut short. "Much as I enjoy visiting with our darling Tristan," she explained to anyone who would listen, "we have too many things we must accomplish before the wedding to waste our time in bucolic pleasures."

"Not the least of which is the reading of the banns in St. George's for three Sundays," Caleb Harcourt added. "I want this wedding to take place as soon as you can make the proper arrangements, dearest lady."

Maddy didn't demur. As far as she was concerned, the event was like scheduling a tooth extraction—the sooner the painful business was over, the better. She had said her good-bye to Tristan. There was nothing left to hold her at Winterhaven.

Thus, one week to the day after the Ramsden party left London, they returned—all except the earl, who elected to spend another fortnight at Winterhaven helping Tristan with the renovations.

To their surprise, droves of invitations for balls and routs, masques and musicales, picnics and Venetian breakfasts, had already arrived at the townhouse addressed to the earl and his betrothed. Caleb Harcourt was ecstatic. "Now you see how right I was about this marriage," he declared that evening when he, Lady Ursula, Maddy, and Lady Carolyn sat in a small salon on the second floor of the London townhouse.

He waved the sheaf of invitations in Maddy's face. "The doors of the finest houses in London are open to you, Maddy girl. You'll be hobnobbing with earls and dukes, maybe even a prince or two—everything that was denied you as a mere merchant's daughter."

Maddy turned a page of the book she was reading without looking up from the text. "You are confusing me with my mother, sir," she said coldly. "It was she, not I, who set such store by titles." They were the first words she'd spoken to the old tyrant since he'd posted the announcement of her engagement in the *Times*.

"Still moping about, are you?" he asked, obviously not the least bit fazed by either her silence or her caustic words. "Well, just wait until you've waltzed with a duke and had your hand kissed by the Regent himself. You'll sing a different tune then, my girl."

"Dear Caleb is right, Madelaine," Lady Ursula interjected, setting aside the list of wedding guests she was writing and rising to her feet. "Once you're over your initial shyness, you'll find this world to which you've gained entrée more exciting than your wildest dreams. Just think, my dear, with your father's money and your new title, you could easily become one of the *ton*'s most prominent hostesses. And what a feather that would be in all our caps."

"And so she will be, with you to guide her, dearest lady," Caleb Harcourt purred, rising to stand beside her. "Now let us adjourn to the book room to make our plans for the wedding." He offered his arm to the diminutive countess. "I want this to be the grandest affair of the Season, and I defer to you in all matters of taste."

"You are too kind, dear Caleb," the countess simpered, and arm in arm they departed the room, beaming happily at each other.

"When did my father become 'dear Caleb' and the countess his 'dearest lady'?" Maddy asked Lady Carolyn when the two of them were out of earshot. "How have I managed to miss this interesting development?"

Carolyn looked up from the scarf she was embroidering. "I believe you've had other things on your mind. The two of them have been inseparable ever since the announcement of the engagement of their children."

She flushed. "Do not think too badly of Mama for falling in with your father's plan, Miss Harcourt. You must understand. the only way she could survive thirty years with my rakehell father was to turn a blind eye to the nightmare of reality and pretend her life was happy and serene. Self-delusion has become such a habit with her, she has already convinced herself that you and Garth are ideally suited. I feel certain that by the day after tomorrow she will believe you are deeply in love and this marriage was your idea, not Mr. Harcourt's."

"You are wise beyond your years, Lady Carolyn," Maddy said, setting her book aside. "And your compassion for your mother does you credit." She hesitated. "I shall need a sage friend to help me through the ordeal ahead," she added tentatively. "I would hope you would be that friend as well as my sister. Can we not seal that pact by agreeing to call each other by our given names from now on?"

Carolyn nodded solemnly. "I would deem it an honor to be both friend and sister to the woman my brother, Garth, marries—and my brother, Tristan, loves."

Maddy's heart skipped a beat. "Tristan has spoken to you?"

Carolyn nodded. "He confessed his love for you before he left for Winterhaven. But only to me. Neither Mama nor Garth are aware of his feelings. It would upset them dreadfully to know he is made unhappy by your marriage."

"As it has upset you. I know now why you have turned into a watering pot this past fortnight. And I suspect at least half of your tears are for your brother, Garth, and the lady he loves."

Lady Carolyn's face went blank with surprise. "You know about Sarah?"

Maddy turned down the corner of the page she was reading and set her book aside. "I didn't know her name, but it was not difficult to see the earl was nursing a broken heart."

"Garth and Lady Sarah Summerhill, the daughter of our neighbor Viscount Tinsdale, pledged themselves to each other when they were but children. There has never been anyone else for either of them, and they are so much in tune with each other, it almost seems as if they are one person, not two," Carolyn said, threading her needle with dark green embroidery thread.

"Sarah is four and twenty. Way past the marrying age," she continued, jabbing her needle into the scarf and pricking her finger in the process. "But she turned every suitor down and waited for Garth all the years he was on the Peninsula as Wellington's aide. It nearly killed him to have to tell her that her waiting had been in vain."

Maddy regarded her companion with solemn eyes. "I assume Lady Sarah's family are in the same serious financial straits as the Ramsdens then."

"Lud, no. Viscount Tinsdale is as rich as Croesus."

"Then why didn't he help your brother?"

Carolyn looked up from her embroidery, the sadness in her eyes making her resemblance to her brother more apparent than ever. "For one thing, Garth didn't ask for his help. For another, while Viscount Tinsdale is a loving husband and father, he is also a high-stickler; I imagine he considered a man tainted with financial scandal to be beneath his daughter's notice."

Her eyes filled with tears. "I just wish both Sarah and you could be my sisters, and for the right reasons. I cannot bear to see my brothers and the ladies they love so unhappy. And all because of our fathers. Mine, who cared nothing for anyone but himself—and yours and Sarah's, who care so much, they are blinded by their ambition for their daughters."

She brightened suddenly. "Maybe Mr. Harcourt will develop a tendre for Mama. Surely he wouldn't send the son of a lady he was courting to debtor's prison."

Maddy grimaced. "You mean by withholding the funds to pay his creditors."

Carolyn's eyes widened with shock and the scarf, threads and scissors slid off her lap and landed in a tangled mess on the carpet. "Oh dear, I thought you knew," she wailed, pressing her fingers to her lips.

"Knew what?"

"I dare not say. Garth told me in strictest confidence and made me promise I wouldn't breathe a word of it, lest it upset you unduly."

Maddy watched the color recede from Carolyn's face. "But you must tell me this thing I should know and obviously do not. It may be information I can use to advantage. Perhaps there is yet a solution to this dreadful riddle in which we find ourselves."

Carolyn hesitated, obviously wrestling with her conscience over betraying her brother's confidence, and Maddy felt her heart thud ominously in her breast. Her woman's intuition told her this information Carolyn possessed could well be the clue she needed to extricate herself and the earl from the stranglehold her father had on them.

"Tell me, Caro. I must know," she urged.

"Garth has only one creditor," Carolyn said finally, her voice sinking to a whisper. "Mr. Harcourt bought up all my father's gambling vowels and the mortgages he took out on the Ramsden estates—"

"And blackmailed Tristan into bringing me back from France, and Garth into promising to marry me," Maddy finished for her. An icy rage swept through her, chilling yet another of the newly kindled sparks of warmth she felt toward her father. "*Nom de Dieu,*" she muttered under her breath. "No wonder the old tyrant is the richest merchant in England; he has no scruples when it comes to accomplishing his own aims."

Rising to her feet, she paced to the pianoforte and back again, deep in thought. "But maybe we can beat him at his own game if I can lay my hands on the records of the earl's debts."

She pressed her fingers to her temples. "Where would my father keep them? I have been in every room in his house and een no sign of a safe." She stared into space, envisioning the ouse in Bloomsbury Square. "He often sits at his desk in the ook room, working on his accounts. They could be there in a ocked drawer I suppose."

Carolyn's worried gaze followed Maddy's pacing. "It is nore likely they're in his office on the waterfront. That was where he showed them to Tris and Garth. But how could you earch for them there? No lady would dare be seen on the Billingsgate docks." She frowned. "And what will you do with he papers if you find them? I'm not certain it would be enirely honest to destroy legal documents."

"It would be entirely dishonest, as a matter of fact. But then ow honest is blackmail?" Maddy sighed. "But you have a oint. Knowing Tristan and the earl as I do, I shall probably ave to find some honorable way of disposing of the records f the debts. Well, I shall worry about that after I locate them. At least they will be rendered harmless in my possession."

She stopped her pacing to stand before Carolyn, her arms olded across her chest. "First I'll search my father's desk at he house. But if they're not there, then we'll have no choice; we'll have to pay him a visit at his place of business."

"*We?*" Carolyn blinked. "You mean you and *me?*"

"Of course. I shall need you to create a diversion. You now, swoon or some such thing, while I search the desk in is office," Maddy said, hoping she had not been mistaken in hinking Carolyn was a creature of spirit.

"Oh, my goodness. I really don't think I could." Carolyn's oice cracked. "I mean, what would Mama say? Besides I ever swoon. I shouldn't have the slightest idea how to preend I had."

She hesitated, a mischievous smile tilting the corners of her retty little mouth. "Still, even Mama has often remarked that could have made my living on the stage, had I not been born lady."

The papers were not in the desk at the house in Bloomsbury quare. Maddy had held out little hope they would be, so she was not too bitterly disappointed. But before she could divulge er plan to Carolyn on how they should lay siege to the

Billingsgate office, she was caught up in a series of fittings fo her bride's clothes which took all of three precious days.

She dared not refuse to submit to Madame Héloïse's pin ning and draping, but she took so little interest in the fabric and designs of the proposed frocks, Lady Ursula threw up he hands in despair. "How shall I ever turn you into a lady o fashion, Madelaine, if you take no interest in your appearance Do you wish to break your poor, dear father's heart?"

Maddy held her tongue, though she longed to say, "He ha shown no compunction about breaking mine." Caro was righ about Lady Ursula. She had closed her eyes to the possibilit that this marriage Caleb Harcourt had arranged was not th perfect solution to all the problems the Rand family face Hiding her frustration beneath a meek smile, Maddy made pretense of studying *La Belle Assemblée* with a view to choos ing the design for her wedding dress.

Then finally, with the fittings at an end, she could set in mc tion her plan to visit Billingsgate. Her father had put a carriag at her disposal and luckily both the coachman and groom he' provided were elderly seamen, whose knowledge of ladies ha heretofore been restricted to ladies of the night. Hence, neithe of them raised a question as to the propriety of two youn women visiting the Billingsgate counting house owned b their employer.

"Do you remember exactly what you are to do?" Madd asked as she departed the carriage at the door of her father' office.

"I remember," Carolyn said. "But I hope I shall not have t sit here too long. If I do, I fear I shall never get the smell o fish out of my garments, and this is my favorite carriag dress."

Maddy gave her a quelling look. "A small price to pay con sidering the future happiness of both your brothers is at stake. Without another backward glance, she marched to the do bearing her father's nameplate.

The discreet buzz of conversation which greeted her as sh opened it ceased instantly, replaced by a communal gasp of as tonishment. She stared at the collection of soberly dressed me of business positioned about the room like so many blackbird in a cornfield and felt a flush of embarrassment heat he cheeks. This was definitely a male milieu that did not welcome female intrusion into its hallowed confines. She took a deep breath, thought of Tristan, and stepped boldly into the room.

The blackbirds scattered before her, all except one odd-looking old fellow who shuffled forward from the midst of the flock. "Here now, miss, I'm afraid I must ask you to leave. This is a house of business—no place for a lady," he said, his thin lips pursed in disapproval.

Maddy stared down her nose at him with the hauteur that had put many an eager young Royalist in his place. "I am Madelaine Harcourt, sir, here to see my father."

"Miss Maddy? Is it really you?" The old fellow peered up at her with rheumy eyes. "I can scarce believe it, though the Cap'n did mention you was home again where you belonged."

The wrinkles crisscrossing his ancient face rearranged themselves into a smile. "I don't imagine you remember me. Lord luv you, you was no taller than this when last I saw you." He held out his hand waist high.

Maddy blinked as long-forgotten memories struggled to the surface of her mind. "Mr. Scruggs? My goodness, don't tell me you're still with my father."

"Aye, that I am, and likely to be until they fit me for a coffin. We're getting old, the Cap'n and me. T'is a good thing you come back to see to his welfare, for he's naught but those two old sea dogs to do for him now."

Maddy felt a brief twinge of conscience as to how she was currently seeing to her father's welfare, until she reminded herself to what lengths he had gone to force her to marry against her will.

"Follow me, Miss Maddy," her father's old clerk said. "I'll show you to the Cap'n's private office. As you've no doubt noticed, we're a bit more elegant now than we was in the old days when you and your mama lived above the Cap'n's shipping office on Fleet Street."

"Indeed you are," Maddy agreed, staring about her at the elegant furnishings and fine paintings.

Crooking his finger, the old fellow beckoned her to follow him to the massive, carved door gracing the far wall of the huge waiting room. He knocked once, then turned the knob.

"Here's Miss Maddy to see you, Cap'n," he said and stepped aside to let her enter her father's office.

"Maddy? What the devil are you doing here? And alone? Good God, girl, hasn't Lady Ursula told you time and again you should never leave the house without a proper companion?"

"But I have a proper companion, Papa," she declared. "Lady Carolyn is waiting outside in the carriage."

"Hell's bells!" Her father leapt to his feet. "The Billingsgate fish market is no place for an innocent child like Lady Carolyn."

"So I found out," Maddy said petulantly. "The missish creature was too terrified to leave the carriage, so I left her to drench the squabs with her silly tears and came in without her."

"The devil you say! Lord, Maddy, I'm beginning to think there's naught but an empty space between your ears." Grim of face, he marched to the door and threw it open. "Don't leave this room. I will fetch Lady Carolyn and then, miss, I will have a few words with you."

No sooner had the door closed behind him than Maddy rushed around the desk and began searching through the drawers. Luck was with her. In the second drawer from the top on the right-hand side, she found the papers she sought. Quickly she stuffed the stack of vowels into her reticule and slid the mortgage documents into the slit she'd made earlier in the lining of her pelisse. Then, closing the drawer, she hurried to seat herself in one of the two chairs opposite the desk.

She glanced about her at the quiet, tastefully decorated room, so incongruous with the noisy, stench-ridden market beyond its walls. Less than two months earlier Tristan and the earl had sat in these very same chairs and listened to her father's ultimatum. In her mind's eye she could see him waving the damning evidence she now possessed in the poor earl's face—demanding he acquiesce to his demands or suffer the humiliation of being thrown into debtor's prison.

She gritted her teeth, envisioning how helpless Tristan must have felt watching his brother squirm; how desperately he must have wanted to help rescue him from the clutches of the powerful cit who held his future and that of his stepmother and sister in his hands. "There is nothing I wouldn't do for them," he had said, and proved the truth of his words by choosing honor over love.

A good ten minutes passed before the door opened and her father led a weeping Lady Carolyn to the chair beside Maddy's. Caro had apparently thrown herself wholeheartedly into the task of stalling their return long enough for a thorough search—and from the looks of it, she was enjoying her theatrical stint immensely.

"I hope you're satisfied with this day's mischief, miss," Maddy's father declared after pouring Carolyn a glass of water from the pitcher on his desk. "This poor child had swooned away before I reached her, and even when she recovered consciousness, she was so terrified, I literally had to pry her from the coach." Like a great bear, he patted Carolyn's heaving shoulders with his mammoth paw, while sobs racked her body and tears coursed down her cheeks.

"It was so dreadful," she wailed, wringing her hands till the knuckles shone white. "All those horrible men whacking the heads off poor, helpless little fish with cleavers the size of Saxon battle axes—and I shall have to bathe in lemon juice from head to toe or smell like something dragged from the bottom of the Thames when I go to Almack's tonight."

The most seasoned actress in Drury Lane could not have played the scene more convincingly, and Maddy was still shaking with laughter when Carolyn and she arrived back at the Ramsden townhouse an hour later.

"So now that we have the papers, what do we do next?" Carolyn asked when the two of them had repaired to her bedchamber to discuss their minor triumph. It was obvious from the tone of her voice she was more than ready for another adventure.

Maddy kicked off her shoes, settled onto the window seat, and drew her knees up to where she could rest her arms on them. "I have a plan," she said, watching the steady stream of carriages and pedestrians in the street below. "But first, you must arrange to introduce me to Lady Sarah Summerhill, for I shall need her help."

"In that case, your plan will be certain to fail. Sarah is a dear soul, but the shyest, most retiring creature alive. She couldn't say 'boo' to a baby in leading strings, much less your father."

Maddy frowned. "I thought you said she was in love with your brother. I'm a firm believer that any woman can find the courage she needs to fight for the man she loves. Now what must I do to meet this shy, retiring lady?"

"She'll be at Almack's tonight. Her mama has dragged her there every Wednesday night since she's been back on the marriage market."

Maddy groaned. "Then Almack's it is, and for the good of the cause, I shall even do my best to be civil to the very uncivil Lady Jersey."

Almack's was a shock. Maddy had expected this most exclusive social club in London to be elegant in the extreme. The large, overheated room into which Lady Ursula led Caro and her was, in fact, rather tacky with its swags of dingy velvet and sagging balconies supported by columns too ill proportioned to claim close kinship to their Greek ancestors.

"Don't make the mistake of eating or drinking anything," Caro whispered behind her fan. "Almack's is noted for its stale cake, salty ham, and warm lemonade."

"Then why is it considered such an honor to be invited to this ugly place?" Maddy whispered back.

"The seven patronesses are the most powerful hostesses in the *ton*. One word from them and a person will never again receive an invitation to any affair of importance." Caro shrugged. "Actually, Emily Cowper and Lady Maria Sefton are quite nice, but the rest of them . . . well, you've met Lady Sally Jersey. The other four *grande dames* are more of the same, except they don't talk as much."

Lady Ursula glanced nervously over her shoulder. "Shhhh, girls. Behave yourselves. It is absolutely essential that Madelaine make a good impression on her first visit to Almack's."

Behind her mother's back, Caro made a moue and Maddy fought the urge to giggle. "Do you see Lady Sarah?" she asked Caro as they made their way through the crowd of hopeful debutantes and their mothers gathered to see and be seen at London's famous marriage mart.

"She's across the room, standing at the edge of the dance

floor with her father and mother," Carolyn answered. "I'll waylay her and take her to the ladies' retiring room. You can join us there."

Maddy glanced in the direction indicated. But her view of Lady Sarah was cut off by an exceedingly fat woman, dressed all in purple, who was bearing down on them. With a white ostrich feather topping her purple turban by a good two feet, she looked for all the world like a mammoth purple frigate in full sail. Trotting beside her was the redoubtable Lady Jersey.

"Ah, Lady Ursula. We've not seen you in an age," the purple frigate declared in a voice that carried the length and breadth of the vast room. She raised a lorgnette encrusted with amethysts and studied Maddy from head to toe. "So this is the chit Rand's chosen to pull his fat from the fire."

Lady Ursula blanched. "May I present my son's fiancée, Miss Madelaine Harcourt, Your Grace," she said, one word tripping over another in her nervous agitation. "Madelaine, dear, make your curtsy to Her Grace, the Duchess of Sherbourne."

Maddy dropped into a graceful curtsy; though, in truth, she would as lief have cut the rude old woman dead, and her haughty companion with her.

"Humpf! Too scrawny for my taste, but surprisingly good bone structure for a cit's daughter." The duchess lowered her lorgnette, but continued to study Maddy as if she were a filly at auction. "So, miss, we know who your father is, but what sort of woman was your mother? Never heard Harcourt was leg-shackled; now all at once he's purporting to be a widower."

"My mother was the daughter of le Compte de Navareil," Maddy said, staring down her nose with true de Navareil hauteur at this impossible creature who dared impugn her lineage. "She did not find London to her liking and returned to my grandfather's home in Lyon six years after her marriage."

"Impudent chit," the duchess grumbled. "I suppose you think that with old Harcourt's money behind you, you'll make quite a splash in London society as the new Countess of Rand."

"The thought had not occurred to me, Your Grace," Maddy said demurely. Raising her fan in the manner she'd been practicing since observing Tristan's Austrian archduchess, she leaned forward and remarked *sotto voce*, "I am accustomed to my grandfather's salon, which attracted the most brilliant political minds in Europe, you see. I believe I should find anything less stimulating to be utterly boring."

The duchess drew back as if she'd been stung by a wasp. For one instant, her already florid face turned as purple as the turban topping it. Then she threw back her head in a guffaw that had all eyes in the room riveted on her. "You've spirit, gel, I'll say that for you. What say you, Lady Jersey, has your precious Almack's seen the likes of this cheeky baggage before?"

Lady Jersey made an indistinguishable sound and the duchess returned her basilisk gaze to Maddy. "Take my arm, gel," she commanded. "We'll promenade the room together and I'll introduce you to a few people of consequence."

Reluctantly, Maddy slipped her hand through the old harridan's plump arm. She had acted in a moment of pique; now she was trapped by her own reckless tongue into being introduced to people in whom she had no interest whatsoever—for the only person she really wanted to meet was Lady Sarah Summerhill.

One face blurred into another as they slowly made their way around the perimeter of the dance floor to the accompaniment of a great deal of curtsying and bowing whenever the old lady stopped to chat with an acquaintance. Lady Ursula, Lady Jersey, and Carolyn trailed behind like the duchess's retinue.

"Ah, Viscount Tinsdale, and how are you and your lovely ladies tonight?" The duchess stopped before a small, somewhat portly middle-aged man whose face was frozen in an expression so haughty, it looked as if even a hint of a smile might crack it into a thousand pieces. He was flanked by two petite blondes—one young, one not so young.

Maddy registered the look of distress on the face of the younger of the two and suddenly she knew why she had been singled out to go on the strut with the duchess. The old she-cat was undoubtedly taking great pleasure in the pain and embarrassment her cruel public introduction of the Earl of Rand's fiancée was causing his former sweetheart.

Caro, God bless her, left her mother's side to embrace Lady

Sarah warmly. "How wonderful to see you," she exclaimed. "We are long overdue for a cozy chat." Turning her back on the duchess, she wrapped an arm about Lady Sarah's slender waist and hurried her toward a nearby door which Maddy assumed led to the ladies' retiring room.

"Well I never!" the duchess exclaimed. "Someone should teach that gel of yours a few manners, Lady Ursula." She yanked her arm from Maddy's grasp. "I've had enough of this ridiculous walking about. I suddenly find I am unbearably fatigued."

Maddy smiled benignly. "I imagine you are, Your Grace. It has been my observation that exhaustion often sets in once the sport is ended."

"Well I never!" the duchess said again, and stalked off in an obvious huff.

"Oh, my dear, what have you done?" Lady Ursula withdrew a handkerchief from her reticule and mopped the beads of perspiration from her forehead. "You have been most foolish. And Carolyn as well. I fear you have both made a powerful enemy."

"Nonsense," Lady Jersey said. "It's time someone put the evil old besom in her place—and so cleverly too. Bravo, Miss Harcourt. It was exactly the sort of thing I'm famous for saying myself. For what it is worth, you have made a friend as well as an enemy, and I flatter myself I wield every bit as much power in the *ton* as the duchess."

She gave Maddy a hearty kiss on the cheek. "Now, if you'll excuse me, I cannot wait to spread the titillating *on-dit* of how a slip of a girl squelched the dreadful duchess." She smiled engagingly. "Would you care to join me, Lady Tinsdale?"

Utterly befuddled, Maddy stared after the two women, who left arm in arm. There was simply no understanding the English.

Viscount Tinsdale remained where he was, looking more than ever as if he had spent the last ten minutes sucking a lemon. He raised his quizzing glass to stare at Maddy. "Your defense of my daughter places me in your debt, Miss Harcourt. If ever I may be of service to you, please feel free to call upon me."

Maddy smiled sweetly at the little viscount. "Thank you, my lord," she said with utmost gravity. "You may be certain I shall remember that in days to come."

She looked about her for Caro, but neither she nor Lady Sarah were anywhere in sight. She turned to ask Lady Ursula where she might find the ladies' retiring room, but the older woman's answer was lost in the confusion of a hoard of nattily dressed dandies descending on them. All demanded an introduction to Maddy and a good half of them scribbled their names on her dance card despite her protest she only knew two country dances.

Luckily, the next set was the Sir Roger de Coverley, one of the two dances her instructor had taught her, and with an experienced partner, she survived the ordeal of her first public appearance on a ballroom floor quite nicely.

Before her next partner could claim her, she slipped behind one of the columns, waited until the set began, then searched out the ladies' retiring room. As she'd suspected, it was here that Caro and Lady Sarah were hiding out.

"I've told Sarah everything I know," Caro whispered, to keep from being overheard by the only other occupants of the room—a woman and her daughter repairing the damage the girl had sustained to her hemline in the last dance set. "You were right about women in love," she continued with a smile. "Sarah said she will do anything you ask her to if it means there's the slightest chance Garth and she can marry."

Lady Sarah gave Maddy a shy smile, so like that of the earl, Maddy liked her instantly. She returned Lady Sarah's smile with one of her own, then held her finger to her lips to caution the two young women gazing at her so hopefully to keep silent until the woman and her daughter completed their repairs and left the room.

"I've thought long and hard about what we should do, and I've come up with an idea," she said once the three of them were alone. "It's a wee bit daring, but my father is a stubborn man. Nothing short of Draconian measures will convince him to relinquish his plan to make me a countess."

Maddy studied the pale, taut faces of her co-conspirators. "Are you game, ladies?"

Without a moment's hesitation, two blonde heads nodded their agreement.

"Very well. Then here is what we must do first . . ."

Fourteen

Carolyn's brief note addressed to Garth was delivered to Winterhaven by one of the grooms from the Ramsdens' London townhouse. It arrived just as Tristan and he sat down to an early dinner on a rainy Friday evening the week after the rest of the family had decamped from the country estate. Garth broke the seal and read it aloud:

> My dearest Garth:
> Mama has been persuaded to give a prenuptial dinner honoring Maddy and you Friday week at eight o'clock and has asked me to write you requesting your presence at the affair. Also, please make certain to bring Tristan with you. The success of this endeavor depends, to a great extent, on both of you attending. It is terribly important that you do not fail us in this.
>
> Your loving sister,
> Caro

Garth folded the letter neatly and slipped it beneath the rim of his plate. "Now what the devil do you make of that?" he asked. "It sounds more like a summons to a council of war than an invitation to dinner."

He frowned thoughtfully. "And who could have persuaded Mama to host yet another dinner celebrating my wedding? I distinctly remember forbidding her to commit me to any social events except those absolutely mandatory to preserve the proprieties. Doesn't the woman realize she is pushing me beyond my limits?"

"Harcourt is probably the instigator," Tristan said bitterly. "He is bound and determined to make this wedding the most extravagant social event of the Season."

Absentmindedly, Garth toyed with his fork, his fair brows drawn together in a frown. "I suppose we have no choice but to do as Caro requests."

"So it would appear," Tristan said, though it boggled his mind to contemplate attending the miserable event. With the utmost effort, he managed to hide his lacerated feelings beneath a reassuring smile; Garth had enough to contend with without listening to his problems as well.

He pushed aside his plate of braised lamb shanks and new potatoes, one of Mrs. Peterman's specialties, to which he'd been looking forward just half an hour earlier. Now the very thought of choking down a morsel of food gagged him. "You will have to return to the city soon anyway to be fitted for your wedding clothes," he reminded Garth. "I suppose Friday is as good a day as any to do so."

His brother nodded his agreement. "You are right, of course." He speared a piece of meat with his fork, only to return it to his plate uneaten. "And you must be fitted as well. It would never do to have my best man making a shabby appearance at the most elegant wedding of the Season."

Until this moment, Tristan had managed to keep too busy with the renovation of Winterhaven to dwell on the prospect of his part in the coming nuptials. Now all at once he was faced with the reality of standing before the altar of St. George's and watching the woman he loved become his brother's wife.

"Very well," he said grimly. "We will go to London and let Weston and his fellows outfit the both of us. But, on second thought, I believe I shall forego Lady Ursula's dinner and devote the evening to quizzing the lads at Whitehall on the latest news of the Corsican."

"But Caro made it very clear in her note that it is urgent both of us attend," Garth said, sounding near to panic. "Do so for my sake, if nothing else. Please, Tris, I need your support. I cannot face this blasted dinner or any of the other prewedding celebrations alone."

It was too much. Something inside Tristan snapped. The emotions he had held in check all the long, frustrating weeks he'd spent with Maddy, overflowed like a swollen creek flooding its banks at spring runoff. "Devil take it, Garth, you ask more of me than I have to give. Do you think you are the only man who has ever known the pain of heartbreak?"

Shock. Disbelief. Stunned realization. In rapid succession the feelings spawned by Tristan's impassioned words played across Garth's ashen features. "Dear God," he moaned. "How could I have been so blind? All this time I have been wallowing in my own self-pity, you have been suffering as well. Why didn't you tell me you were in love with Miss Harcourt?"

Tristan opened his mouth to protest that his affections were not attached, but closed it again instantly. He could see from the look on Garth's face that it was too late to deny the truth he had inadvertently blurted out.

"What would I have accomplished with such a confession?" he asked, cringing at the anguish in his brother's eyes. "What have I accomplished now with my stupid outburst, except add to your misery?"

Garth rested his forearms on the table and pinned Tristan with a look that demanded nothing short of the complete, unexpurgated truth. "Does Miss Harcourt know how you feel about her?" he asked quietly.

"Yes."

"And does she feel the same about you?"

Tristan slumped in his chair and stared morosely at the food congealing on his plate, unable to meet his brother's penetrating gaze. "I have reason to believe she does."

"I'm sure you do. How I missed it, I cannot imagine. Now that I think about it, every word she's uttered since our first meeting has pertained in some way to you."

Garth pounded his fist on the table. "The cit and his threats be damned. I will cancel my engagement to Miss Harcourt and find some other way to put my affairs in order. Nothing could induce me to save my own skin at the expense of my brother's happiness."

Tristan bolted upright. "You will do no such thing. Your magnanimous gesture would be for naught. Harcourt would never agree to his daughter marrying a nameless bastard, much less an impecunious one. I have resigned myself to the fact that Maddy can never be mine; I am only grateful that in marrying you, she will be spared the cruelty and abuse suffered by most women who are married solely for their dowry."

Grimly, he folded his serviette and placed it on the table beside his plate. "Her courageous spirit has survived the tyranny of her grandfather and the foolish scheming of her father; I could not bear to see it trampled beneath the heels of a blatant opportunist who saw in her nothing more than the means of getting his hands on a fortune."

The sudden flush suffusing Garth's cheeks reminded Tristan he had just verbalized the very reason why his brother had agreed to the marriage in the first place. "You know what I mean," he finished lamely.

"And you know full well no woman will ever experience anything but kindness and respect from me. But I doubt that will make Miss Harcourt any happier to become my bride." Garth searched Tristan's face with troubled eyes. "Nor, I think, will it ease your loss sufficiently to make you wish to spend the rest of your life watching her be wife to your brother. I know I could not stand to see Sarah once she wed another."

"Lord Castlereagh has asked me to represent him in either Vienna or Paris once Bonaparte is put to rout. I have agreed," Tristan said simply.

"As I thought." Bitterness sharpened Garth's voice. "In gaining the solution to my financial problems, I shall lose the two people I love most in the world—Sarah and you. I am beginning to think the price of being the Earl of Rand is too dear to pay."

"But one you will pay, nevertheless, because the alternative is even more unthinkable." Tristan rose from his chair and clapped a hand to Garth's shoulder. "Be of stout heart, my brother. I am told time heals all—even broken hearts. In the meantime, we can but take it one day at a time."

He managed a halfhearted smile. "What say we ride up to the city tomorrow morning instead of waiting till Friday? We can dispense with the tedious business at Weston's, then take rooms at the Clarendon and live the life of carefree bachelors for the balance of the remaining days—and nights. It has been years since we have enjoyed the pleasures of London together."

He shrugged. "Who knows, I may even agree to accompany

you to Lady Ursula's dinner once my mind is sufficiently fogged with brandy and exhaustion."

The hour of eight had come and gone by the time Tristan and Garth arrived at the Ramsden townhouse on Friday evening. But then, time had become so blurred during the se'nnight they'd been on the town, they had long ago ceased to distinguish day from night.

A bit worse for wear, they departed the hackney coach they'd hired to transport them from the Clarendon. Standing together at the base of the stairs, they regarded the imposing door of the townhouse with a certain amount of trepidation.

Garth was the first to break the uneasy silence. "We must be more than an hour late. Mama will be furious. She is a stickler where promptness is concerned."

"Not to worry. Lady Ursula is a dear soul who will excuse our tardiness when we explain the reason for it," Tristan said with far more assurance than he actually felt.

Garth looked skeptical. "What *is* our reason?"

Tristan racked his exhausted brain for a plausible answer to his brother's weighty question, but the effort proved to be beyond him. "I shall think of something if the subject arises," he said vaguely. "Which I doubt it will. There are always so many people at these affairs, we have probably not yet been missed."

He glanced about him, suddenly aware that the multitude of carriages which normally lined the street when a member of the *ton* entertained was nowhere to be seen. He recognized one of the only two drawn up before the townhouse as Caleb Harcourt's landau, but he could not place the fashionable black barouche that sat behind it.

"This is Friday, isn't it?" he asked, as a suspicion dawned that in their frantic, and fruitless, pursuit of pleasure since arriving in London, they might have managed to outrun time itself.

"I feel quite certain it is." Garth rubbed his temples as if the very act would stimulate his sluggish brain. "In fact, I know it is. I distinctly remember one of the porters at the hotel mentioning as much."

"Then this is either a very small dinner party or we are, in fact, early rather than late." The thought was so heartening, they immediately advanced up the stairs arm in arm, raised the brass door knocker, and gave it a resounding rap.

The footman who answered the door was the young Irishman whom Lady Ursula had insisted on bringing up to London from Winterhaven. Relief was apparent on his freckled face. "T'is glad I am to see you, milords. You're the last to arrive. The other guests are all in the small salon off the dining room."

"All of them?" Garth raised an eyebrow. "It's a small dinner party then."

"Very small, milord. A table of nine to be exact."

"Nine? That in itself is odd. In fact, this dinner party grows odder by the minute." Garth glanced uneasily at Tristan. "Mama is usually so careful to perfectly balance her guest lists. I cannot understand what she is thinking of."

"Actually, t'is Lady Carolyn who's done the invitin', with Miss Harcourt's help, of course," the young Irishman vouchsafed. A pixie-like grin tipped the corners of his generous mouth. "Lady Ursula has had other things on her mind, if you take my meanin'."

Tristan surmised he referred to the upcoming wedding. He couldn't imagine what else could be occupying the countess's mind with the event but three weeks off.

The footman relieved them of their hats and gloves, then ushered them down the hall. "I'll be announcin' you meself if you've no objections. For t'is that anxious the two young ladies are, and I'll not keep them waitin' for old Frobisher, the butler, to do the honors."

So saying, he threw open the door to the salon and announced, "T'is them as you've been waitin' for, milady."

"Garth! Tristan! Thank heavens you've finally arrived." Lady Ursula left Caleb Harcourt's side to glide toward them, a euphoric smile wreathing her face. "Cook just informed me she cannot keep dinner back one more minute and Frobisher is positively incensed over the disruption to his household schedule." She blew them each a kiss, sent one Harcourt's way as well, and glided on to the bell pull hanging beside the door jamb. "I'll ring the testy old grouch to let him know you're here," she said with what sounded suspiciously like a giggle.

Tristan exchanged a quizzical look with Garth. He could

scarcely believe the fey creature who'd greeted them so blithely was the same prim and proper woman he had known since a lad of six. Nor could he equate the huge man regarding her with a moon-calf grin on his face to the stern-featured cit he had dealt with in the past.

But a minute later, he forgot both the countess and Caleb Harcourt. Like a homing pigeon gone to roost, his gaze flew to Maddy, to the exclusion of everyone and everything else. She was standing against the far wall, talking to Caro, and she was wearing the same leaf-green frock she'd worn when they'd said their good-byes at Winterhaven. The sight of her literally took his breath away.

His woolgathering was interrupted by a strangled, keening sound, much like that of a mortally wounded animal. Startled, he realized it emanated from Garth, who stood beside him in the doorway, his gaze riveted on three people seated on a jade-green Kentian settee a few feet from where Maddy and Carolyn stood.

Tristan blinked, unable to believe his eyes. The stiff-necked gentleman in wine-colored satin evening attire who was perched in the exact center of the lion-clawed monstrosity was Viscount Tinsdale, and the two ladies flanking him were his wife and his daughter, Lady Sarah Summerhill.

"How could she be so cruel?" Garth gasped, his rigid fingers gripping Tristan's arm like an eagle's talons. But whether he was asking how his sister could be so cruel as to invite her, or how Lady Sarah could be so cruel as to attend a party celebrating his betrothal to another, was not immediately apparent.

A helpless, smoldering rage consumed Tristan. Protocol dictated that, as his brother's best man, he must expect to be subjected to social contact with Maddy until this blasted wedding was over; but there was no earthly reason why Garth should have to endure the pain and humiliation of seeing Sarah.

Instinctively, he sought Maddy's eyes, fearful of what he might see. But far from looking bewildered or downcast by this bizarre collection of guests, she appeared defiant—even militant, if the fire in her amber eyes could be believed.

Caro stood beside her, her expression equally combative—and beyond them sat Lady Sarah, looking more like a small, determined bulldog about to lock its teeth around a bone than her usual timid self.

A shiver crawled along Tristan's spine and somewhere in the vicinity of his stomach a hard, cold knot formed. It was a reaction remarkably similar to the one that had foreshadowed his entrance into the tortuous *traboules* of Lyon. Something equally dark and secretive was brewing here. In truth, he felt as if he were sitting on a keg of gunpowder just inches from a lighted flint.

With a few long strides, he crossed the room to confront Maddy and Caro. "What the devil is going on here? And which one of you is the sadist who planned this hellish party?" he demanded in a hoarse whisper only they could hear.

Two sets of eyes—one pair amber, the other blue—regarded him with stoic recalcitrance. Neither owner of said eyes deigned to answer him.

"Speak up, you two. What is going on here?"

"The party is my doing," Maddy declared defiantly. "I have gathered this particular group of people together in order to right a wrong done your brother by my father."

"Maddy has an idea to thwart her father's plan," Caro explained.

Tristan groaned. He had witnessed enough of Maddy's efforts at righting wrongs to be aware that someone usually ended up with his head bashed in. This time it could very easily be Garth.

"Did it never occur to you that you are playing with fire here, Maddy?" he asked, barely managing to control his temper. "Your father is a stubborn, opinionated man who firmly believes he is doing the right thing. It is beyond foolish to tamper with such a man and his objectives when he holds all the cards."

Maddy elevated her chin a notch higher. "But he doesn't— hold the cards, that is. I do."

"She stole them," Caro said. "With my help."

Tristan stared from one flushed face to the other, the knot in his stomach tightening by the second. "She did *what*?"

He received no answer to his urgent question for the simple reason that at that very moment Frobisher, the butler, appeared in the doorway to announce, "Dinner is served."

Conversation at the dinner table was desultory, to say the least. But Maddy had expected no less considering the odd collection of guests Caro and she had assembled in Lady Ursula's name.

Caro was no help whatsoever. She was jumpy as a flea on a hot rock, and the enormity of the project facing them before the evening ended had rendered her virtually tongue-tied.

Viscount Tinsdale was grimly silent, devoting all his energy to gorging himself on the incredibly mediocre *turbot fillets Sauvignon* and *woodcock flambé* served up by Lady Ursula's so-called French chef. Lady Tinsdale, on the other hand, ate little and said less, but merely watched her daughter with worried eyes.

As well she might. Sarah had done nothing but stare soulfully into Garth's eyes since the moment they entered the diningroom. In retrospect, Maddy realized it had been a serious mistake to seat the two of them across the table from each other. Unless Sarah pulled herself together, she would be of even less help than Caro in the confrontation to come.

Maddy found herself wondering if Tristan would ever again look at her with his heart in his eyes. He had reverted to his old, surly self once she had confessed her plan to do battle with her father, and the looks he was casting her way at the moment were anything but soulful.

She sniffed. But wouldn't the ungrateful wretch sing a different tune once she'd accomplished her mission!

Surreptitiously, she stole a guilty glance at her father, wondering if he had any inkling what was in store for him. It was all too obvious, from the ridiculous look on his face, that he had nothing on his mind except his silly flirtation with Lady Ursula—and the countess appeared every bit as engrossed in him.

This came as no surprise. Caro had warned earlier, "Do not count on Mama to side with us against Mr. Harcourt. The two of them have been smelling of April and May ever since they announced the betrothal of their offspring."

Maddy sighed. She could plainly see that if anything was to be accomplished this evening toward convincing her father to see reason, she would have to be the one to accomplish it. So be it, then. The weeks since her grandfather's death had taught her she was made of stern enough stuff to face any challenge.

Finally, the interminable dinner was over and the service

plates removed. Maddy swallowed the lump of fear filling her throat, took a last furtive look at Tristan's handsome, scowling face, and with Father Bertrand's cross clutched tightly in her fingers, rose to her feet. Clearing her throat, she launched into her shocking edict before Lady Ursula could suggest the ladies withdraw to leave the gentlemen to their port and cheroots.

Fifteen

"I have two announcements to make," Maddy said in a clear, strong voice, though her knees were knocking so badly, she had to brace her hands on the table to keep from dropping back into her chair.

All eyes turned toward her, and the halfhearted conversation that had sprung up once the last of the frothy *crème chantilly* had been consumed ceased immediately. The incredulous expressions on the various faces around the table reminded her this kind of public display was not what was expected of a well-bred young lady. But with dogged determination, she plowed on.

"First, I have come to the conclusion that I am one of those 'heaven forbid bluestockings' both the earl and Lady Ursula find so unacceptable," she continued, "and, as such, I flatly refuse to attend any more of the boring social affairs of the *ton*, except possibly the Ladies' Book Review Club and the Friends of the British Museum Society."

A cumulative gasp rose around the table, with the exception of Caro and Lady Sarah, who smiled their agreement, and Tristan, of course, who showed no reaction whatsoever. Maddy ignored her mixed reception and continued. "As far as I can see, such things as amateur musicales, Venetian breakfasts, and especially those dreadful Wednesday evening affairs at Almack's are a complete waste of time for an intelligent woman."

"Stow it, Maddy," her father growled. "I'll have no such blasphemy spoken in the presence of refined gentlewomen."

"Hush, my dear. Let me handle this." Lady Ursula laid her small white hand over Caleb Harcourt's large tanned one. "I understand your feelings in this matter, Madelaine. Naturally, the lifestyle of the British aristocracy is much more demanding than that to which you have been accustomed and you will have to put forth a certain amount of effort to fit in. But one must look at such things sensibly. How can you hope to be a proper Countess of Rand if you refuse to fulfill your social obligations?"

"My point exactly, my lady. I have been doing my best to persuade both you and my father that I am not at all suited for the position. But neither of you will listen to me."

"You'll do just fine," her father insisted. "All you need is a few of the lessons Lady Ursula suggested . . . and a change of attitude."

"My attitude is not going to change, Papa, and I cannot think of a single accomplishment required of a proper lady of the nobility that is of the slightest interest to me. Why should I take lessons to learn how to do things that bore me to flinders?"

"But my dear Madelaine, think of Garth," Lady Ursula exclaimed, looking ready to burst into tears. "Surely you would not want to disgrace him."

"Of course not. I am very fond of the earl," Maddy declared, secretly congratulating herself that she had so cleverly maneuvered the countess into saying exactly what she wanted to hear. "Which leads me to my second announcement." She turned to face Garth, who looked even more pale and unhappy than usual. "I hereby release you from the offer of marriage which my father coerced you into making me, my lord."

A flush suffused the earl's cheeks and his mouth opened and closed, then opened again, but not a sound passed his lips.

"Sit down and behave yourself, Maddy," her father ordered in a voice that in its day had sent a shipload of sailors scurrying up the rigging of one of his brigantines. "We have had this discussion before. I told you then where I stood; nothing has happened since to change my mind about pursuing certain actions should this marriage fail to come about."

He shrugged. "And as for the earl, he will just have to be patient until his mama can take some of the rough edges off you. After all, he made his choice of brides of his own free will. No one held a pistol to his head."

"Of his own free will, eh?" Maddy knelt down and retrieved

the stack of debts accrued by the Fourth Earl, which she had hidden beneath her chair earlier in the day. "And what of these interesting documents, which have all been endorsed over to you by the original note-holders, Papa? Did they not play some part in his decision?"

Her father's eyes widened in astonishment, as did those of the earl and Tristan. "Devil take it, you devious little baggage, where did you get those?" he bellowed.

"She stole them from your desk with my help," Caro said, leaping to her feet. "And how dare you call Maddy devious, you . . . you blackmailer."

Maddy watched her father's face turn a virulent purple, and she held her breath, afraid he might have an attack of apoplexy. Whatever havoc he had wrought with his foolish plan, he was still her father, and she loved the stubborn old tyrant.

"Caleb dear, do not overset yourself," Lady Ursula urged. "I am certain this is all just a misunderstanding that can be cleared up with a simple explanation."

Her voice hardened to a tone Maddy had never before heard her use. "Sit down this minute, Carolyn," she demanded. "And you, too, Madelaine. I don't know what the two of you have done, but it sounds terribly wicked and I am certain you owe dear Caleb an apology."

"I will not sit down and I will not apologize, my lady," Maddy declared. "It is my father who should apologize to me and to the earl for trying to force us into a marriage neither of us wants. If he had truly loved me, as he claimed, he would have destroyed these records of the old earl's debts and set us both free to marry where our hearts lie."

She stole a look at Tristan to see his reaction to her telling statement, but the scowl on his handsome face was anything but encouraging.

"I, too, refuse to apologize," Caro said in a show of stubborn support that gladdened Maddy's bruised heart. "I stand with Maddy. Mr. Harcourt should be ashamed of himself for playing God with other people's lives." She folded her arms and glared defiantly at the table in general.

"Dear, oh dear, what a coil." Lady Ursula slumped in her chair and promptly dissolved into tears.

"I also stand with Maddy." Lady Sarah rose to her feet. "And Mr. Harcourt is not the only person at this table who should be ashamed of himself."

"Sit down, Sarah! Immediately!" Viscount Tinsdale raised his quizzing glass to stare coldly at his daughter. "What has possessed you to act in such a manner? This tasteless business is none of your concern. In fact, I believe it is high time we took our leave of this ill-begotten gathering."

Sarah tossed her head defiantly. "I will not sit down, Papa, and I will not leave. I have never before disobeyed you, but in this you are wrong. Anything to do with Garth Ramsden is very much my concern. I am twenty-four-years old and I have waited for him since we made our pledges to each other when I was but fourteen—"

"Sarah, darling, don't do this. I cannot bear it," Garth cried, covering his face with his hands.

Sarah stared at Garth's bowed head for a moment, her eyes bleak. Then she faced her father anew. "You knew I loved Garth. Yet, when I begged you to help him, you said you couldn't spare the money because you had contracted to buy a series of expensive paintings for your famous collection. I wish you joy of them, Papa. For if I cannot have Garth, I will have no man. I will go to my grave a spinster, and you will never have a grandson to cheer you in your old age."

Viscount Tinsdale dropped his quizzing glass—and his mouth. He stared at his normally sweet-natured, biddable daughter as if she had suddenly grown two heads. "Demme, Harcourt, this is all your doing," he said turning his baleful gaze on the object of his derision.

"He's right, Caleb. This whole, dreadful mess is your fault." Lady Ursula dabbed at her brimming eyes with a soggy handkerchief. "How could I have been so taken in by your charms as to believe I had come to care for a man who was blackmailing my poor son?"

"Devil take it, Ursula, nobody told *me* the earl was promised," Harcourt grumbled. "I was just looking to acquire my daughter a title the easiest way possible."

"And a fine mess you've made of things trying to climb above your station." Viscount Tinsdale stared down his nose at the offending cit, his expression that of a man who had just taken a whiff of something unspeakably foul. "This is a prime example of why we of the old aristocracy oppose the infiltration into our ranks of bourgeois commoners."

"Why you overstuffed little pipsqueak!" Harcourt half rose from his chair with an obvious intent to throttle the little viscount. But Tristan, who heretofore had merely sat back and watched the proceedings, reached across the table and restrained him with a hand on his arm and a few brief but expressive words, which earned him scathing looks from both the combatants.

"Elizabeth, Sarah, we are leaving!" the viscount declared haughtily.

Lady Tinsdale pushed back her chair and stood up, her usually placid eyes blazing and two bright spots of color highlighting her pale cheeks. "You may leave if you wish, Horatio, but I stand with my daughter. I have lived with your selfish, tight-fisted ways for thirty years, but I can live with them no longer. Harcourt's methods may be unscrupulous and his judgment faulty, but at least he had his daughter's welfare at heart; you put the acquisition of a few Rembrandts and Vandykes above the happiness of your only child. For that, I cannot forgive you."

Viscount Tinsdale's eyes fairly popped from his head. "Elizabeth!" he gasped. "Have you lost all sense of propriety, to speak to your lord in such a manner?"

"I have lost nothing, Horatio, except my respect for you." Lady Tinsdale's expression remained defiant, though her lips trembled noticeably. "And while you are out and about making your expensive acquisitions, you'd best look into acquiring yourself a mistress, for I fear I have developed an excruciating headache which will prohibit my according you your husbandly privileges at any time in the foreseeable future."

Before Maddy's eyes, Viscount Tinsdale wilted like a flower deprived of its source of sunshine and water, and she recalled Caro's claim that despite his selfish ways, he loved his wife and daughter dearly. "What is it you want of me, Elizabeth?" he asked with obvious resignation.

Lady Tinsdale's expression softened a fraction. "I want you to help the earl out of the financial problems he inherited from his ne'er-do-well father so Sarah and he can marry."

"And how, pray, am I supposed to do that when Harcourt holds all his notes?"

As if the viscount's peevish question were the cue she'd been waiting for, Lady Ursula dried her tears and rose to her feet. "I believe Mr. Harcourt is going to destroy those dreadful notes, my lord," she said, her voice deceptively calm. "For if he doesn't, he will find that he, too, will be deprived of certain unnamed privileges which he has been enjoying recently." She glared at the recipient of said privileges. "And as my late, unlamented husband was wont to say when he held a winning hand, 'on that I stand pat.'"

"Why, Mama, surely you're not implying . . ." Carolyn blushed furiously. "I knew you were fond of Mr. Harcourt, but it never occurred to me you were . . . I mean, you're much too prim and proper to . . ."

"Don't be a ninny, Carolyn. I'm not *that* prim and proper." Lady Ursula leveled her gaze on the big man sitting beside her. "So, Caleb, what are you going to do about those notes Madelaine is waving under your nose?"

"This is blackmail," he said indignantly, then had the grace to flush when he met Maddy's knowing gaze.

"Some might call it that," Lady Ursula said. "I prefer the term 'tit for tat.'"

Maddy watched her father glance around the table, a bemused expression on his handsome, age-weathered face. Every woman was standing; every man seated. He scowled. "Devil take it, madam, between you and my scapegrace daughter, you leave me little choice." Reaching across the table, he snatched the documents from Maddy's hands, dropped them into the silver centerpiece, and lighted them up with a candle from one of the candelabra.

"There," he declared as the flames licked the edges of the epergne. "I've done my part and more for the House of Rand, if you add the cost of this bonfire to all the money I've poured into this townhouse and that mausoleum you call Winterhaven. Now, let's see how much blunt the skinflint viscount is willing to part with."

"I suppose I could manage to advance sufficient funds to see the Rand estates back on a paying basis," the viscount said grudgingly.

Between the laughing and crying and chattering that followed the viscount's statement—and the frantic efforts of Frobisher and the footmen to keep the conflagration from setting the table on fire—general pandemonium reigned for the next few minutes.

Maddy was hugged and kissed and thanked with heartfelt sincerity, first by Lady Tinsdale, then by Lady Sarah and the earl once they had stopped gazing into each other's eyes long enough to do so. Viscount Tinsdale was not so appreciative. He mumbled something about foreigners corrupting the thinking of decent Englishwomen and promptly departed with the other three to make plans for his daughter's future.

Maddy smiled sentimentally as she watched them go. The earl really was a sweet man and he deserved the kind of loyal, loving wife Lady Sarah would make him.

"So, daughter, you've had your way after all," her father said, giving her an affectionate thump on the back, "and though it's cost me dearly, I've no regrets. If I'd not embarked on my scheme to make you a countess, I'd never have won the heart and hand of a fine woman like Lady Ursula."

Maddy smiled up at him. "She is truly a lovely lady, and I wish you nothing but happiness, Papa."

"And I you, daughter. You're a clever one for sure; too clever for your own good, to my way of thinking. I hope, for your sake, this lucky bastard you're so fond of is brave enough to take a managing woman like you to wife. For there's not many as would do so."

He leaned forward, gave her a kiss on the cheek, and whispered in her ear, "If by chance he should balk at the leg shackles, you have my permission to remind him you bring an impressive dowry to the marriage bed."

So saying, he gathered Lady Ursula on one arm and Caro on the other and departed the dining room. A few minutes later, the servants followed suit, carrying the still smoking epergne with them.

The moment Maddy had both prayed for and dreaded had finally arrived. She was alone with Tristan at last. Suddenly, all her bravado evaporated like a puff of smoke in a windstorm.

Except for that one brief moment when he'd kept her father

from attacking Viscount Tinsdale, Tristan had remained so detached from the drama she'd initiated, one might think it in no way affected him. Even when she'd won her point and the three other men had come forward to declare their undying love for the ladies of their choice, he had silently retreated to the shadowy window recess at the far end of the room.

Was her father right? Had she frightened him off with her managing ways?

As if to corroborate her suspicion, he stepped from the shadows, his right hand raised to his forehead in a crisp military salute. "Well done, Madame General. Wellington himself couldn't have rallied his troops around him more effectively. Though in winning the battle, you may well have dealt your own fortunes a death blow."

Maddy tensed, uncertain of his meaning. "I am not normally a managing kind of woman," she protested, trying to read his expression. "I only did what had to be done to stop my father from ruining four lives."

"With *his* infernal managing." Tristan sighed deeply. "I'm firmly convinced it's a family trait. I am also convinced that had you decided to try your hand at managing the French army, Bonaparte would even now be occupying Mad King George's throne."

Maddy felt her temper flare. How dare he ridicule her after all the trouble she had gone to for him. "And, of course, it goes without saying, you do not want a managing wife."

"There may be worse fates, but offhand I cannot think of one," Tristan said matter-of-factly.

"Well, that is that then." Maddy's heart lay like a heavy stone in her breast. "I suppose if I really had my mind set on marrying you, I could promise I'd never try to manage *you*," she ventured hesitantly.

"Why not promise to make the Thames flow backward? You'd have a better chance of being believed." Tristan shook his head sadly. "I know you, Maddy Harcourt. You are a deucedly clever and devious woman. I shudder to think how many times you've maneuvered me into doing something I swore I would never do in just the same way you brought your father and Viscount Tinsdale to their knees tonight. With a few well-chosen words."

"I had a great deal of help in accomplishing my objective," Maddy declared indignantly. "Have you forgotten that four other women played a part as well?"

"Hah! Think you I was fooled by the performances of such timid creatures? They were simply marionettes speaking your words with their voices. No, my dear, it was very apparent who had orchestrated the plot of tonight's little drama." Tristan's knowing smile made her long to brain him in the same way she had the young Royalist who had taunted her so cruelly.

"Papa predicted you would balk at marrying me," Maddy said bitterly. "He said you would find the idea of marrying a managing woman too frightening by half. Fool that I was, I refused to believe you such a coward."

"Your father was wrong as usual." An indefinable expression that looked almost like amusement flickered momentarily in Tristan's unusual eyes. "For, it does not frighten me, my dear; it positively terrifies me. I do not believe I have ever before fully appreciated the awesome power of a determined female—even one who was, for all practical purposes, cutting her own throat."

He walked to the table, poured himself a glass of wine from a cut-glass carafe, and studied the shimmering, golden contents in the light of a candle. "The plain truth is, Maddy, no man in his right mind would consider marrying a woman like you."

Maddy's spirits dropped to somewhere between her ankles and the soles of her slippers. "Not even a man who loved me?"

"Ah well, now that's a horse of a different color, isn't it?" He took a swallow of wine, set the glass on the table, and moved toward her. "The poor sod suffering from that affliction would already be a candidate for Bedlam, so we could scarcely expect him to act rationally."

He stood close now. So close, she could feel the heat of his strong, lithe body, smell the lemony scent of his freshly starched cravat. Did she just imagine it, or was that laughter glinting in the rakehell's eyes? By all that was holy, if he had simply been teasing her all this while . . .

"What are you saying?" she asked, her heart thumping so loudly in her breast, she felt certain he could hear it.

"I'm saying I suspect you of being a practitioner of the art of witchcraft, Maddy Harcourt, for I have most certainly been bewitched since a particular moonlit night at a French grist-mill. Nothing else could explain the fact that I long to marry a woman with the figure of a boy and the tongue of a wasp—a woman who is so foolish as to maneuver herself out of inheriting one of the largest fortunes in England by marrying a name-less bastard."

Maddy felt as if the weight of the world had suddenly been lifted from her shoulders. "Oh, Tristan," she marveled, "is it true? You want me even without my fortune?"

He drew her into his arms. "I want you, little witch. Only you. Without so much as the slippers on your feet or the dress on your back." He nuzzled her neck. "Especially without the dress on your back."

Maddy felt a hot flush suffuse her cheeks at the thought of the untold pleasures his wicked, provocative words portended. She snuggled against him and raised her arms to encircle the strong column of his neck. Tenderly, he kissed the tip of her nose, the curve of her cheek, the sensitive flesh of her earlobe until, frustrated beyond belief, she pursed her lips, mutely beg-ging him to once again claim them in a searing kiss.

He didn't. Instead, he raised his head to search her face with anxious eyes. "Understand me, Maddy, I can provide for you, but not in the lavish manner of your father. I believe I have a future in England's diplomatic corps, but in the beginning my salary as an embassy attaché will be but a pittance."

"I understand. We shall survive very nicely. I am a good housekeeper and an excellent cook," Maddy declared, making a snap decision to withhold until later the information that her father still intended to provide her with a generous dowry. Until much later. Sometime after she had Tristan's ring on her finger.

It was not that she meant to deceive him. Heaven forbid! But the dear fellow seemed so inordinately pleased with the thought that he would be the breadwinner of the family, she could not bring herself to tell him that she was bringing a for-tune to their union after all.

It had something to do with his honor, she felt certain. He put great store in his honor.

She strongly suspected it also gave him a feeling of control. If there was one thing she'd learned from living with her grandfather, it was that men liked to think they were in control.

"Now that we have that settled, my love, do you think you could kiss me?" she asked, smiling meekly up at him. "For if you do not, I fear I shall be forced to collect the kiss you still owe me."

She sighed dramatically. "Since that outstanding debt appears to be my only fortune at present, I'd rather not spend it just yet."

With a joyful chuckle, he complied with her request at once with a tender, yet demanding passion that claimed her as his forever. Just exactly as she'd known he would.